The Works of John Steinbeck:
In the Magic Light of "Celtic Twilight"

The Works of John Steinbeck: In the Magic Light of "Celtic Twilight"

Edited by Yasuhiro Sakai

Osaka Kyoiku Tosho

The Works of John Steinbeck: In the Magic Light of "Celtic Twilight"

Yasuhiro SAKAI

Osaka Kyoiku Tosho
1-25, Nozaki-cho, Kita-ku, Osaka 530-0055, Japan
email   daikyopb@osk4.3web.ne.jp

First pubulished 2024

Printed in Japan at Osaka Kyoiku Tosho, Osaka

ISBN 978-4-271-21086-3 C3098

Author's Preface

Here I have decided to publish *The Works of John Steinbeck: In the Magic Light of "Celtic Twilight."* I am convinced that this book is the result of over 40 years of research on Steinbeck, which I have spared much time doing the research while doing school duties.

It all started with an incident in 1993. In the spring of that year, Professor Kenji Zenimoto (deceased) at Shimane University requested me to give a lecture titled "Comparative Cultural Studies" to the third-year students of the Faculty of Education at Shimane University. This is a perfect opportunity to test my own research results.

Ten years earlier, in 1983, I had joined the John Steinbeck Society of Japan, the Chu-Shikoku American Literature Society, the American Literature Society of Japan, and the English Literary Society of Japan. In addition to my school duties, I had dreamed of the happiness of being able to teach the students in my specialized field someday at a Research Institute called a University. And that was the moment when it came true.

However, a big test of lack of ability was waiting for me. I myself had studied American literature to some extent on my own, but I had no idea which culture to compare it with, and I continued to worry for nearly half a year. What was more, it was too much of a burden, not just literature, but culture other than American culture, which I didn't even know much about. At that time, Mr.Zenimoto invited me to a "The Chieftains" concert. The world-famous Irish folk music band that played BGM in the movie *Barry Lyndon* had come to Shimane Civic Center and gave a concert. I loved folk music, so I bought a ticket and went to the concert.

When I listened to their music at the concert, I was surrounded by a lingering feeling and excitement that I didn't get from the LP sound. "This is an American folk song," I thought. The '4-7 (*yona*)*nuki* sound,' unique to folk music, resounded deeply. Then, the sounds found in American folk songs and the musical form called "reel" in the Celtic music made me think, "This will be a research of the culture for my comparative culture research," as if I had been taught by God in Izumo. This may be called '*En*' or Good Luck. Since then, I had bought and read books on Celtic culture and listened to CDs on Celtic music. Chieftains and Enya are still my favorite artists. At this very encounter, I thought it was Steinbeck's Irish-Celtic case.

It is no exaggeration to say that my research on Celtic culture began thanks to this professor. It must be some kind of luck that this book will be published 22 years after the professor passed away. After all, on March 26 in 2002; in the year Zenimoto passed away, I was watching the musical "Oklahoma!" on Broadway in New York when my watch suddenly stopped working. I sent it for repair, but the battery was not dead. I wondered if the Celtic fairies had told me about Zenimoto's passing, and while praying for his soul, I am very glad that this book has been published in this way. Luckily, in the first year of 1993, I gave a comparative lecture on "American culture" and "Celtic culture" from the second semester to the students at Shimane University.

Thus began my association with Celtic culture. In the latter half of the 1990s, the movie *Titanic* was released, and in the chapter "Party in the Third Class," there is a scene in which Leonardo DiCaprio, the main character, performs an Irish dance (Riverdance). As a result, this "Irish-Celtic" culture had come to be known all over the world. I was forced to read many books about the influence of "Celtic culture" on "Irish-Celtic culture," and I was able to make historical considerations about the relationship between "Celtic culture" and "American culture." As for me, I felt like a fish in the water.

At the end of the 1990s, Professor Zenimoto said, "I want to read Steinbeck's works. Please lend me your two favorite books." I lent him *The Grapes of Wrath* and *Cannery Row*. He said, "These two are Celtic." When I asked him, "What do you mean?" he replied, "The former highlights the Irish land problem. The latter is somewhat similar to the light imagery of the poet W.B. Yeats, who is my specialty." At that time, I had a very strong impression that I would have been able to read *The Grapes of Wrath* in that way. This is exactly what Professor Hideo Inazawa pointed out.

This book, to be exact, consists of two parts. Part I contains the work theory that I considered on the Steinbeck novels including the introductory chapter. Part II, if I may refer to it a little, contains the excellent papers of my dearest colleague scholars who gave me inspiring my long research and commemorating my retirement as an English teacher. I would like to express my deep gratitude to them.

Finally, I would like to thank all the teachers who taught me English, especially Professor Takahiko Sugiyama (deceased), who invited me to study American literature during my university days, and Professor Kenji Zenimoto, who invited me to study Celtic culture.

I would also like to express my deep gratitude to President Tetsuya Yokoyama, his wife, Michiko Tsuchiya and all the staffs at *Osaka Kyoiku Tosho* Publishing Co. Ltd., who have been very supportive of the publication, and my family, who have supported me strongly behind the scenes.

Contents

****

Part II

Introduction:
Steinbeck Literature from the Celtic Viewpoint

With this chapter as a starting point, we will read and understand the literature of Nobel Prize-Winner John Steinbeck from the perspective of "Celtic Culture" over the next 11 chapters. Until now, little attention has been paid to the relationship between Steinbeck and Celtic culture. However, in Japan, there was a scholar who took notice of this perspective early on. It was Hideo Inazawa.

In his book titled *Sutainbekku-Ron (Steinbeck View)* (Shichosha, 1967), Inazawa argues that "It is indisputable that Steinbeck's being of Irish stock consciously or unconsciously greatly influenced his work. This at some times erupts with roars of laughter in *Tortilla Flat*, and at other times it takes the form of a heavy contemplative mood in *East of Eden*. The origin of this tinge of sweet sentimentality that hovers over so many of his works is also partly to be found here..." (p.17 Translation Mine). As is well known, Steinbeck is of Irish-Celtic descent, because his mother, who read to him when he was a child, had a great influence on him, and it was undoubtedly his mother's skills as a story-teller that made Steinbeck acquire his writing ability.

It is possible to speculate which works Mr. Inazawa refers to as "many of his works," but this time, the author of this book spotlighted 10 works by Steinbeck and read them from various perspectives of Celtic culture. This book is the culmination of the author's long-term study on Steinbeck Literature from the Celtic Viewpoint. Then a brief overview can be presented from now on.

It is an undeniable fact that there are various viewpoints regarding Celtic culture. Among them, the following three points of view stand out in relation to Steinbeck Literature. Firstly, the Legend of the Holy Grail that appears in the so-called Legend of King Arthur and its motifs. In fact, this Legend of King Arthur originated in *The Mabinogion*, a book about Celtic culture written in medieval Welsh. Secondly, Light Imagery and Fairy Tales used and written by Irish poet, W. B. Yeats. Thirdly, the presence of the "Druids," which represents the priesthood and the rituals. Of course, we must not forget the existence of animals, especially those related to the "Celtic Culture," which deifies animals such as "pig," "cow," "cat," and "snake."

In any case, Steinbeck's reading volume is enormous, and it can be said that he has extensive knowledge. Looking at the books introduced in Robert J.DeMott's *Steinbeck's Reading: A Catalogue of Books Owned and Borrowed* (New York: Garland, 1984), his reading area is so wide that it is difficult to describe. Having read so many books, it is not surprising that his imagination is extraordinary. Then his major works will be introduced one by one.

First, Steinbeck's first novel *Cup of Gold* has many story developments that are likened to "King Arthur Legend." Merlin, an old sage who also appears in *Le Morte D'Arthur* and is reminiscent of the Druid, appears in many works, and the characters are often compared to Celtic fairies. For a maiden work, it should be highly praised for experimentally portraying the writer's own identity. Steinbeck would be given high marks for calculating the historical background of the 1920s in the United States and also properly expressing the entertainment value of an adventure novel. The *Pirates of the Caribbean* series, produced as if to commemorate the 100th anniversary of the writer's birth and produced by a film production affiliated with the same Irish-American film director Walt Disney as Steinbeck, is still popular and is still being produced even today.

Next is a critical essay on *The Pastures of Heaven*. The story stage that appears in this work has a very similar atmosphere to that of Ben Bulben, which actually exists in Ireland. Ben Bulben still has a strange atmosphere at night, and there are many Irish people who still believe that fairies roam there. When the author of this book visited Ben Bulben, there was something of a fairyism. Therefore, the characters who appear in this work are deliberately compared to Irish fairies walking around Ben Bulben. W. B. Yeats's patriotism for his native Ireland, and his willingness to protect Ben Bulben's atmosphere from development, are similar to Steinbeck's efforts to protect rural areas from being destroyed by capitalism in 1930s in the United States. The author of this book would like to read this work as a "curse" woven by Irish fairies which protest rural development.

In chapter 3, we will discuss *To a God Unknown*. The theme of "pagan gods" in Celtic culture stands out throughout the work. In other words, Steinbeck's identity as a Celt represents itself everywhere in this work. Furthermore, if we decipher the red blood motif, we could decipher the orange and the green imagery of the color of the national flag of Ireland in which Joseph committed suicide in relation to Celtic culture. There are also many images of Celtic Light. The image of "gray" is that of Celtic Twilight, and in this Light Image we can decode the idea of Celtic Utopia "Tír na nÓg." Was Joseph able to choose a happy death?

Chapter 4 deals with a critical essay on the controversial work titled *Tortilla Flat*. This work was banned in Ireland as its publication. The reason is wine addiction and bad behaviors of the characters. A depiction as "good people" of many characters that appear in the work connotes the ambiguity of Celtic fairies deeply-rooted in Celtic culture. It is such a great masterpiece that in the author's mind, re-evaluating this work is a first priority.

Chapter 5 deals with a critical essay on *Saint Katy the Virgin*. This work sold surprisingly well when it was first published. This masterpiece was later included in *The Long Valley*. The seemingly incomprehensible final ending could be interpreted from the Celtic viewpoint. If we analyzed the symbolism of a "pig," and the phonological considerations of Katy linking to Cathy/Kate's naming that later bore fruit in *East of Eden*, there could also be something seen in the final ending by considering in the light of *The Mabinogion*, a book written in medieval Welsh.

In chapter 6 and 7, *The Grapes of Wrath* is discussed. The former critical essay was completed thanks to TRAVEL GRANT Scholarship conferred by the English Literary Society of Japan in 2001 and the latter one was based on the Symposium Presentation delivered at the annual conference of the John Steinbeck Society in 2019.

Celtic "Diaspora" is especially focused in the critical essay in chapter 6. The "land problem" is also a major problem that has been traumatized by the Irish since the days of British rule. In *The Grapes of Wrath*, the tragedy of the Joads, who were forced to emigrate from Oklahoma to California, is presented in the form of "Diaspora" as the psychological trauma of many Irish people who were forced to emigrate to the New World in the 19th century.

Celtic music is clearly discussed in chapter 7, in which musical notes of the traditional Irish air "Chicken Reel" are included, which the author of this book struggled to listen and write, and also which Steinbeck really used as an "Irish Tune" in *The Grapes of Wrath*. The dance, based on the Irish dance in *The Grapes of Wrath*, could be interpreted as a "Song of Joy" and "Song of Manself," not "Song of Myself."

In chapter 8, unlike the writing order, the author picked up *The Wayward bus*. This is the author's arbitrary idea, because the two works : *The Grapes of Wrath* and *The Wayward Bus*, so-called "Road Narrative," are placed in confrontation with chapter 6, 7 and 8, that is, the 1930s (Great Depression Period) vs. the late 1940s (After the Second World War Period). So that in this position the situation in the United States could be well compared and contrasted. By this standard, in chapter 9, we can read *Cannery Row*, which depicts America during World War II, and *Sweet Thursday*, which could be said to be a sequel that depicts America after the Korean War in the 1950s, to be well confronted.

The Wayward Bus was published in 1947 in the late 1940s as was mentioned earlier. It is a masterpiece that comically portrays a daily life in the midst of the development of transportation to the suburbs, and the circumstances surrounding hotels and other lodging facilities, in a medieval drama style. In this work the "Angus Cows" flowing down the San Ishidro River are compared to the "gods" of Celtic mythology, and the "oak tree" is reminiscent of the "Druids." In the depiction of "Celtic Twilight" such as "twilight" and "dawn" tinged with "gray"

4

as the image of the light of the city, the daily life of the bus passengers centered on Camille Oaks is well woven into a slapstick comedy. It is elaborately drawn as the device that symbolizes these Celtic Culture in the development of the story. Will the bus make it to its destination safe and sound, and that through the heavy rain?

In chapter 9, two works: *Cannery Row* and *Sweet Thursday* dared to be listed. The reason is that the author of this book interprets the latter as a sequel to *Cannery Row*. Also by listing the two works at the same time, we could see how well Steinbeck's philosophical thought grew. Furthermore, as was mentioned earlier, these two works also give us a glimpse of the situation in the United States in the 1940s and 1950s.

Two works set in a certain region of California (the writer's hometown) during and after World War II, or after the Korean War, are slapstick comedy weaving with Mack and his friends, with Doc at the center. Chapter 14 in *Cannery Row* clearly describes Celtic representations as "Time of Twilight Magic." In addition, many "oak trees" appear in the two works to symbolize the "Druids," and play an important role in the development of the story.

In *Cannery Row*, Steinbeck's philosophies of "Non-Teleological" thinking and "Group-Man" theory stand out in places where they clearly appear. These thoughts, as the music of Doc's mind, developed from "Gregorian Chant" (monophony) to "Fugue" (polyphony). It is elaborately connected with Steinbeck's "Non-Teleological" thinking and "Group-Man" theory. Here we can read the growth of the writer's own mind and the high quality of his writing ability.

Chapter 10 deals with a critical essay on *East of Eden*. At over 600 pages length, it is the work closest to the title of this book. Steinbeck himself, as a story-teller, clearly mentions Ireland. The story-teller also depicts Irish-Americans. There are also many Celtic representations in this work. The depictions of "twilight" and "dawn" symbolizing "Celtic Twilight" and the frequent use of "oak trees" are widely seen throughout the work.

5

Steinbeck is responsible for the development of the story with careful calculations. The author of this book focuses on Cathy/Kate, an American Eve-like being, and makes an attempt to examine her from the starting point of whether she is really evil, because she is Eve who supports Adam in the Old Testament. The consequence was almost the same as that of women advocacy in feminist criticism. This is clarified in chapter 10. However, it is a consideration from the Celtic viewpoint, not from the feministic viewpoint.

Finally, chapter 11 deals with a critical essay on *The Winter of Our Discontent*. This work is said to be Steinbeck's last novel. In the author's opinion, in this work, Hawley as a protagonist, that is to say, Steinbeck himself appears as the "Druid." The "Druids," from generation to generation, have handed down their teaching to their sons, but they are destined to be betrayed by their sons. The modern Druid, Hawley also admonishes his son in this work, but he is also betrayed by his son Allen II in the form of "plagiarism."

Celtic representations of the "oak tree," "Hawley's Own Place" linking the sea and the land symbolizing "Tír na nÓg," "twilight" and "dawn" are well connoted as "Celtic Twilight." As is seen in other Steinbeck's works, the imagery of "gray" colors and "light" is also used extensively in this work, and plays an important role in the development of the story.

It is appropriate for the final work as a family heirloom that saves Hawley from suicide. The "Philosophers' Stone" appears as a talisman in this work. Steinbeck's interest in the Middle Ages is unparalleled and in this final novel, he describes the "Philosophers' Stone" as a result of alchemy that draws "immortality" in conjunction with the Legend of the Holy Grail. The story development of this work could be elaborately designed, thanks to the magic-like writing techniques by John Steinbeck himself. This is so much so in fact that his magic would influence the *Harry Potter* series based on the similar Celtic representations as are considered in Steinbeck Literature.

Part I

Chapter 1

Cup of Gold :
The Irish Pirate Henry Morgan and Steinbeck's Maiden Voyage as a Writer

Introduction

This chapter deals with Steinbeck's first work *Cup of Gold* (1929) from the perspective of Celtic culture. As has often been pointed out, the writer became interested in Sir Thomas Malory's *Le Morte d'Arthur* from an early age, especially when his mother read it to him. It can be considered that his writing style is influenced consciously or unconsciously by his mother's story-telling techniques.

In *Steinbeck: A Life in Letters* (1975), despite the demeaning statement that "I am finishing the Henry ms out of duty [*Cup of Gold*, a fictionalized biography of Henry Morgan, the pirate] but I have no hope of it any more" (*SLL* 11), Steinbeck wrote "for the purpose of getting all the autobiographical material out of my system," (*SLL* 17) defiantly saying, "I can write about other people" (*SLL* 17). In other words, this work was completed in the writer's own words, under the name of an "immature experiment" (*SLL* 17).

For Steinbeck himself, rather than making his debut in the literary world, it seems that he wanted to search for his own "identity" by introducing many "experimental" attempts in this work. The writer believes that what he wanted to identify as one of the elements of that "identity" was the "Celticity" of his ancestors. First of all, the beginning of the work is the Wales of England, a region where Celtic culture appears strongly. In addition, the Celtic fairy "Tylwyth Teg" (20) and the Celtic keyword "Druid" (21) are too numerous to mention.

The presence of Merlin can be mentioned as a particularly important character in this work. Merlin was one of the heroes for Steinbeck in early age and he appears also in this work as the same name of the character as in *Le Morte D'Arthur*, which was read to him by his mother since childhood. He is the Druid who is responsible for the secret of King Arthur's birth and advises Arthur on his fate, playing an important role closely related to the King. However, in this work, although he is depicted in a Druid-like manner, Merlin is "a fortune-teller with supernatural powers, not a magician" as is stated by Kiyoshi Nakayama (Nakayama 29 Translation Mine).

Because this work is Steinbeck's maiden work, and because the style has many elements of "immature experiment", it has not been highly evaluated by critics and researchers until now. Among them, Kingsbury highly evaluates this work and concludes that "Steinbeck's own language of the twentieth century and the language which mainly occurs in the direct speech of Steinbeck characters, which is an attempt to reproduce the language of seventeenth-century English" (Kingsbury 32-33), demonstrating Steinbeck's interest in the Middle Ages. The significance of this paper in pushing forward Steinbeck's research is extremely apparent. In addition, Timmerman was the first researcher to analyze "Holy Grail Legend" in earnest about this work. He states that "Apparent everywhere in the novel, finally, is the influence of the Grail Quest of Malory's *Morte D'Arthur*." (Timmerman 1986, 53-54)

Furthermore, as has often been mentioned in the past, the symbol of the "Cup of Gold" is none other than Panama. Lupack indicates Panama as "a city of great wealth" (Lupack 187) in his book. Couldn't this idea connect with the concept of "El Dorado"? It is true that Panama is not part of the Western United States, but as is also represented in "The Leader of the People" and in Steinbeck's main work *The Grapes of Wrath*, Steinbeck would think of projecting the motif of "Wild West" into his work. Could it be possible that *Cup of Gold* is the beginning? Furthurmore, would it be possible to regard this "Westering" on the same level as the quest of the "Holy Grail"?

As is mentioned above, the author desires to read this work from a new perspective of "Celtic Culture." In other words, the author would like to examine the "Celtic fairies" from the perspective of "twilight and dawn" when they are active. The author believes that analysis from these perspectives allows us to consider this novel more deeply.

From a different point of view, while considering the impact this novel had on a series of Hollywood blockbuster films, *Pirates of the Caribbean* (2003~) series were produced as if they were waiting for the 100th anniversary of Steinbeck's birth. The author would like to consider how to depict Henry Morgan, the main character of this work, which is said to be different from the original figure, and would also like to consider the significance of Steinbeck's writing modes of *Cup of Gold*.

I

In this work, the story begins with a depiction of a mystical night, reminiscent of Celtic magic.

> It was a preternatural night; a time when you might meet corpse-candles gliding along the road, or come upon the ghost of a Roman legion marching at a double quick to reach its sheltering city of Caerleon before the full storm broke. And the little misshapen beings of the hills would be searching out deserted badger holes to cover them from the night. (6)

The word "preternatural," which suggests the supernatural phenomenon symbolizing the Celts in this scene, the word "a Roman legion," which suggests the ancient Rome that was founded by driving out Gael and Gaul, as well as its ghost, and the use of the term "misshapen beings of the hills", which is reminiscent of Celtic fairies: these are very Celtic. Furthermore, the scene where Dafydd appears, inviting Henry to travel to the West Indies, and a description of "A faint sound of footsteps came along the highroad—a sound that might have been the wind or those walking things which cannot be seen" (7) are also a depiction reminiscent of a kind of "ghost." Therefore, it is thought that these Celtic depictions are helpful for the development of the story Steinbeck adds Celtic fairies to the story at several points to spice up the work. The first is Tylwyth Teg (20), a Celtic fairy which appears in the scene where Morgan goes to see the old sage Merlin before he leaves. According to Briggs, this fairy "very much admire golden-haired children, whom they carry away into Fairyland if they can. They live under green hills or under water and love dancing, singing and music like other fairies" (Briggs 150), so it can be interpreted that Elizabeth, who becomes Morgan's wife, is also the alter ego of this fairy. In particular, it can be said that all the women who influence Henry Morgan are depicted in sexual and fairy images.

First, we will consider how to portray Elizabeth as a fairy. In the Elizabeth's scene, music is one of the reasons. Music plays a role as background music in movies and dramas as well. In addition, it also has the effect of making the work more visually exciting. Young Elizabeth is portrayed as a fairy image: "a thing in mystery" (29), and when she reunites Henry Morgan in chapter 5, she assumes the form of a splendid woman. It can be interpreted that she has become an adult fairy.

> She [Elizabeth] looked shyly at him [Henry Morgan]. "I'll play for you, if you like,"she said.
> "Ye-es—you, do."
> "Now this is the Elves' Concourse. Listen! You can hear their little feet pattering on the grass. Everybody says it is sweet and pretty." Her fingers methodically worked at the strings.   (240-241)

A description of Henry Morgan admiring her beautiful fingers playing the Irish harp follows, but the song "Elves' Concourse" shown here is Irish Air. After this performance scene, Elizabeth, on a whim, proposes to Henry Morgan a temporary "marriage" (244) for the rest of her life.

The second reason why the author considers Elizabeth to be Tylwyth Teg, a fairy in human form, is that Elizabeth is described as a "a small girl with yellow hair" (45), which fits Briggs' description above.

The third reason is that it is easy to live with a human male as a husband for a certain period of time. Soon after Elizabeth has finally married Henry Morgan in the final chapter, her husband Henry will soon be in his dying bed, so the marriage period is considered to be very short.

This period may seem short, but it may be long. As Briggs said, "a hundred years of mortal time has passed in what he [Tylwth Teg] believed to be less than a hundred minutes" (Briggs150). By incorporating this idea, Steinbeck seems to adopt a method that allows the reader to freely think about the length of the marriage, the happiness of marriage, etc.

The ultimate scene to interpret Elizabeth as a fairy is the dying bed scene at the end of Henry Morgan's lying in the bed. It is a scene that Elizabeth expresses her true nature as a fairy.

> He [Henry Morgan] was still in a reclining position, and the Long grotto was sliding past him. Of a sudden, the movement stopped. He was surrounded by strange beings, having the bodies of children, and bulbous, heavy heads, but no faces. The flesh where their faces should have been solid and unbroken. These beings were talking in dry, raucous voices.
>
> (266-267)

The 'child-bodied' fairy shown here can be interpreted as either the Celtic fairy "Changelings" (Briggs 45-47) or the fairy Tylwyth Teg which appears in the work. The story teller continues the description in the dying scene of Henry Morgan as follows. It is as if Elizabeth alludes to the fairy Tylwyth Teg.

> Then he [Henry Morgan] saw that the little beings were crouching before an approaching form. They turned toward the form and cowered, and at

length fell on their knees before it and raised trembling arms in gestures of supplication.

Henry strained his attention toward the figure. Why, it was Elizabeth coming toward him—little Elizabeth, with golden hair and a wise young look on her face. She was girdled with cornflowers, and her eyes were strangely puzzled and bright. With a little start of surprise she noticed Henry.

"I am Elizabeth," she said.   (267-268)

The author considers not only Elizabeth but all women related to Morgan depicted as fairies.

Next we will consider Paulette, who appears as a Creole slave girl. Paulette has "a golden, golden skin" (89), worships "wood spirits" (89) and sings low chants "in honor of the Great Snake" (89).

The ultimate is described metaphorically as "a fairy to mend my [Morgan's] shoes" (93), reminiscent of the Celtic fairy "Lepracaun." This "shoe-mending fairy" Lepracaun is, according to Briggs, "the fairy shoemaker who is supposed to have won great wealth for himself" (Briggs 111), and also because Morgan's description that "his [Morgan's] hoard was not great enough" (88), it is unclear whether Morgan is counting on Paulette's fortune, or whether Paulette will contribute her fortune to Morgan but the two of them unite each other unconsciously.

Lastly, La Santa Loja in Panama ("The Red Saint" in English) is compared with the image of Elizabeth whom Morgan admired and fell in love with since childhood. This woman, who is depicted in parallel with Elizabeth, is represented as an admirable existence for Morgan.

As is mentioned in the introductory chapter, Steinbeck is thought to use the image of "Celtic Twilight," which W.B. Yeats uses as a symbol of the Celts, as one of the methods of story progression in this work. It is used to describe the conquest of Panama, La Santa Loja, and the feat of making Ysobel his own

14

woman.

Panama is conquered in chapter 4 in this novel. In his mystical depictions such as "a yellow dawn crept out of the little painted hills of Panama" (189), and especially in the description of Ysobel captured in chapter 6, the expression "gray twilight" (216-217) is used. It is used continuously and repeatedly. And this has a great implication of making Henry aware of himself and his thoughts on materialistic desires, leading to a scene depicting the greatest theme of this work.

> "I [Henry Morgan] find I am tired of all this bloodshed and struggle for things that I will not lie still, for articles that will not retain their value in my hands. It is horrible," he [Henry Morgan] cried. "I do not want anything any more. I have no no lusts, and my desires are dry and rattling. I have only a vague wish for peace and the time to ponder imponderable matters."
>
> "You will take no more cups of gold," she [Ysobel] cried. (222)

This scene seems to represent the main theme of this work. Panama, which Morgan portrays as a symbol of Cup of Gold, is mainly seen as "unsatisfactory conquests" (222). The depiction in this citation that "I have only a vague wish for peace and the time to ponder imponderable matters" is Morgan's greatest theme of self-enlightenment. He looked calmly at his ridiculous actions and was able to realize the foolishness of what he did just to get rich. After these ponderations, Morgan returned to the port town of Port Royal, where he was acclaimed by those around him for his feat, and even got married to Elizabeth, but he was not satisfied with what he had done. He was lying in vain in his dying bed.

II

Henry Morgan with his subordinates, conquering Cup of Gold, that is, Panama is the story of the Holy Grail Quest, as is mentioned in the introduction.

In Steinbeck's research, Lisca was the first to discuss the "Holy Grail Legend" in this work, but Timmerman gave a more detailed consideration. Timmerman, in his book, refers to "those specially marked by God for its [Grail's] pursuit" (Timmerman 1986, 54) and "the task of maintaining order in the kingdom" (Timmerman 1986, 54).

The real name of La Santa Roja (Spanish for The Red Saint), a mysterious woman whom Morgan met in Panama, and Elizabeth, whom Morgan has admired since childhood, is Ysobel (Spanish for Elizabeth), and this is a "last, futile attempt to ground his [Morgan's] dream in attainable reality" (Timmerman 1986, 54). Steinbeck himself states that "Malory's self-character would be Launcelot. But being an honest man he found faults in himself, faults of vanity, faults of violence, faults even of disloyalty and these would naturally find their way into his dream character" (*SLL* 553). Kimie Imura, a prominent researcher of Celtic culture, seems to support this Steinbeck's idea.

> Malory, like the French writer Chrétien de Troyes, did not make Sir Percivale the subject, but put Sir Galahad in the main. However, Sir Galahad is the alter ego of Sir Launcelot, who lives in this world from beginning to end, and it is Sir Launcelot that forms and concludes the story.
>
> (Imura 307 Translation Mine)

There are many literary works with the motif of the legend of the Holy Grail, so the author of this book will refrain from adding considerations to each one here, but in this work, *Le Morte D'Arthur* is a hint for the development of the story. There is a scene where "Captain Morgan sat behind a broad table of which each leg was a curious carved lion, and around him, seated on stools, were the thirty leaders of his fleet and army" (163); Morgan is clearly considered to be King Arthur. Furthermore, the number "thirty" in this scene is a phonological association with the number "thirteen."

As is mentioned in the introduction, in order to interpret Steinbeck's works from the perspective of Celtic culture, we have to do an analysis of *The Mabinogion*. This is because *The Mabinogion* is an introduction to Celtic culture written in medieval Welsh. It is believed that the so-called "Arthurian Legend" is based on the romance story contained in this, and in *Steinbeck: A Life in Letters (SLL)*, we can read the fact that Steinbeck himself is considered to be quite familiar with this *The Mabinogion (SLL 360)*.

Satoko Morino mentions in her book that "the origin of the legend of the Holy Grail is Perceval" (Morino 485). This Perceval is Percivale in the so-called "Arthurian Legend." From this fact, the hero of "Holy Grail Legend" is considered to be Percivale, and simply by applying this scheme, Morgan, the hero of *Cup of Gold*, is thought to conquer Panama following Percivale. Namely, in *King Arthur and His Knights of the Round Table*, a boys' and girls' edition of *Le Morte D'Athur*, in the chapter "The End of the Quest for the Grail," Percivale finds the "Lady Blanchefleur" (French for "White-Flower Lady"). She eventually marries Percivale, after which Percivale becomes 'king' (Green 310-311). This story development is very similar to that in *Cup of Gold*, in which Morgan reunites Elizabeth and Ysobel, and gets married to the former and gets blissful wealth from the latter. Therefore, in the author's opinion, the hero depicted in "Holy Grail Legend" motif in *Cup of Gold* is not Launcelot but Percivale, also known as Perceval, shown in *The Mabinogion*.

Seen in this way, the fact that some of Steinbeck's early works set in France can be considered excellent as one of the themes of the writer's writing. The title of this novel was changed later, but Steinbeck was unconsciously attracted to the title of the uncompleted work *"The Green Lady" (SLL 14)*, which would be relevant to the "Lady Blanchefleur" that Percivale was looking for. An image very similar to this is associated with the color image of the word "green" lady. This is based on the fact that the writer Steinbeck would have used the original hero of *The Mabinogion*. The author believes that this is a proof that Steinbeck continued to stick to the title conscious of Percivale and his story.

Morino continues, "A 'graal' made of pure gold inlaid with precious gems and emitting a strong light means 'hollow dish' as a common noun (DEAF), but the contents are sacred rice cakes. So, it is the only food that has extended the life of the Fisher King" (Morino 486 Translation Mine). The image of this chalice, especially the golden imagery, matches the title of the work *Cup of Gold* ("Golden Chalice"), and the Fisher King is thought to be Pwyll.

Panama is depicted as a symbol of "wealth" in this work, and is so-called "El Dorado." According to Turner, "wave after wave is rolling westward; the real Eldorado is still farther on" (Turner 13), and the dream of "exploiting the west" gave birth to so-called American dream.

In *Cup of Gold*, there appears an expression of "Puritanism" (163). It is just before the conquest of Panama in the story, and just after the depiction imitating "Knights of the Round Table" motif. Therefore, ideologically, the expansion of the west toward California was similar to the "determination of peace and war with the Indians, the regulation of Indian trade, the purchase of Indian lands, and the creation and government of new settlements as a security against the Indians" (Turner 10) at the time, and the act of oppressing Panama and also the people there was on the same level. However, in *Cup of Gold*, as Turner points out that "the attempts to limit the boundaries, to restrict land sales and settlement, and to deprive the West of its share of political power were all in vain" (Turner 19), Morgan could seemingly attain such power control. Internal conquest will not be possible, and the story ends without Morgan's satisfaction.

Considering this, the acquisition of "El Dorado" was achieved in the course of the struggle against the Indians at that time. It can be said that it is one of the "Holy Grail Legends" that has been achieved.

We can also read the conquest of Panama in terms of Celtic culture. It is a country located in the Caribbean Sea to the west of Ireland, and the origin of the "Westering" is that Puritans from England traveled to America. Panama, located in the Caribbean Sea, could be thought of as a Celtic Utopia, "Tír na nÓg."

According to Delaney, it is "the Land of the Young, as green and sunny as

Eden" (Delaney 85). Therefore, the conquest of Panama also meant reaching Morgan's utopia, "Tír na nÓg."

By the way, at the time of the publication of this work, it seems that the writer Steinbeck had not a few ideas in common in 1920s. This would be because of the background of the decades, or because of the influence of other writers, such as Fitzgerald's *The Great Gatsby* (1925). One of the ideas is the concept of "decadence." In other words, "dreams and wealth once acquired" fall into the abyss, leaving only despair behind. Gatsby also gains wealth, but falls out of love and chooses to die.

In Steinbeck's later short story "The Leader of the People" (1938), Jody's grandfather, old man Gitano, lamented, "No place to go, Jody. Every place is taken. But that's not the worst—no, not the worst. Westering has died out of the people. Westering isn't a hunger any more. It's all done. It is finished" (303). Steinbeck's own idea that "Dreams, wealth and fame will crumble and degenerate" is a major theme of *Cup of Gold*.

III

Steinbeck had a strong desire to make *Cup of Gold* into a movie. The work was published in 1929, the year of outbreak of the Great Depression.

The 1920s was a period of great development for the film industry. *Jazz Singer* (1927), the first "talkie," revolutionized the film industry. In addition, S.M. Eisenstein's representative work *Battleship Potemken* (1925), which was the first in the world to use "Montage Theory," also shown in the United States, and the famous actor Douglas Fairbanks starred in *The Mask of Zoro* (1920). It was also a decade of film development, such as adventure action dramas and above all, the success of the silent movie actor Charles Chaplin.

In such an era, Steinbeck himself made works with an awareness of action adventures, and he was aware of the movie adaptation of *Cup of Gold*. Even in 1949, twenty years after its publication, Timmerman wrote, "he [Steinbeck] still thought *Cup of Gold* had smashing possibilities as a film" (Timmerman 1990, 22).

Coincidentally or by chance, Steinbeck had the opportunity of the 100th anniversary of his birth to having made it to reality. His dream has finally come true. It is *Pirates of the Caribbean* series (five films in total, the sixth film is currently in preparation), which began as an idea and concept in 2002, has been serialized since 2003, and continues to be produced as a movie. The original of this movie is said to be *Monkey Island* (an entertainment as a TV game), but there are many parts that are very similar to *Cup of Gold*: story progression, characters, and even locations.

The first *Pirates of the Caribbean: The Curse of the Black Pearl* was released in 2003, the 101st anniversary of Steinbeck's birth. A woman named Elizabeth appears as the heroine in the characters.

This Elizabeth appears until the third *Pirates of the Caribbean: At World's End* (2007). In *Cup of Gold*, the eponymous Elizabeth is portrayed as the hero's eternal heroine. In addition, the location of the stage is "Port Royal," which matches the location of the stage of the final chapter of *Cup of Gold*.

The fourth work, *Pirates of the Caribbean: On Stranger Tides* (2011), is based on the Celtic folktale "Fountain of Youth" suggested in the introduction. Also, in this 4th film, there appears so-called "Blackbeard," the real pirate Edward Teach, who competes with the fictional main character Jack Sparrow. Steinbeck also mentions this "Blackbeard" (117) in *Cup of Gold*, and the connection between the two works is very interesting.

Looking at it this way, it could be said that the *Pirates of the Caribbean* series is heavily influenced by Steinbeck's *Cup of Gold*.

Although there are currently no papers or criticism comparing the two, the author claims that since the production company of *Pirates of the Caribbean* is the Walt Disney Company, the Irish-American Walt Disney and Steinbeck's way of representing Celtic culture have been linked to each other. It seems that the blood relationship between the two works unconsciously connects them.

In conclusion, *Cup of Gold* may be a crude work of Steinbeck just embarking on his maiden voyage as a writer, but as we have seen, it is a pioneering adventure novel with his own keen insight. It has had an extraordinary impact on the Hollywood movie *Pirates of the Caribbean* series and the Japanese ocean adventure romance *manga* series, *ONE PIECE* (1999-). Overall, it can be said that *Cup of Gold* is worthy of a Nobel Prize-winners first novel, and that, for a virgin work, it is an excellent work that fully anticipates the future of Steinbeck's writing activities.

Works Cited and Referred Bibliographies

Anonymous, trans. Lady C. Guest. *The Mabinogion, From the Welsh of the Llyfr Coch O Hergest*. London: Bernard Quaritch, 1877.

Brekilien, Yann. *La Mythologie Celtique*. Paris: Édition du Rocher, 1993.

Briggs, Katharine. *Abbey Lubbers, Banshees and Boggarts*. London: Routledge, 2003.

Cunliffe, Barry. *The Celtic World*. London: McCraw-Hill Book Company, 1979.

Curran, Bob. *The Creatures of Celtic Myth*. London: Cassel & Co., 2000.

Curtin, Jeremiah. *Myths and Folktales of Ireland*. New York: Dover Publications, 1975.

Delaney, Frank. *Legends of the Celts*. London: Hodder & Stoughton, 1989.

Frazer, James George. *The Golden Bough: A Study in Magic and Religion*. New York: Oxford University Press, 1994.

Green, Miranda J. *Celtic Myths*. London: British Museum Press, 1993.

_____. *Exploring the World of Druids*. London: Thames & Hudson Ltd., 1997.

Green, Roger Lancelyn. *King Arthur and His Knights of the Round Table: Retold out of the old Romances*. New York: Penguin Books Ltd., 1953.

James, Simon. *Exploring the World of the Celts*. London: James and Hudson Ltd., 1995.

Kingsbury, Stewart A. "Steinbeck's Use of Dialect and Archaic Language in the *Cup of Gold*" in *Steinbeck Newsletter*. Volume II, Number 2. Ed. Tetsumaro Hayashi et al. Muncie: Ball State University, 1969.

Lisca, Peter. *The Wide World of John Steinbeck*. Reprinted, New York: Viking Press, 1981.

Lupack, Alan and Barbara Tepa Lupack. *King Arthur in America*. Cambridge: D.S.Brewer, 1999.

Malory, Sir Thomas. *Le Morte D'Arthur*. Caxton Edition. London: Macmillan & Co., Limited, 1912.

[Imura, Kimie, trans. *The Story of King Arthur* IV. Tokyo: Chikuma Shobo, 2006]

Steinbeck, John. *Cup of Gold*. New York: Robert M. McBRIDE COMPANY, 1929.

_____. *In Dubious Battle*. New York: Covici-Friede, 1936.

_____. "The Leader of the People" in *The Long Valley*. New York: Viking Press, 1938.

_____. *The Grapes of Wrath*. New York: Viking Press, 1939.

_____. *Steinbeck: A Life in Letters*. Ed. Elaine Steinbeck and Robert Wallsten. New York: Viking Press, 1975.

Timmerman, John H. *John Steinbeck's Fiction: The Aesthetics of the Road Taken*. Norman: University of Oklahoma Press, 1986.

_____. *The Dramatic Landscape of Steinbeck's Short Stories*. Norman: University of Oklahoma Press, 1990.

Turner, Frederick. J. *The Frontier in American History*. New York: Frederick Turner Classics, 1921.

Zakzek, Iain. *Chronicles of the Celts*. London: Collins & Brown Ltd., 1996

Hara, Kiyoshi. *Spiritual History of Ethnic Origins: Brittany and Modern France*. Tokyo: Iwanami Shoten, 2003

Kimizuka, Junichi Supervised and Edited by The Society of English Studies. *America in the 1920s: The Light and the Shadow of the Roaring Twenties*. Tokyo: Kinseido, 2004.

Kimura, Masatoshi, ed. *65 Chapters for Understanding the Celts*. Tokyo: Akashi Shoten, 2018.

Morino, Satoko, ed. and trans. *Welsh Translation of the Original Mabinogion*. Tokyo: Hara Shobo, 2019.

Nakayama, Kiyoshi. *A Study of Steinbeck Literature: California Period*. Osaka: Kansai University Press, 1989.

Nakazawa, Shinichi, Mayumi Tsuruoka et al., *Celtic Religion Druidism*. Tokyo: Iwanami

Shoten, 1997.

Tsuruoka, Mayumi and Kazuo Matsumura. *Illustrated Celtic History: Reading Culture, Art, and Mythology.* Tokyo: Kawade Shobo Shinsha, 1999.

Green, Miranda J. *Dictionary of Celtic Myth and Legend.* London: Thames and Hudson Limited, 1992.

The Oxford English Dictionary. First Edition. Oxford: At the Clarendon Press, 1933.

Chapter 2

The Pastures of Heaven:
Various Curses Caused by the Celtic Fairies

Introduction

Many scholars and critics point out that in Steinbeck's *The Pastures of Heaven*, there exists something of a "curse." This "curse" exerts its influence throughout the book and is deeply related to the psychology and behavior of the characters in this work.

In Japan Noboru Shimomura, the scholar who first referred to this "curse," analyzed it and concluded that "Steinbeck showed his earlier interest both in man's primitive fear of misfortunes caused by the so-called curse, and in the irony caused by the gap between appearance and reality" (20-21) in his study titled *A Study of John Steinbeck: Mysticism in His Novels*.

Peter Lisca pointed out that "If it is kept in mind that although the Munroes are an 'evil cloud,' as Steinbeck puts it, they never commit 'a really malicious act nor an act [. . .] not dictated by honorable expediency or out and out altruism,' it becomes obvious that these stories are given further unity by their common preoccupation with irony—the evil results of the Munroes' innocent actions" (59-60), and he concluded that "Each story revolves around this kind of irony" (62), in *The Wide World of John Steinbeck*.

The storyteller says "Bert Munroe came to the Pastures of Heaven because he was tired of battling with a force which invariably defeated him. He had engaged in many enterprises and every one had failed, not through any shortcoming on Bert's part, but through mishaps, which, if taken alone, were accidents. Bert saw all the accidents together and they seemed to him the acts of a Fate malignant to his success" (20-21). According to this description, the "curse" in this work seems to be something of "a Fate" and something of "an

25

Accident."

In this paper, I will analyze the "curse" as something formed of Fate and Accident underlying this work from a Celtic viewpoint: consciously or unconsciously, it is true that Steinbeck's attitude toward writing, the formation of his thinking and character formed in his childhood were mainly influenced by his mother, of Irish origin, who taught him how to read and write. Therefore, one hypothesis might be that in *The Pastures of Heaven* also, some Celtic elements could be embodied in some way or other.

I

The "evil-cloud," as Steinbeck put it, is considered to be a "curse" exerting its influence throughout the story and its essence seems to have its origin in Celtic Fairy Tales based on Celtic Culture. Manfred (Manny) in the second chapter. Tularecito in the fourth chapter, Hilda in the fifth chapter and the dead baby in the eleventh chapter may be described as "changelings." Changelings, according to Katherine Briggs, are "the things that were left to take the place of human babies or nursing mothers stolen by the fairies" (Briggs 45); they are very feeble and strange. It is also reported that they sometimes have a unique power beyond humans. Manfred in the second chapter was "a serious child of seven, whose face was pinched and drawn by adenoids" (20) and Hilda in the fifth chapter "had begun to tell lies" (82) caused by her neurotic breakdown. The second baby Alicia conceived in the eleventh chapter "is dead" (262) before its birth.

As to these "changelings," Steinbeck depicts the so-called half-witted Tularecito in the fourth chapter powerfully by making Miss Morgan (considered his mother's other self) tell about the lack of Fairy Culture in America: "part of America's cultural starvation was due to its boorish and superstitious denial of the existence of fairies" (68).

Chapter four may be said to be the chapter in which Steinbeck depicts fairies in the Celtic Folklore most effectively. First of all, the appearance of Tularecito meaning "a little frog" sounds weird and each syllable of the word seems to have its strange and unique effect on the story itself. Tularecito himself sounds like a gnome and one of the changelings.

> And sure enough he [Pancho] found a tiny child lying in a clear place in the sage. It was about three months old by the size of it, Pancho thought. He picked it up and lighted a match to see just what kind of a thing he had found, when—horror of horrors!—the baby winked maliciously and said in a deep voice. "Look! I have very sharp teeth." (58)

The storytelling of Steinbeck about the weirdness and the horror of Tularecito reaches something of a climax when the writer uses the technique of having the boy Tularecito come to listen to the stories earnestly for the first time after Miss Morgan tells the fairy tale of the gnome. Therefore, Tularecito in particular is truly a changeling of the gnome sent to the human world as the writer suggests to us in the cited part below.

> Now a change came over Tularecito. Gradually, as Miss Morgan read about elves and brownies, fairies, pixies, and changelings, his interest centered and his busy pencil lay idly in his hand. Then she read about gnomes, and their lives and habits, and he dropped his pencil altogether and leaned toward the teacher to intercept the words. (68)

This description shows that Tularecito recognized his own 'identity' as a gnome after all, leading to him searching for the gnome in the orchard as a climax.

> Bert Munroe walked out before breakfast to look at his trap again, and he found the open hole. "The little devils!" he cried. "They're keeping it up, are they? I'll bet Manny *is* in it after all."
>
> He studied the hole for a moment and then began to push dirt into it with

the side of his foot. A savage growl spun him around. Tularecito came charging down upon him, leaping like a frog on his long legs, and swinging his shovel like a club. (76)

We must notice the words "I'll bet Manny *is* in it after all" uttered and misunderstood unconsciously by Bert Munroe. As I have already pointed out, this seems to be a scene in which Steinbeck describes Manfred on the same level as Tularecito as one of the changelings.

Alice in the third chapter is a daughter of "Shark" Wicks. She has been very beautiful from childhood but as the Wicks "knew that their lovely daughter was an incredibly stupid, dull and backward little girl" (34), we might put her into the same category as Tularecito and Manfred, as changelings. However, her beauty is so full of mysticism that she also seems to be put into another category: the category of fairies called "selkies."

The reason may be that after she turned fourteen years old, "Shark" Wicks extraordinarily rules her in everything. He interferes with his daughter in everything in order to protect her purity. He "knew the dates better than she did. 'Is she all right?' he asked wolfishly" (36).

According to Briggs, the female selkies were "content with their own husbands, but they used to come on to the smooth sands to dance, and they would take off skins and lay them aside, and quite often it happened that a mortal would see them and fall in love with one. Then he had only to steal away her skin and she was a captive and was forced in the end to marry him" (Briggs 142). In this chapter when "Shark" Wicks left Salinas for his aunt's funeral and his ruling power did not influence his daughter. Alice danced with Jimmie Munroe for the first time at the school dance. And at this school dance Alice's would-be husband Jimmie and Alice kissed each other and Alice danced with him and lost her purity after she "had taken off her coat" (45). That is, Alice, if considered as a "selkie," would never be allowed to return back to the sea of 'Purity' without "her coat" (45) and is described ironically as having lost her purity.

Junius Maltby and his son Robbie also remind us of something with Celtic background, although the "changeling" image and its description cannot be found in this chapter. Robbie is not a changeling because he "grew up gravely" (113). His manners and his way of leading a life grow looser and looser owing to his father's idleness. This is so much so in fact that something of a hermitage they live in looks like the dwellings of fairies. This seems to have something to do with Celtic culture as I said above.

> Fences reclined tiredly on the ground under an overload of bramble. The fruit trees stretched bare branches clear of a forest of weeds. Wild blackberry vines clambered up the apple trees; squirrels and rabbits bolted under her [Morgan's] feet, and soft voiced doves flew away with whistling wings. In a tall wild pear tree a congress of bluejays squawked a cacophonous argument. (127)

Other things with Celtic background can be seen here: the relevance between Junius Maltby in the sixth chapter and Billy Duffy in the Irish folktale "The Three Wishes" as to laziness; the relevance between the Lopez sisters in the seventh chapter and the Irish folktale "The Doomed Sisters" as to their destined situations; the relevance between Molly Morgan in the eighth chapter and Morgan Le Fay in *Le Morte D'Arthur* as to both of them being full of mystery; the relevance between the punishment of death told in the ninth chapter and the Irish folktale "Daniel O'Connell" as to the Irish fondness of the murder fantasy of death; and the relevance between Pat Humbert in the tenth chapter and the Celtic myth of Naoise in the Ulster Myths as to the failure of the accomplishment of love.

Considering and analyzing these intertextualities brings to our attention some Celtic characteristics Steinbeck uses to make known his identity of his Irish stock. Junius Maltby in the sixth chapter is the one "sometimes they [the people of the valley] hated with the loathing busy people have for lazy ones, and sometimes they envied his laziness" (110), and Billy Duffy in "The Three Wishes" is "the best hand at doing nothing in all Europe" (Carleton 292). Both of the two are driven away from their homeland toward the end of the story because of their laziness.

Rosa and Maria in the seventh chapter and Jane and Anne in "The Doomed Sisters" are cursed and doomed from the beginning, although there is a small link between the two stories. Rosa and Maria are forced to close their doors and are also driven away from their homeland by Bert Munroe's innocent joking words, "Did you [Mrs. Munroe] see that old woman-killer with Maria Lopez?" (154), while Jane is caught by an old woman who "'suddenly started out of a thicket" (Maturin 34) and has been ill since then. Anne, the elder sister, is destined to get married to a bridegroom with a face as "pale as that of a corpse" (Maturin 40). This Irish tale is therefore something of a horror fantasy, an element which is one of the Celtic characteristics. However, both of the two stories have an incessant theme of Curse and Fate.

As is pointed out by many scholars and critics, Molly Morgan in this work and Morgan Le Fay in *Le Morte D'Arthur* have some similarities. Molly Morgan is described as a woman full of mystery. The storyteller's descriptions such as "Miss Morgan, the new teacher, was very young and very pretty; too young and dangerously pretty" (65-66) and "She [Molly Morgan]'s too pretty to be around that fool of a Bill" (177) are such cases in point. Moreover, she is depicted as a woman who hopes to conceal her bitter past and to delete it from her memory full of enigma.

The ways of describing Morgan Le Fay, King Arthur's sister, are also full of mystery, which is an everlasting theme in *Le Morte D'Arthur*. The description, "When she [Morgan] saw that she must be overtaken, she shaped herself, horse and man, by enchantment, unto a great marble stone" (Malory 86), will make us recognize that she has some kind of supernatural power and in the last scene that King Arthur was hurt and was brought into a ship, there were three queens and "that one was King Arthur's sister queen Morgan Le Fay" (Malory 481) who took good care of him. This description will call to mind Steinbeck's mother, of Irish origin.

The murder fantasy is said to be one of the favorite tendencies of the Celts and this "murder" theme materializes itself in the ninth chapter of this work and in the Irish folktale "Daniel O'Connell." Raymond Banks in the ninth chapter becomes excited to hear of the punishment of death, but with the appearance of Bert Munroe he happened to realize his ambivalent state of mind: the like and the dislike of the punishment of death.

The protagonist in "Daniel O'Connell" is a well-known political leader Daniel O'Connell himself and this folktale is full of wit and humor. This story also deals with the punishment of death but the theme is expressed with humor. Daniel's words, "Ye [Lordship] can't, according to English law as printed in that book in black and white, sentence a man to be both burned, beheaded, and hung. Prisoner, prisoner, you're free at liberty to go free" (MacManus 94), are full of wit and humor, although it is far from the Celts' fondness of murder und death fantasy.

Pat Humbert in the tenth chapter is somewhat reminiscent of Naoise, who loved Dréidre but whose love was not fulfilled by their fate and destiny. Like Naoise in the Ulster Myth, Pat is described as a decent gentleman but is described as rather a shy character in this work. His character is characterized by the description "Pat never became a part of any group he joined. Rather he hung on the fringes, never speaking unless he was addressed" (238). Owing to this shy character Pat seems not to be destined to win the love of Mae, a daughter of Bert Munroe, by his fate and the Munroe family as a catalyst.

II

In the Celtic culture, there was an old traditional custom of 'druidism' by which the Celts worshiped the oak tree as a god. The druids built sacred places in the woods, held ceremonial worshiping of the oak tree and secluded themselves in a mountain hermitage. In *The Pastures of Heaven*, as the story develops, an oak tree seems to appear as a Celtic metaphor and as druidism underlying the Celtic culture. There are so many of them in this work and I will pick up two significant "Oak Trees" as a metaphor.

First, as to the bars put on some of the windows of Hilda's house, it is stated that "Guess what they [the people in the house] got on some of the windows—bars! Not iron bars, but big thick oak ones" (87). Those bars are used to force Hilda into a serious nervous breakdown to stay in the house. The old Celtic superstition indicates that they have to keep the doors and the windows of the house open in order for fairies to return the original body as a human being through these openings and, if it is in fact based on this superstition, for Hilda to get well again. However, in the last part of the fifth chapter she died after all without realizing her dream of getting healthy for the reason that all the windows were shut with oak bars! Therefore this seems to be considered a tragedy based on Celtic superstition.

Second, an "Oak Tree" appears in the earlier part of the eleventh chapter when Richard Whiteside came to the Pastures of Heaven in the 1850s and heard the so-called "Divine Revelation."

> He [Richard Whiteside] looked into the sky, but it was clean of both birds and clouds. Then the breeze that blows over the hills in the evening sprang up. The oaks made furtive little gestures toward the valley, and on the hillside a tiny whirlwind picked up a few leaves and flung them forward. Richard chuckled, "Answer! Many a fine city was founded because of a hint from the gods no more broad than that." (247)

This is the part closely resembling the scene in which Brigham Young led his people to Utah in 1847 and exclaimed "This is our Land!" Similarly the words Richard Whiteside uttered signify the Pastures of Heaven as an "American

Pastoral" and the "Oaks" as "druidism."

Now we should take a look at the time of occurrence of "curses" in this work. See the following table below. The "curses" in this work mostly occur at dawn, in the late afternoon, in the twilight, or at night. I will consider these facts in the light of the Celtic culture.

The first part of this work begins with a symbolic depiction of a herd of deer browsing on "a long valley floored with green pasturage" (2) and the appearance of deer and of the long valley symbolizes the fairyland suggestive of the countryside in Ireland. A deer is Phouka in this first chapter that brings a Spanish corporal "good fortune and health and happiness" (Briggs 133).

Originally there was no tale like "Genesis" in the Celtic myths. Therefore it seems that Celtic myths were born in the Mother Earth. In this sense there appear many fairies including changelings, selkies, and also the gnomes Tularecito searched for in the holes of the orchard in the last part of the fourth chapter.

Imura said as follows:

> As for the strong faith in the Sun as a symbol of immortality, a direction of its vector is contrary to that of the normal: not that "The sun rises in the morning and sets in the evening" but that "The sun that set in the evening rises in the darkness of "Death" and the following day, will rise with the meaning of "Reincarnation," as it were, "from Death to Reincarnation" and "from Darkness to Light." (Kamata and Tsuruoka 47; my translation)

Samhain, the beginning of the Celtic Year and the coming of the Dark, is a keyword to a Celtic calendar and it seems to have a close link to fairies. Toulson said that "This [*Samhain*] is the thinnest time of the year, the season at which the veil between time and eternity can easily become transparent. It is now, when the darkness overtakes the light" (Toulson 21). Danaher clarified the existence of fairies by claiming that "Our [The Celts'] ancients looked on the night as the end of the year's growth, and fairies were let loose to visit every growing plant and with their breath blast berries and hedge-rows, field blossoms, ragworts and late thistles" (Danaher 200). The phrase "veil between time and eternity" by Toulson is something of a crevice of time in *Samhaim* and the Celts seemed to think this crevice of time with dim light symbolizes something of mysticism. That is, at this crevice of time, especially at dawn or in the twilight, it is supposed that many fairies hover about around them. Therefore, one hypothesis may be that *The Pastures of Heaven* is full of mysticism based on this Celtic superstition. Almost all the times of occurrence of the "curses" in this work are at dawn, in the late afternoon, in the twilight especially in the twelfth chapter, or at night as I describe in the table below. These are the hours with dim light or with no light, and as to the hours with dim light, W. B. Yeats creates an image of "Tír na nÓg" in the poem titled "Into the Twilight" of *The Celtic Twilight*: as a "Utopia" beyond space and time of the Celts.

III

W. B. Yeats, a poet very popular in Ireland, reconstructed Celtic folktales and legends as Folk Literature and contributed to the so-called "Irish Restoration" in terms of Nationalism.

In his letter to John O'Leary in 1892. he proclaimed his idea about Irish Nationalism by stating "Let them [the projected series] be done by good Irishmen who can write and they will be read" (Wade 203) and in this situation he made a strong pledge as to writing fairy tales, stating also in his letter that "My [Yeats'] own *Irish Fairy Stories* will be out very soon now with two drawings by Jack" (Wade 199).

He published *The Celtic Twilight* in 1893. As we are aware, this work is not so much a story or a collection of Celtic folktales or legends as writing which incorporated his views into original folktales or legends.

Chapter 39 in *The Celtic Twilight* is a short story titled "By the Roadside," in which there is one excellent scene with the best twilight image of "the spiritually virtuous Celt" (Sugiyama 76); in the Irish air one old man singing attracts the people and their horses around him.

> The voices melted into the twilight, and were mixed into the trees, and when I thought of the words they too melted away, and were mixed into the generations of men. Now it was a phrase, now it was an attitude of mind, an emotional form, that had carried my memory to older verses, or even to forgotten mythologies. (Yeats 138)

The Celtic fairy tales representative of the Celtic tradition are said to have a great influence on the literary movement. Ben Bulben in Sligo where Yeats spent his boyhood, and his *The Celtic Twilight*, a collection of fairy tales which an old man Paddy Flynn talked about in his leaking hermitage, were milestones; according to Ellmann, "He [Yeats] makes a collection of fairy tales in which he asserts that the Irish peasants, because of their distance from the centers of the Industrial Revolution, have preserved a *rapport* with the spiritual world and its fairy denizens which has elsewhere disappeared" (Ellmann 119). This statement will lead to Sugiyama's indication that "Out of the twilight, he [Yeats] began to write of contemporary social and political events in Ireland" (Sugiyama 6-7) by depicting "the hidden Ireland" (Sugiyama 6).

Ben Bulben, which W. B. Yeats used as a setting for writing *The Celtic Twilight*, has been a mental image for him from his childhood. The Pastures of Heaven (Corral de Tierra) is also influential in Steinbeck's mind. This is so much so in fact that we can say Steinbeck uses the Pastures of Heaven. Corral de Tierra, as his symbolic setting to the same degree Ben Bulben is used by Yeats. These two will make us perceive the similar sense of place of landscape and atmosphere.

Chapters	Victims of Curse	Catalysts of Curse	Time of Occurrence	Suggestive of Celtic folktales & legends
1	A Spanish corporal	The Pastures of Heaven	Late afternoon	phouka=deer
2	Manfred	T. B. Allen	Night	changelings
3	Alice	"Shark" Wicks	Night	selkies
4	Tularecito	Bert Munroe	Night	gnome
5	Hilda	Helen Van Deventer	Night	changelings
6	Junius Malthy	John Whiteside	Night	"Three Wishes"
7	Lopez sisters	Bert Munroe	Afternoon	"Doomed Sisters"
8	Molly Morgan	Bert Munroe	Night	Morgan Le Fay
9	Raymond Banks	Bert Munroe	Night	"Daniel O'Connell"
10	Pat Humbert	Bert Munroe	Night	Naoise
11	The Whitesides	Bert Munroe	Dawn	changelings
12	One old man	The Pastures of Heaven	Twilight	*The Celtic Twilight*

Conclusion

We have witnessed and analyzed John Steinbeck's *The Pastures of Heaven* featuring Irish Fairy tales and Folktales. In this last chapter I will state some conclusions in the light of this Celtic viewpoint and American Culture.

The economic situations were much worse than bad been expected at that time after the Great Depression in California. This phenomenon is revealed clearly by Gregory's description that "From the start of the Depression, state officials tried to discourage newcomers from heading west. Anxious to head off the migration of job seekers, authorities spread the word that economic conditions in California were deplorable" (Gregory 22).

Therefore, the economic conditions were also deplorable when Steinbeck began to think of writing this novel for the first time as *Dissonant Symphony* in his letter to his friend Carl Wilhelmson in the early 1930s stating that "I am putting five hours every day on the rewriting of this one and in the evenings I have started another [*Dissonant Symphony*]" (Steinbeck and Wallsten 22). Nevertheless, the writer seemed not to worry about the deplorable state of the Californian economy, judging from the following statement of the same letter. "I have the time and the energy and it gives me pleasure to work" (Steinbeck and Wallsten 22).

It was only on the eighth of May in 1931 when Steinbeck disclosed the structure of *The Pastures of Heaven*, stating in his letter to Mavis McIntosh that "They [People in Corral de Tierra] were ordinary people, ill-educated but honest and as kindly as any. In fact, in their whole history I cannot find that they hove committed a really malicious act nor an act which was not dictated by honorable expediency or out-and-out altruism" (Steinbeck and Wallsten 42-43) and added that "I think the plan at least falls very definitely in the aspects of American life category" (Steinbeck and Wallsten 43).

Whatever his idea and attitude towards writing this collection of short stories might be, it was sure that Steinbeck tried to disclose these "aspects of American life category" by describing Californians in their ways of life and their economic situations during and after the Great Depression as a monster of industrialization and capitalism. In this sense the Pastures of Heaven (Corral de Tierra) was an "American Pastoral" where "wilderness" and "civilization" co-existed and it seemed a hazard to Steinbeck that his homeland would be at the mercy of this "monster."

To conclude, as we have seen. *The Pastures of Heaven* is a great milestone of John Steinbeck's writing career where we are able to notice the 'curse' and 'decadence' in the Pastures of Heaven (Corral de Tierra) as an "American

Pastoral" suffering under the agricultural situation during and after the Great Depression in his country.

Works Cited

Briggs, Katherine. *Abbey Lubbers, Banshees and Boggarts*. London: Routledge, 2003.

Carlton, William. "The Three Wishes." *Irish Folktales*. Ed. Henry Glassie. New York: Pantheon Books, 1985.

Danaher, Kevin. *The Year in Ireland: Irish Calendar Customs*. Dublin: Mercier Press, 1972.

Ellmann, Richard. *Yeats: The Man and the Masks*. London: W. W. Norton, 1978.

Kamata, Toji and Mayumi Tsuruoka eds. *Keruto to Nippon (Celt and Japan)*. Tokyo: Kadokawa Shoten, 2000.

Gregory, James N. *American Exodus: The Dust Bowl Migration and Okie Culture in California*. London: Oxford UP, 1989.

Lisca, Peter. *The Wide World of John Steinbeck*, 1958. New York: Gordian Press, 1981.

MacManus, Donegal Seumas. "Daniel O'Connell" in *Irish Folktales*, ed. Henry Glassie. New York: Pantheon Books, 1985.

Malory, Sir Thomas. *Le Morte D'Arthur*. The Text of Caxton. London: Macmillan, 1912.

Maturin, Charles Robert. "The Doomed Sisters" in *Great Irish Tales of Horror: A Treasury of Fear*, Ed. Peter Haining. London: Souvenir Press, 1995.

Shimomura, Noboru. *A Study of John Steinbeck: Mysticism in His Novels*. Tokyo: Hokuseido Press, 1982.

Steinbeck, Elaine, and Robert Wallsten, eds. *Steinbeck: A Life in letters*. New York: Viking Press, 1975.

Steinbeck, John. *The Pastures of Heaven*. New York: Brewer, Warren & Putnam, 1932.

Sugiyama, Sumiko. *Yeats: Fatherland and Song*. Kyoto: Yamuguchi Shoten, 1985.

Toulson, Shirley. *The Celtic Year: A Month-by-Month Celebration of Celtic Christian Festivals and Sites*. Shaftesbury. Dorset: Element Books Limited, 1996.

Wade, Allan, ed. *The Letters of W. B. Yeats*. London: Rupert Hart-Davis, 1954.

Yeats, W. B. "The Celtic Twilight" in *Mythologies*. London: Macmillan Press, 1959.

Chapter 3

To a God Unknown:
"God" as Polytheism

John Steinbeck's early masterpiece, *To a God Unknown* (1933), has attracted many scholars and critics. As has been pointed out, there are psychological, philosophical, and religious aspects in this work. French says, "Steinbeck does suggest that there is something superhuman about Joseph's extraordinary self-consciousness" (French 49), and in his book, Balaswamy analyzes from Indian philosophy to deal with the major theme of sacrifice, which is "integral part of the individual's union with the universe" (Balaswamy 49-50). Through his approach, he concludes that "man is an inseparable part of Nature" (Balaswamy 66).

Among these previous studies, Peter Lisca, a pioneer scholar of Steinbeck studies, points out regarding the first epigraph of this work, "Steinbeck combines five and six, seven and eight, as well as omitting the first and last stanzas. The omissions are significant" (Lisca 41), although the original hymn has ten stanzas.

This consideration leads to the analysis of Kiyoshi Nakayama who says, "While praising the supreme Deity who stands above God as Polytheism, and because of the unknown, it is a profound hymn that signifies a quest for the 'sacrificing deity.' And the supreme Deity suggested here is not that of Christ, but a pagan Deity" (Nakayama 333-334, trans. Mine).

This idea is almost in line with the idea of God in Celtic culture. This is because the gods in Celtic culture are also "gods as polytheism" and there are many pagan gods. The reason why this work has a Celtic color is none other than Steinbeck's high writing abilities. Steinbeck's literary ability was strongly influenced by his mother, who read to him during his childhood and boyhood. It can be assumed that Steinbeck's mother is of Irish stock and had a great influence upon Steinbeck consciously or unconsciously.

This chapter deals with the Celtic tradition of the oak tree symbolizing

"Druidism," Fairy Culture, and Steinbeck's "Phalanx Theory." The author would like to try a consideration from Celtic perspectives.

I

In this work, the "oak tree" has a very important implication in the development of this work. The story begins just when Joseph settles in search of land in the west.

> Two miles away he [Joseph] could see, beside a gigantic lonely oak, the white speck of his tent pitched and left while he went to record his homestead. A long time he sat there. As he looked into the valley, Joseph felt his body flushing with a hot fluid of love. "This is mine," he said simply, and his eyes sparkled with tears and his brain was filled with wonder that this should be his. (12)

The main point of focus in this settlement scene is Joseph's "Oak Tree Worship" or "Druidism." It is a place where his 'Celtic identity' is glimpsed. Of course, the problem of land is also a common problem among various ethnic groups in the multicultural nations of America. This is a surviving problem for the Irish people, especially as a result of the long British rule.

"Oak Tree Worship" can be seen countless times in this work. If we think that it is symbolically depicted, it can be thought that it allegorically symbolizes "Jesus Christ," so it can also be depicted as a Celtic paradox that a pagan god also lives in Joseph. If there is anything that is particularly important in the development of the story, it is Joseph's relationship with Elizabeth.

Elizabeth is the daughter of a saddlery merchant, and her mother is "a highland woman" (59). This depiction reminds us of highland mountains of Scotland, one of the Celtic regions. In this work, when Joseph introduces to her an "oak tree," she "leaned against the tree and stroked its trunk. 'There could be a seat up in the tree, you see, Joseph, where those limbs start out from the trunk. Will you mind if I climb the tree, Joseph?'" (84). While others treat the "oak tree" as pagan, Joseph and Elizabeth touch it without hesitation. Especially Elizabeth works to strengthen her marital relationship with Joseph.

Another scene is, Joseph's strong faith of "oak tree" in the child of Joseph and Elizabeth who will be born soon, as follows:

> "I[Joseph]'ll make a seat for the baby up in the crotch. When he's a little older I may cut steps in the bark for him to climb on."
> "But he might fall and hurt himself."
> "Not from that tree. It wouldn't let him fall." (202)

In this scene, although the baby ends up hurt, it will be suggested that Joseph's and Elizabeth's faith in "oak tree" symbolizing "Druidism" will be well handed down to their children. This is a very important part of the work, as in the scene are well depicted the narrator's and even the writer's own dreams of inheriting Celtic culture and living robustly in "American Culture."

It is also very interesting that Joseph's elder brother Burton, also has Irish elements. He is portrayed as "one whom nature had constituted for a religious life" (38), somewhat reminiscent of St. Patrick, who condemns "Druidism" as heresy.

> Burton did not move. "You are lying, Joseph. You think you have been secret, but I have watched you. I've seen you make offerings to the tree. I've seen the pagan growth in you, and I come to warn you." Burton was excited and his breath came quick. (172)

The writer, through the narrator, portrays the character Burton as St. Patrick, suggesting to the reader the historical fact that "he [St. Patrick] confronted and defeated the Druids on Tara in the Holy Land" (Hara 206, trans. Mine). This seems to give the work a rich and Celtic layered flavor.

The ultimate act of disrespect that Burton did to his younger brother Joseph was having cut the severing life of the "oak tree" which Joseph so desperately needed. With the "oak tree," signifying "alter ego" cut off, Joseph was forced to see what the surrounding land was like. In the end, the worst situation develops: Elizabeth loses her life together with Joseph on a trip called "picnic" (225). Moreover, in the end, even Joseph commits suicide and becomes "rain" (322) and "the rush of waters" (322) and saves "the dying land" (310). So much so in fact, Burton's role as a catalyst is considered to be very important. This can be understood from the following quotation.

Joseph knelt down beside the hole and saw a chopped path on the trunk. "What did it?" he demanded angrily.

Thomas laughed brutally. "Why, Burton girdled your tree! He's keeping the devil out."

Joseph frantically dug around with his fingers until the whole path of the girdle was exposed. (216)

II

Next, we will discuss the relationship between Elizabeth and fairies. Fairies are one of the considering aspects of traditional "Celtic Culture." In Sligo in Ireland, W. B. Yeats was born and spent his childhood at the foot of Ben Bulben. His book titled *The Celtic Twilight* (1893) was published: a book of a collection of fairy tales told by Paddy Flynn who lived in a leaky hut. Kimie Imura states in the commentary section of its translated version, regarding its significance, "When it was published, it awakened the love of the Irish people for their homeland and nature, which gradually gave them the conviction and pride of being a Celtic people. It eventually rose to the Irish literary revival movement. This fairy tale strengthened the ethnic consciousness of the people and lifted them from love for their land to love for their nation " (Imura 244, trans. Mine).

Beyond the academic standpoint, it can be interpreted that fairy tales had a very important significance in the rise of nationalism in all Celtic cultural spheres, including Ireland. In *To a God Unknown*, there are two referred quotations of "fairies," both of which are about Elizabeth, a projected figure of Steinbeck's mother.

This is one of the depictions of Elizabeth, which is thought to be a projected figure of Steinbeck's mother as is stated above. Although the harness dealer's father condemns, "Your [Elizabeth's] mind is closed. You have no single shred of reason. Take your mother, now, a highland woman and straight from home— her own father and mother believed in fairies" (59), she insists on the "Celtic identity" that runs in her blood, saying,"There's things that won't stand reason, but are so, just the same." (59)

Secondly, in the passage "Elizabeth told some stories she had from her mother, tales of the Scottish fairies with their everlasting preoccupation with gold or at least some useful handicraft" (140), some of the "Celtic Culture" is expressed.

In addition, there is also one referred quotation of "Druidism" as follows: "'Do not let this thing pass through me into my child, Lord Jesus. Guard me against the ancient things in my blood.' She [Elizabeth] remembered how her father said his ancestors a thousand years ago followed the Druidic way" (183).

By the way, Joseph who devotes himself to "Druidism," has just one short scene that reminds us of fairies. Immediately after arriving and settling in California for the first time, Joseph utters these lines.

> "It's mine," he[Joseph] chanted. "Down deep it's mine, right to the center of the world." He stamped his feet into the soft of the earth... For a moment the land had been his wife. "I'll need a wife," he said. (14)

In this quotation, from Joseph's depictions of "the land had been his wife" and "I'll need a wife," it is possible to connect his future wife Elizabeth to "the earth" through the "Celtic Fairies." It is a very Celtic mythology-like depiction, suggesting to us that Joseph will marry Elizabeth through the "Celtic Fairies." Also, in Joseph's another depiction of "into the soft of the earth...," it can be said that it is clearly a way of depicting "Celtic Fairies" consciously.

According to the Celtic calendar, a year begins on the day when fairies leave the "bottom of the Earth" and go out to the "surface" through a "cave." This is called "*Samhain*."

In the Celtic world, *Samhain* is defined as "a period in which the conventional boundaries of space and time were temporarily suspended and where the spirits of the Otherworld mingled freely with the living" (Green 36). *Samhain* in the Celtic calendar is depicted in this work as follows.

> Rama drew her chair forward so that she could put her hands on Elizabeth's knee. "This is a strange time," she said softly. "I told you at the beginning that a door is open tonight. It's like an All Soul's Eve, when the ghosts are loose." (120)

This is the scene where Rama, wife of Joseph's brother Thomas, tells Elizabeth about Benjamin's death. It evokes the image of Celtic fairies emerging from their caves to the surface of the earth on an All Soul's Eve, and the sound of the name Benjamin (when associated with 'Benji'), who was murdered and passed away, is associated with Banshee, a Celtic fairy who "foretells the death of someone specially great or holy" (Briggs 22).

In this way, Steinbeck skillfully incorporated the cultural device of "Celticity" into his major works including *To a God Unknown*. Therefore, it seems that the work is made more multi-layered by Steinbeck's incorporating "Celticity."

III

As the story develops, in the final climax, Joseph cuts open the "vessels of his wrist" (321). The act of saving the earth by making it rain has been discussed by many researchers and critics, but the descriptions in chapters 10 to 11, which have not been discussed so far, could be focused on Celtic culture. It seems to be a very important part that should be called the climax of the first half. Because after Joseph and Elizabeth's wedding, they took a train from Monterey to King City, then a horse-drawn carriage from King City to Nuestra Señora, which could be considered a Celtic Utopia, "Tír na nÓg." In this mysterious period such as a very relaxed "hypnotic time" (104), each of them has a new start. This is because they talk about their views on life This chapter 10 is a key chapter where we can read the writer's own philosophy through the narrator. It is considered to be an extremely important scene.

In chapters 10 and 11, the expressions like the image of "crossing the pass" are often used. This is one of the clues to understand the work. It is in the evening, when the sun was "quartering to the westward" (94) that Joseph and Elizabeth went "up a long slope" (94), which is the most important time zone when we think of Celtic culture.

Kimie Imura states that "For the Celts, the time when the fairies begin to move is "the time before rebirth," that is, "the twilight time before dawn," and the time after "rebirth" returning to "darkness" (Kamata and Tsuruoka 47, trans. Mine). Based on this idea, as Fujimoto points out, this time period is called both "before dawn and twilight" (Fujimoto 741, trans. Mine). It can be thought of as two "twilight hours." As for the "night" that governs the darkness, Imura states that "Designing image of 'death' in the earth, the ethnic and mythical aspects of fairies are being revived as 'eternal memories from the past to the present'" (Kamata and Tsuruoka 47-48, trans. Mine). Therefore, two of these twilight hours are, as Fujimoto points out, thought to be the Celtic paradise "Tír na nÓg," where those escape who are fed up with the world dominated by the notions of good and evil, and which transcend time and space" (Fujimoto 742, trans. Mine). Although there is some resistance to the expression "fed up with the world," What Fujimoto is talking about here is, in short, a "mysterious period of time."

By quoting the third and the fourth stanzas of the poem of W. B. Yeats' "Into the Twilight," we will consider the significance that seem to be related to the interpretation of this work.

Come heart, where hill is healed upon hill:
For there the mystical brotherhood
Of sun and moon and hollow and wood
And river and stream work out their will;

And God stands winding His lonely horn,
And time and the world are ever in flight;
And love is less kind than the gray twilight,
And hope is less dear than the dew of the morn. (Finneran 59)

In this poem, the word 'mystical' in the third stanza, and the words of "sun, moon, hollow, wood, river, and stream" all live according to their own will; furthermore, in the line of "love is less kind than the gray twilight" in the fourth stanza, Elizabeth's "hypnotic time" (104) is elaborately expressed in her love for Joseph when applied to this work from this Celtic aspect.

Furthermore, what the author of this book would like to emphasize is the story exhibition spanning two chapters in *To a God Unknown* in the "twilight hours" of traditional "Celtic Culture," although fairies do not appear.

In addition to its literal meaning of "through the pass" (95), it can be interpreted as a metaphorical and spiritual meaning, and here it can be interpreted as a "turning point in life." For Joseph, it was his duty to see if he could transcend "a boundary" (96), as in "Christ nailed up" (96), and for Elizabeth, it seems to mean "to be a woman" (98): from a child to a full-fledged woman. For Joseph, first of all, this "pass" is a "space between the real and the clean" (96) and a "boundary" (96).

Yesterday we were married and it was no marriage. This is our marriage—through the pass—entering the passage like sperm and egg that have become a single unit of pregnancy. This is a symbol of the undistorted real. I have a moment in my heart, different in shape, in texture, in duration from any other moment. (96-97)

What the author of this book would like to focus on here is the passage of "a moment in duration from any other moment", which is reminiscent of "Tír Na nÓg" peculiar in "Celtic Culture," and the term of "a single unit." In particular, the latter term "a single unit" reminds us of Steinbeck's "phalanx theory." As was mentioned earlier, Joseph is assimilated with the earth, and Elizabeth is assimilated with the earth through fairies. As was mentioned in the quoted part, by passing through this "pass" and becoming one with the "earth," it is possible to create a mythical and multi-layered depiction of "their true marriage."

As for Elizabeth, "to be a woman" (98) means giving birth to a child as a woman. Raising a child and becoming a full-fledged mother can be thought of as the act of going "through the pass" (95). In giving birth to a child, in the end, it was a "hard birth" (196), but she exerted all her strength towards the birth, until at last "the baby lay in its basket-crib" (195). The first stage of the process of becoming a mother was successfully passed.

In addition, the writer's narrative, which spans these two chapters, has been used in many of his works, such as the painting technique that can be seen in an impressionistic way, and the scene depiction, that is, from the red of the sun to the yellow of twilight, and from gray to black toward darkness. The story progresses in the symbolic scene depiction that he is most good at. This is the true value of Steinbeck's way of his story development.

IV

Many researchers and critics have already challenged Steinbeck's "phalanx theory." According to Benson, the theory was not originally unique to Steinbeck, but he "produced his account of the social (and ultimately cosmic) theory under the symbolic title of "Phalanx" (Benson 268).

It can be seen that this theory was developed by Steinbeck under the influence of W. C. Allee, biologist and ecological theorist, and a professor of philosophy, John Elof Boodin at U.C.L.A. Especially when it comes to "God," Steinbeck seems to have been influenced by the professor Boodin's theory.

> He[Boodin] shared Brown's enthusiasm for scientific method, and his pragmatism, but differed from the materialist in that he also wrote of a "cosmic idealism" in which matter responds to the control of Form (that is, God), which coexists with matter. What most interested Steinbeck were Boodin's ideas concerning the juncture of individual minds brought together to form a larger whole with properties of its own. (Benson 267-268)

Regarding "Phalanx Theory," in the recollection of Richard Albee, professor Boodin's disciple as a younger brother of Steinbeck's friend writer, Benson states as follows:

> "We [Ed Ricketts, Dick Albee and John Steinbeck] talked together more than once, but it was after one transcendent session that John produced his account of social (and ultimately cosmic) theory under the symbolic title of "Phalanx." (Benson 268)

Benson further noted that Albee and Steinbeck had a strong interest in ancient European history. As for the word "phalanx" meaning "shield" in Steinbeck's term of "phalanx theory," Benson indicates that the ancient Romans called this "phalanx" tortoise.

> When the men pulled their shields together and advanced in lockstep,

they became one moving "animal," something like a modern tank in its advance on enemy positions. After reading Steinbeck's essay, Albee commented, "Did you know the Romans called the phalanx a tortoise? It's a wonderful symbol." (Benson 269)

This is a hypothesis that this "phalanx theory" is based on Steinbeck's Celticity presumed to be of Celtic origin. The word "phalanx" means the image of the 'shield,' invented "by Philip of Macedon, refined and made famous by Alexander the Great" (Benson 269). It is very interesting that the famous depiction of the "turtle," (*GOW* 20-22) which is described in almost all the pages of chapter 3 of Steinbeck's representative work *The Grapes of Wrath*, has its origin in the Celtic culture of the Gaul, associated with the ancient Roman army. Even if they are blown away by a small truck, turtles wear shield-like "armored tail" (*GOW* 21), get up and march, which is a symbol of the Celtic culture of the Gaul, associated with the ancient Roman army.

Another hypothesis is that Steinbeck's "phalanx theory" originates from the medieval European ideology described in Arthur O. Lovejoy's *The Great Chain of Being* (1936). The book contains too much amount to consider that it is impossible to analyze all of them, but in short, the view of the thought stated in this book is that "there exists a chain of existence that begins with God and descends to humans and animals" (Lovejoy 60), and when considered from this philosophical view, it seems to be linked to the Celtic view of life that Kenichi Kihara states as follows:

The Celtic view of life is characterized by one large, continuous, changing form: belief in the flow of life. They have expressed the tide of life that springs out of the ground as a spiral whirlpool. This vortex is signified as one Cosmic World that connects all individual lives that return to the soil and regenerate. Tales of ever-changing fairies and reborn heroes are also born from this continuum of life. (Kihara 353, trans. Mine)

Lovejoy argued that there was a process in which this continuous view of the universe gradually evolved from an immature one, citing Leibniz's writings at the end of the 17th century, and reached the conclusion "that the world is as yet incomplete, that the Chain of Being must be construed as a process in which all forms are gradually realized in the order of time" (Lovejoy 256).

Celtic view of life is consistent with the concept of this developing stage presented by Lovejoy. In other words, the Celtic view of life exists as an aggregate in the relationship between the earth and the underground. This is because when Christianity began to spread in the Celtic world, the Celtic gods were said to be "the gods who were chased by the newly arrived humans and came to live underground" (Hara 45, trans. Mine). On this point, I quote from *To a God Unknown*. It can be seen that the description is about the "land" motif such as mountains and the earth, never the stars.

> "...there are times when the people and the hills and the earth, all, everything except the stars, are one, and the love of them all is strong like a sadness."
>
> "Not the stars, then?"
>
> "No, never the stars. The stars are always strangers—sometimes evil, but always strangers. (103)

I would like to draw your attention to the part of this quotation that says "never the stars." Celtic myths and folktales about the stars are none or few.

Therefore, Steinbeck's "phalanx theory" was originally based on Celtic thought, but through "meeting Ed Ricketts in October 1930" (Benson 184), this "aggregation of the earth and the underworld," which coincides with Ed Ricketts' view of life of "seeing each marine animal along the shore within the scheme of the shore as a whole" (Benson 187), gives rise to a hypothesis that this "Whole Body" has expanded into the realm of marine organisms. And it is a well-known fact that the first work dealing with this "phalanx theory" in marine organisms was "The Snake" in *The Long Valley*, first published in 1935.

One conclusion and future challenges

As we have seen, there are so many "Celtic" elements in this work. The question of the relationship between the Indian Vedas adopted into this work and Celtic culture cannot be answered in a few words. Kotsuji states that "the common feature of Celtic folktales and Indian tales is their eloquence of storytelling" (Kotsuji 114, trans. Mine). It seems to be very difficult to demonstrate it.

Matsumura, in his essay "Truth as Salvation," takes up G. Dumezil's theory of "trifunctional system" of the Indo-European languages and writes as follows:

> The contrast between the laws of nature true and those false, which underlie the ancient Iranian views of salvation, is similar to that of the ancient Indians, the Germanic peoples, the Celts, and the ancient Greeks, even though the terms are different. In a nutshell, it is making aware the 'order' that exists in the universe, and by matching the rhythm, the gods, the king, and the people can escape from disaster and be saved. (Matsumura 189, trans. Mine).

This idea is almost identical to that of Lovejoy's *The Great Chain of Being*. For, according to Lovejoy, in this macrocosm, "order," whether biological, environmental, or spiritual, exists as one and the same cosmic aggregate. Steinbeck's view of the universe was also born from this "order" and through his friendship with other biologists and philosophers, he seems to have his "phalanx theory" developed into something "holistic." In addition, it seems that Celtic thought is related to Joseph's bloodshed at the end of the story. In Steinbeck's other work, such as *Of Mice and Men*, Lennie is shot in the back of the head by George at the end of the story and dies.

The writer depicts its foreshadowing scene in which the old man Candy's old dog is also shot in the back of the head and dies. The scene of Joseph's "bloodshed, death, and salvation" is also a foreshadowing scene of the bloodshed before Elizabeth's death, and is also the bloodletting of pigs by an old man as a ritual sacrifice. If these are the writer's foreshadowing styles, which are his forte and unique to him, then the final scene is also convincing.

First of all, Celtic thought also appears in the ritual of a pig sacrifice. The old man's words, "I[The old man], through the beast, am the sun. I burn in the death" (266). This line connotes exactly, "The sun that died and set gives rebirth" (Kamata and Tsuruoka 47, trans. Mine).

Now, Elizabeth's death and Joseph's death have something in common. Both bloody red blood where rain falls on green rocks and green earth. The first time Elizabeth went into the woods, "her hands were scratched and her hair pulled down when she came at last through the bramble wall and straightened up" (180), and she died an untimely death when she penetrated deep into the forest for the second time. It is a mysterious way of dying that is thought to be killed by the fairies who come to pick her up from the cave.

What is common to the two scenes: both in Elizabeth's death scene and in Joseph's last scene, "He watched the bright blood cascading over the moss" (321), is that red color (of the blood) assimilates the green color (of the moss). These two colors seem to be of great importance in "Celtic Culture." Of course, it should be considered that it is used as a symbol and the hint to solve this problem can be found in W. B. Yeats' poem and Oscar Wilde's short story (both Irish works).

"The Nightingale and the Rose" is a short story by Oscar Wilde in which a nightingale dyes a pale rose red with her own blood in exchange for her life. "The Nightingale pressed closer against the thorn" (Wilde 295) and the green Rose turns red with the Nightingale's blood, and the Nightingale is sacrificed to the Rose.

Also, in W. B. Yeats's poem "The Rose Tree," the last two lines "There's nothing but our own red blood/ Can make a right Rose Tree" (Finneran 183) can be interpreted as a parallel with this Joseph's last scene.

Regarding the last two lines of this Yeats' poem, Jeffares quotes Pearse's idea that "Bloodshed is a cleansing and sanctifying thing" (Jeffares 194). It seems that Joseph's "Blood and Salvation Theme" is inspired by this Celtic thought. In other words, it seems to be the same plane as the Celtic idea of "blood."

In general, there is so many Celtic aspects in *To a God Unknown* that it seems to be a work with the deepest religious and philosophical theme among the Steinbeck's works. As for my future research, I will focus on the "intertextuality" (similarities between works) of Vedas and Celtic Mythologies through a comparative study of Gaelic (an archaic language indigenous to Ireland) and Sanskrit.

Works Cited and Referred Bibliographies

Balaswamy, Periaswamy. *Symbols for Wordlessness: A Study of the Deep Structure of John Steinbeck's Early Novels.* Chennai: Ramath Academic Publishes, 2005.

Benson, Jackson J. *The True Adventures of John Steinbeck, Writer.* New York: Viking Press, 1984.

Briggs, Katherine. *Abbey Lubbers, Banshees and Boggarts.* London: Routledge, 2003.

Finneran, Richard J. ed. *The Collected Poems of W. B. Yeats.* New York: Simon & Schuster Inc., 1996.

French, Warren. *John Steinbeck.* 2nd ed. Boston: Twayne Publishers, 1975.

Green, Miranda. *Exploring the World of Druids.* London: Thames & Hudson Ltd., 1997.

Jeffares, A. Norman. *A New Commentary on the Poems of W. B. Yeats.* London: Macmillan Press, 1984.

Lisca, Peter. *The Wide World of John Steinbeck.* Reprinted, New York: Gordian Press, 1981.

Lovejoy, Arthur O. *The Great Chain of Being.* Harvard University Press, 1936.

Steinbeck, John. *To a God Unknown.* New York: Robert O. Ballou, 1933.

_____. *Of Mice and Men*. New York: Covici-Friede, 1937.

_____. *The Grapes of Wrath*. New York: Viking Press, 1939.

Wilde, Oscar. *The Complete Works of Oscar Wilde*. Leicester: Galley Press, 1987.

Yeats, W.B. "The Celtic Twilight" in *Mythologies*. London: Macmillan Press, 1959.

[Yates, W.B. *The Celtic Twilight*. translated by Kimie Imura (Tokyo: Chikuma Shobo, 1993)]

Fujimoto Reiji "Yeats" Uesugi Fumiyo ed. *Light Imagery: English Poetry in Tradition*. Tokyo: Kirihara Shoten, 1985.

Hara, Kiyoshi. *Celtic Water Veins*. Tokyo: Kodansha, 2007.

Kamata Toji and Mayumi Tsuruoka eds. *Celt and Japan*. Tokyo: Kadokawa Shoten, 2000.

Kihara, Kenichi. *Yeats and the Mask: The Paradox of Death*. Tokyo: Sairyusha, 2001.

Kotsuji, Umeko. *Thoughts on Celtic Celts*. Tokyo: Shakai Shisosha, 1998.

Matsumura, Kazuo. "Truth as Salvation: Focusing on Ancient Iran." Yasushi Yoshida ed. *Various Aspects of Salvation*. Tokyo: Yamamoto Shoten, 1990.

The Oxford English Dictionary. First Edition. Oxford: At the Clarendon Press, 1933.

Chapter 4

Tortilla Flat:

An Epilogue of the Folk Song *Danny Boy* and a Feast of the Celtic Fairies

Introduction

In Steinbeck's early novels, especially so-called California trilogy: *The Pastures of Heaven* (1932), *To a God Unknown* (1933), *Tortilla Flat* (1935), the maternal lineage, Celtic cultural traditions are particularly prevalent. The author of this book analyzed The *Grapes of Wrath* (1939) at the National Conference of the American Literature Society of Japan in 1998 and considered *The Pastures of Heaven* (1932) at the International Conference of John Steinbeck Society of the United States in 2005.

This chapter deals with the final novel in the California trilogy, *Tortilla Flat.* It is considered from the perspective of "Celtic Culture."

Steinbeck's unfolding novel *Tortilla Flat* is one of his unique slapstick stories that can be glimpsed in the post Great Depression period in California. Because of the height of Steinbeck's literary ability in childhood and adolescence, this novel is one of the masterpieces that can also be analyzed from Celtic culture. The influence of his mother, who read to him over the course of his life, was very strong. Steinbeck's mother was originally from Northern Ireland and it seems that she transplanted her "Celticity" into Steinbeck. This is why it can be assumed that Steinbeck was unconsciously influenced by "Celtic Culture."

By the way, this *Tortilla Flat* is the masterpiece that first made Steinbeck famous. Despite being an original work, there seems to be surprisingly little previous research on it: mainly from the "King Arthur" perspective and the *paisano's* "Collective Phalanx Theory" viewpoint seem to be the main research approaches so far.

Peter Lisca, a pioneer scholar in Steinbeck research, said that "one is not quite certain that it is 'different'" (Lisca 88) although "these characteristics [of drinking wine and looking healthy] do make clear the 'strong' philosophic-moral system" (Lisca 88) and concluded that "Steinbeck uses the comic spirit of *Tortilla Flat* to criticize certain aspects of society, but there is no indication that the life depicted in its pages, though it has its virtues, is the ideal for which man should strive" (Lisca 91): a negative but realistic criticism.

In another criticism, Alan and Barbara Lupack stated that "it seems natural that he [Steinbeck] should use an overlay of Arthurian allusion to transform the lives of the nearly penniless inhabitants of Tortilla Flat into something as noteworthy as the lives of the noblest of knights" (Lupacks 195) and went on to say that "there is an American tradition of democratizing the Arthurian legends by parodying the figure of Arthur or downplaying his power" (Lupacks 195), referring not only to Steinbeck studies but also other writers' studies such as Bridges, Twain, and Beard.

The fictitious space of Tortilla Flat which is the story stage of this work, is a similar Celtic place image to an Irish land of Ben Bulben where Irish poet W. B. Yeats valued its atmosphere and wrote many poems behind the scene of the land.

I

As the main characters in this work, Torrelli who sells wine as a moonshiner during the Volstead Act period, Danny, the protagonist, who continues to be loved while causing trouble to others, and others surrounding him, including Pilon, a retired infantry soldier, Jesus Maria, a religiously strong-hearted character depicted allegorically, an infantry-trained Big Joe, Pablo who happened to meet with Pilon and joined living with Danny after living in prison and Pirate who saved 25 cents a day by selling firewood.

The town hadn't changed much, except for prohibition; and prohibition hadn't changed Torrelli's. Joe traded his overcoat for a gallon of wine and went out to his friends. (123)

In particular, it seems that Torrelli is one of the most important supporting characters, not limited to alcoholic beverages. He is a very important presence in this work as a purveyor of alcoholic beverages. However, in this work, he is depicted as a "bootlegger" (270) during the Volstead Act period as was stated before.

In addition, in this work, the method of depicting Rupert Hogan, "the seller of spirits" (67) that appears in Chapter 5, etc., and especially wine, seem to be heavily involved in the development of the story.

There are nearly 140 descriptions of wine in the work, including gin, brandy, whiskey; in addition, all descriptions of bottles, glasses, etc., associated with these alcoholic beverages all told.

When combined, the number easily exceeds 160, and in total, i.e., the number appears 2 out of all the 317 pages. When calculated like this, there is at least one description in one page.

Bredahl wrote in the article "The Drinking Metaphor in *The Grapes of Wrath*" as follows:

> Bottled alcohol receives its major attention in the early section of the novel and, unlike coffee, is associated with isolation. Though the consuming of liquor usually connotes good fellowship, in *The Grapes of Wrath* it is always consumed apart from the group. (96)

It is thought that the same indication as this Bredahl's analysis applies to *Tortilla Flat*. At the beginning of the story, wine is described as something that releases Danny from "the weight of responsibility" (17). Unable to let go of the wine, he drives himself to death, and at the end of the story narrates the story-teller, "They [Danny's friends] looked at one another strangely, and then back to the burned house. And after a while they turned and walked slowly away, and no two walked together" (317).

> When Danny thought of the old lost time, he could taste again how good the stolen food was, and longed for that old time again. Since his inheritance had lifted him, he had not fought often. He had been drunk, but not adventurously so. Always the weight of the house was upon him; always the responsibility to his friends.
>
> Danny began to mope on the front porch, so that his friends thought him ill. (261)

At the end Danny dies a violent death, but at the beginning of the story, after the First World War, he somehow managed to survive and return to his hometown, but he could not live up to his status.

As is sung in the second chorus of the Irish folk song *Danny Boy* and the imaginary story that follows, it implies that even if he returns home safely, Danny's fortune will change for the worse as if there were the lyrics of the second chorus, in which the thoughts of Danny's mother are prayed for her son's safety, as follows:

> But if ye come, when all the flowers are dying,
> If I am dead, as dead I well may be.
> Ye'll come and find the place where I am lying,
> And kneel and say an Ave there for me.
> But come ye back when summer's in the meadow.
> Or when the valley's hushed and white with snow.
> T'is I'll be here in sunshine or in shadow.
> Oh, Danny Boy, O, Danny Boy, I miss you so. (Cited from www. eigouta. com)

Chapter 4

There were two houses in Danny's inheritance, but it was even a burden. For Danny, who lives in "freedom" (261), this "freedom" (261) is hindered. The story-teller describes the existence as the "Enemy" (300).

> Danny drew himself up. It is said that his head just missed touching the ceiling. "Then I will go out to The One who can fight. I will find The Enemy who is worthy of Danny!" (300-301)

This "Enemy" is symbolically depicted and replaced with "The One who can fight" (300) and another expression of "Danny's Opponent" (301). It makes the story richer and more mysterious. After this, Danny, as if possessed by this "Enemy," faces "death" (305) and the story comes to an end.

First, I mentioned the previous research on Steinbeck's depiction of alcoholic beverages, but it is clear that "wine" plays the most important role in the development of the story. However, it seems that the motif of this wine has not been talked about much in the previous research. When we think of wine, the first thing that comes to our mind is the blood of Christ. Here, I quote one of the masterpieces of the Irish poet Yeats', "Her Vision in the Wood" (1926), which uses wine as a motif.

> Dry timber under that rich foliage,
> At wine-dark midnight in the sacred wood,
> Too old for a man's love I stood in rage
> Imagining men. Imagining that I could
> A greater with a lesser pang assuage
> Or but to find if withered vein ran blood,
> I tore my body that its wine might cover
> Whatever could recall the lips of lover.
>
> And after that I held my fingers up,

59

Stared at the wine-dark nail, or dark that ran

Down every withered finger from the top;

But the dark changed to red, and torches shone,

And deafening music shook the leaves; a troop

Shouldered a litter with a wounded man,

Or smote upon the string and to the sound

Sang of the beast that gave the fatal wound.

All stately women moving to a song

With loosened hair or foreheads grief-distraught,

It seemed a Quattrocento painter's throng,

A thoughtless image of Mantegna's thought—

Why should they think that are for ever young?

Till suddenly in grief's contagion caught,

I stared upon his blood-bedabbled breast

And sang my malediction with the rest.

That thing all blood and mire, that beast-torn wreck,

Half turned and fixed a glazing eye on mine,

And, though love's bitter-sweet had all come back,

Those bodies from a picture or a coin

Nor saw my body fall nor heard it shriek,

Nor knew, drunken with singing as with wine,

That they had brought no fabulous symbol there

But my heart's victim and its torturer. (Finneran 273-274)

In this poem, "I tore my body" is clearly a motif of Christ, and wine symbolically represents "Reincarnation." The depth of this poem is, above all, as follows:

  1. the yearning of an old woman for the figure of a young woman,

  2. the motif of wine as a medium,

3. "Adonis associated with Vision" (Jeffares 329) and

4. darkness: a "Celtic depiction of a scene" that evokes the red wine imagery. Christianity was deeply ingrained in Gaul quite early on. According to the Christ's words at the Last Dinner, wine is the blood of Christ and the material of "Reincarnation" meant to be opened to the "Eternal Life."

From this point of view, when considering *Tortilla Flat*, Steinbeck has not been able to depict wine image as elaborately as W. B. Yeats. Danny that Steinbeck portrays is not 'God' on the same level as 'Christ.' In Danny's description from the climax chapters 15 to 17 of the work, I will quote the part where this is most clearly understood and we will try to consider it.

> Where Danny went, a magnificent madness followed. It is passionately averred in Tortilla Flat that Danny alone drank three gallons of wine. It must be remembered, however, that Danny is now a god. (298)

At the climax of the story Danny is depicted as a god. The word "god" is not "God" in a capital letter but written in a small letter. The difference of whether "capitalized" or not is clearly whether it is the "God Almighty" or "God as Polytheism." That is, the "God" which Steinbeck describes is not "God Almighty" but "God as Polytheism."

Therefore, Danny's drinking of wine does not seem to be assimilated with "Christ" image. Interpreting "God" in a capital letter as "single, unitary, and supreme" (Lambek 120), we cannot analyze the "gods" Steinbeck describes, in general, on the same level as Christ. They should be analyzed on the same plane as folklore, as many words of "gods" are used in *The Pearl* (1947).

II

This work is based on an episode about *paisanos* that Steinbeck heard from Susan Gregory, who was born in Monterey, when he worked in a sugar factory while he was a student at Stanford University. Therefore, it seems that it can be interpreted as a folktale level story, as is stated in the last chapter.

This is very similar to the creative attitude that Yeats completed in *The Celtic Twilight* (1893), a collection of fairy tales, after hearing from an old man named Paddy Flynn who lived in a leaky hut in Ireland. Kimie Imura states the following in the commentary section of the translated version of *The Celtic Twilight*.

> When it was published, it awakened the Irish people's love for their native land and nature, which gradually gave them a belief and pride as Celtic people, and eventually led to the Irish literary revival folklore movement. This fairy tale strengthened the people's national consciousness and lifted them from love for their land to love for their country. (Imura 244, trans. Mine)

How about replacing it with a "propaganda" in the mid-1930s, appealing to "nature" and "the free life of *paisanos*" especially in poor rural regions in America during the New Deal after the Great Depression. It can be said to have been fulfilled. In other words, it can be said that it has contributed greatly to the upliftment from "love for California" to "love for America as a nation," "Holistic" and "Phalanx theory" (holistic group theory, non-teleological thinking theory) against "Fascism" or "Totalitarianism," which leads to a criticism of capitalism that caused impoverishment.

In this chapter, I dare to read this work as a fairy tale. It seems that Danny and the *pisanos* drink wine and deviate from human behavior from late afternoon to evening, or from evening to night, or from night to dawn. The following are the places where these Celtic depictions of the scenes are thought to appear. There are four places in total, but the three places that are considered to have deviated from human behavior are the following three.

First, one of Danny's two houses is destroyed in a fire (Chapter 5). It is a big incident for Danny, but the Celtic scene description that implies it is depicted as follows:

The sun went westering and took on an orange blush. Under the rose bush in Torrelli's yard Pablo and Pilon finished the first gallon of wine. (68)

Next, in Chapter 12, we learn that the dogs owned by the Pirate can see the visions of St. Francis, and that, like Dr. Dolittle, the Celtic depictions of the Pirate who can understand the language of dogs are described. I quote as follows:

It was dusky in the glade, and the air was sweet with pine resin. The trees whispered softly in the breeze. (217)

And finally, I will quote the scene that is the most eminent in chapter 16 about "the Last Death of Danny." This goes like this as follows:

For a long moment the people waited, holding their breaths lest the harsh rush of air from their lungs should obscure some sound. But they listened in vain. The night was hushed, and the gray dawn was coming. (301)

As to why it can be said that these are Celtic depictions of the scenes, the "twilight" hours mentioned earlier, i.e., "the twilight hours when late afternoon changes into night," and "the twilight hours when night turns to dawn," are depicted as one aspect of Celtic culture. This is because it is thought to be a time period reminiscent of the Utopia "Tír na nÓg" and a time period in which fairies can regenerate.

According to Imura, for the Celts, the time when fairies begin to move is "the time before 'rebirth', namely, 'the twilight before dawn,' and the time after 'rebirth,' returning to 'darkness'" (Kamata and Tsuruoka 47, trans. Mine), and from this idea, this time period can be considered to be two "twilight hours" namely "before dawn and twilight" (Fujimoto 741), as is pointed out by Reiji Fujimoto.

Regarding the night which governs darkness, Imura said, "with the image of 'death' in the earth, the ethnic and mythological aspects of fairies are revived as 'eternal memories from the past to the present'" (Kamata &Tsuruoka 47-48, trans. Mine). Therefore, these two hours of the day, "the twilight hours before dawn" and "the twilight hours," are, as Fujimoto points out, "tired of this world dominated by the notions of good and evil. It can be thought of as the Utopia of the Celts, 'Tír na nÓg'" (Fujimoto 742), where people escape from time and space. What Fujimoto considers here is, in short, a "mysterious period of time." It is represented by the word "curious" in "They[*Paisanos*] drank quietly in the late afternoon, that time of curious intermission" (164) in the ninth chapter.

III

In the previous chapter, we talked about the "mysterious time period" during which Danny and other *paisanos* drink wine and become active. Here I would like to present two grounds for thinking of them as fairies.

The first is the use of the word "spirit" to describe alcoholic beverages. In this work, this "spirit," which means "alcoholic beverage," is depicted in the depiction of "Rupert Hogan, the seller of spirits" (67). In other words, in this work, both Hogan and Torrelli are in a position to sell wine, and by selling the "spirit" of wine to a person, it is thought that they are given an invitation ticket to the Land of Fairies (Tír na nÓg).

It can be said that they play a very important role. The word "spirit," not limited to Celtic culture, is synonymous with "alcoholic beverages." It means "fairies," and Danny and other *paisanos* drink wine. The idea that it is because they are transformed into a fairy that they rampage holds true. And that, in that "mysterious space and time" (Tír na nÓg). It can be said that it is a unique way of depicting Celtic culture.

Next, regarding the textual usage of the word "good people" used to describe "fairies," I will consider the way it is used and what it means. Yeats uses the term of "good people" in *Fairy and Folktales of the Irish Peasantry*, in which he states the word "good people" implies "fairies."

> Beings so quickly offended that you must not speak much about them at all, and never call them anything but the "gentry," or else *daoine maithe*, which in English means good people, ... (Yeats 1)

Therefore, *paisanos* in this work are originally "good" people like fairies. In this work there are many descriptions that suggest their "good" human nature underlying fairy-like features. I would like to see them by main characters. The seven scenes quoted below are applied to this idea. (Underlined parts, Mine)

> This story deals with the adventuring of Danny's friends, with the <u>good</u> they did, ... (9-10)

> "Where is Pablo, that <u>good</u> man?" (24)

> Pilon was an honest man. It worried him sometimes to think of Danny's <u>goodness</u> and his own poverty. (36)

> Enough for Pilon to do <u>good</u> and to be rewarded by the glow of human brotherhood accomplished. (99)

> He [Big Joe Portagee] resolved to do something <u>nice</u> for Pilon sometime. (152)

> Jesus Maria Corcoran was a <u>pathway</u> for the humanities. (173)

The Pirate felt that he had been washed in a golden fluid of <u>beatitude</u>. (207)

Conclusion

When we read this work as a fairy tale, the difference between "American Culture" and "Celtic Culture" will be touched on. In the United States, as is known, in order to develop the frontier, trees were cut down, and at the same time, Christian missionaries, as was seen in the Carmel Mission in California (1770) came there and tried to spread Christianity. It was promoting urbanization; generally by cutting down trees, people have been trying to propagate Christianity in the European continent. In the United States also, as in Europe, they tried to propagate urbanization and spread Christianity.

However, St. Patrick, in the missionary propagation of Christiarity in Ireland, while preaching he preserved trees. Celtic traditional thought "Druidism" coexisted with Christianity juxtaposed. Therefore, under this idea, the idea of fairies also remained widely.

When considered in this way, the burning of Danny's two houses plus Danny's death: weren't these a challenge of Celtic culture toward American culture? i.e. Celtic fairy culture against American capitalism during the post Great Depression period of the 1930s, as the resistance of rural culture against capitalism?

It was yet inconceivable at that time that *Tortilla Flat*, as a propaganda novel expressing the idea of "Natura Naturans" vs. "Natura Naturata" in the United States, can be interpreted as a highly evaluated work.

Works Cited and Referred Bibliographies

Bredahl, A. Carl. "The drinking Metaphor in *The Grapes of Wrath*" in *Steinbeck Quarterly* Volume VI, Number 4. Muncie: Ball State University, 1973.

Finneran, Richard J. ed. *The Collected Poems of W. B. Yeats*. New York: Simon & Schuster Inc., 1996.

Jeffares, A. Norman. *A New Commentary on the Poems of W. B. Yeats.* Reprinted, London: Macmillan Press LTD., 1989.

Lambek, Michael. "Provocations from an Anthropology of Religion" in *Religion Beyond a Concept.* Ed. Hent de Vries. New York: Fordham University Press, 2008.

Lisca, Peter. *The Wide World of John Steinbeck.* Reprinted, New York: Gordian Press, 1981.

Lupack, Allan and Barbara Tepa Lupack. *King Arthur in America.* Bury St Edmunds: St Edmundsbury Press Ltd., 1999.

Steinbeck, John. *To a God Unknown.* New York: Robert O. Ballou, 1933.

_____. *Tortilla Flat.* New York: Covici-Friede, 1935.

_____. *The Pearl.* New York: Viking Press, 1947.

Yeats, W. B. "The Celtic Twilight" in *Mythologies.* London: Macmillan Press, 1959.

[Yeats, W. B., Kimie Imura, trans. *The Celtic Twilight.* Tokyo: Chikuma Shobo, 1993.]

_____. *Fairy and Folktales of the Irish Peasantry.* New York: Dover Publications Inc., Revised in 1991.

Fujimoto, Reiji. "Yeats" in Fumiyo Uesugi ed. *Light Imagery: English Poetry in Tradition.* Tokyo: Kirihara Shoten, 1985.

Kamata, Toji and Mayumi Tsuruoka eds. *Celt and Japan.* Tokyo: Kadokawa Shoten, 2000.

The Oxford English Dictionary. First Edition. Oxford: At the Clarendon Press, 1933.

Chapter 5

Saint Katy the Virgin:
A Consideration from a Celtic perspective on "Virginity"

Introduction

Shinichi Nakazawa and Mayumi Tsuruoka, in their book *Celtic Religion Druidism*, write, "Celtic historical heritage stretches from the eastern edge of Europe to the western edge, and modern archeology clarified time and space of the Celts of the Continent of Olden Times and divides and links Bohemia and Ireland; Switzerland and Brittany; Germany and Belgium according to the common dominator of the Celts" (Nakazawa and Tsuruoka 117, trans. Mine).

The works featured from this viewpoint are works set in France written by Steinbeck, at least three: each one from the oldest, *Saint Katy the Virgin* (1936), "The Affair at 7, rue de M—" (1954), and *The Short Reign of Pippin IV: A Fabrication* (1957). The sorcery that can be called magic seen in "The Affair at 7, rue de M—" and the allegorical nature seen in the other two works are influenced by Celtic culture.

France also meant the Gallic region in the olden times, where Celtic culture flourished in ancient times, and Steinbeck started so-called "pilgrimage" to Ireland in 1952 and traveled to France in 1954.

For Steinbeck who is of Irish stock, it can be suggested that lurks in the depths of the soul seem to be consciously or unconsciously intrigued by his mother's Celtic elements. Here I will not go into detail, but since I have taken these works of *The Grapes of Wrath*, *East of Eden* and so on from the viewpoint of Celtic culture, this time I will try to decipher the work *Saint Katy the Virgin* from the perspective of Celtic culture, but it has been paid little attention from critics and researchers so far.

Regarding the work, Lisca describes it as "an altogether delightful tale that even Chaucer's Reeve or Miller would have been proud to present as his claim to the free dinner" (Lisca 94-95), although it seems that other critics' evaluations are not so high.

I

The story begins in the year 13xx. That is, it begins in France in the 14th century.

> In P... (as the French say) in the year 13..., there lived a bad man who kept a bad pig. He was a bad man because he laughed too much at the wrong times and at the wrong people. He laughed at the good brothers of M... when they came to the door for a bit of whiskey or a piece of silver, and he laughed at tithe time. (1-2)

The "Binomial Contrast" of "Good and Evil" that Steinbeck excels in describing may be a regular and an endless theme for the writer, although the "good and evil" that Steinbeck depicts has a very deep connotation. I will discuss this in more detail later. First, we will look at the story.

Evil Pig Katy's mischiefs go beyond description. She "began by stealing most of the milk" (4), "ate them [the rest of the younger piglets]" (5), and "began eating the chickens and ducks" (5) she got from the neighbors.

The climax of the first half of the only 25-page story is Katy's exorcism scene. When Brother Colin and Brother Paul sent out from Monastery M... came to Katy's wicked owner, Roark, to collect the tithe after talking about taking Katy in, Katy bit Brother Colin. After having his calf meat torn off by Katy, Colin escapes and climbs up a tree, and then Brother Paul holds the Cross over Katy to perform exorcism toward Katy.

> Paul paid him [Brother Colin] no attention. He unwound his girdle, and

to the end of it tied the chain of his crucifix; then, leaning back until he was hanging by his knees, and the skirts of his robe about his head, Paul lowered the girdle like a fishing line and dangled the iron crucifix toward Katy.

As for Katy, she came forward stamping and champing, ready to snatch it and tread it under her feet. The face of Katy was a tiger's face. Just as she reached the cross, the sharp shadow of it fell on her face, and the cross itself was reflected in her yellow eyes. Katy stopped—paralyzed. (16-17)

Here the story of the Celtic folklore "Jack O' Lantern" comes to mind. The story goes something like this: Claiming that he should make amendment for his daily misdeeds, Jack asks the devil to climb a tree and fetch apples as his last wish. Then, the cross is pointed at the devil who has climbed the tree, only for the devil to be hindered from coming down from the tree. The devil wasn't able to go to heaven or hell after Jack's death, and he only hollowed out his Soul, Turnip, and continued burning it. At the Halloween festival, this turnip turned into a pumpkin in the United States in modern times.

The original story is an old Celtic folktale. This *Saint Katy the Virgin* can be considered a parody of this folktale. Namely, pointing the cross at the demon pig, the two Brothers descended from the tree. It is thought that the story scene is set to the exact opposite. A different world between the space above and below the tree: this boundary can be interpreted as "*Annwvyn*" according to *The Mabinogion*.

In this way, this work contains a motif of Celtic folktales and the use of words and phrases that evoke Celticity. We will discuss them in detail in the next chapter.

II

This chapter deals with the consideration as to what the "pig" symbolizes and its connection to Celtic folklore. Boars were originally a symbol of fertility in Celtic society, and although they were distinguished from pigs, the boar "represented war and hunting on the one hand and hospitality and feasting on the other" (Green 1992, 44). Kimura states as follows:

> Next to the cow, the pig is also important as a religious symbol in Celtic society, early pigs were smaller and more ferocious than modern pigs. The fruit of the oak tree, sacred to the Celts because they grew up by eating acorns, they were revered as sacred animals. The abundant supply of their favorite meat must have also contributed to the increase in pig worship. In early Celtic society, pigs were associated with the warrior class and were sacrificial animals at the burials of warriors. (Kimura 192, trans. Mine)

In this work, the boar is mostly represented by the word "pig," but it is used only once by the word "boar" (6). This scene depicts Katy's strength and ferocity, and can be thought of as being temporarily elevated to the image of Celtic god of war. After being replaced by the word "pig," the demonic element in Katy is shattered by "prayer" and elevated to a graceful pig: very similar to the Cathy vs. Kate relationship that Steinbeck portrayed in *East of Eden*.

In the first place, generally speaking, it is used for the proto-languages of the world, such as Greek and Sanskrit. Words with an "h" in them, which require pronunciation in the glottal rather than the velar, originally symbolized "barbarous" pronunciation. A similar phenomenon is thought to have been observed in the proto-Celtic and Gaelic languages.

Considering the phonological change from the savage Kathy to Katy, a name on the same level as Cathy, Katy's elegance seems inevitable. Steinbeck never wrote Kathy, but considering this inflection, Katy is considered to be on the same level as Kate.

Next, I would like to analyze the mystique of the "pig." In the 14th-century manuscripts full of mystique of "Celtic Culture," especially its religious tales of medieval Wales, *The Mabinogion*, I will quote several parts of the mystique of the "pig" and its magical properties as follows:

> "Lord," said Gwydion, "I have heard that there have come to the South some beasts, such as were never known in this island before." "What are they called?" he asked. "Pigs, Lord." "What kind of animals are they?" "They are small animals, and their flesh is better than the flesh of oxen." "They are small, then?" "And they change their names. Swine are they now called." "Who owneth them?" "Pryderi the son of Pwyll; they were sent from Annwvyn, by Arawn the king of Annwvyn."
>
> (Anonymous, trans. Guest 414)

'Annwvyn' depicted here means a different world, and a 'pig' is a tribute from another world. The 'pig' was a leading role of a banquet and its taste was very delicious. This tribute "pig" from another world can be therefore interpreted as a sacred animal in "Celtic Culture."

Some hint of deciphering Katy's virginity from Celtic culture is also provided here. I will quote from *The Mabinogion*.

> The maiden came in. "Ha, damsel," said he[Math], "art thou maiden?" I know not, lord, other than that I am." Then he took up his magic wand, and bent it. "Step over this," said he, "and I shall know if thou art the maiden." Then stepped she over the magic wand, and there appeared forthwith a fine chubby yellow-haired boy. (Anonymous, trans. Guest 421)

Except for emergencies, Math could not exist "unless his feet were in the lap of a maiden" (Anonymous, Trans. Guest 413). It is a very interesting interpretation to apply this idea to Katy. There is no "magic wand" in *Saint Katy the Virgin*, but an exorcizing "cross" (16) can be thought of as this magic wand.

By the way, the two Brothers who appeared in this work did not receive "tithe" from Roark but instead they were "too glad to get anything" (10). When this scene is well applied to the Celtic culture mentioned earlier, an expression signifying "A tribute pig from another world is the best gift," the two Brothers had a religious view which was on the same level as "Celtic Culture" under "Christian Doctrine." In this sense, it seems that Steinbeck makes the narrator tell about his religious view more elaborately.

III

Steinbeck's view of religion is generally said to lack coherence. Catholic or Protestant is ambiguous. In *In Dubious Battle* (1937), there is described a prostrating prayer scene on the ground. Around 1932, when *Saint Katy the Virgin* was first written, Steinbeck had not a little interest in religion. Around this period, he wrote *The Pastures of Heaven* (1932), in which there is a story about people dying for their religion. The Carmel Mission dates back to the late 18th century, when it was spread and established by Spanish Catholics who settled in California. "Celtic Culture" features Catholicism; the same plane as the Catholicism in Christianity. This is the author's very bold hypothesis, but it seems that Steinbeck tried to incorporate Celtic culture into his writing, based on Catholicism in Christianity. It is depicted as the pagan aspects of Celtic culture that are more fundamental than Christian doctrines.

Therefore, Steinbeck's religious views are pointed out as naïve by various critics and researchers, but the author believes that the naivety is rather a strength and elegance of Steinbeck as a writer. Considering the way of using many words of "Gods" or "gods," the plural form of God, as are depicted in *The Pearl* (1947), etc., it seems that Steinbeck created works based on the idea of "polytheism."

Finally, we will discuss the climax of the story, Katy's "virginity." Steinbeck seems to affirm the inherent "good" and "bad" of human beings. In other words, it can be considered that he is creating works from the standpoint of the so-called "Sex Theory."

In fact, in most of Steinbeck's works, "good" has a religious connotation.

Chapter 5

Starting with "good" (including images of God), "modesty" (3), "piety" (7), "graces of God"(8), followed by "holy" (18), "bad" (1 and more pages), "wrong" (1), "devil" (4 and more pages), "worst" (4), "sin" (5), "evil" (5 and more pages), "crimes" (17), "wickedness" (23) followed by each word.

Looking at the meaning of these words in detail, first of all, 'good,' which expresses goodness and includes the meaning of God and 'piety.' The same is true for the characters who appear in *Tortilla Flat*. When they take spirits suggesting "alcohol" into their body, they will feel tipsy and become "Good People," and moreover, in "Celtic Culture," it connotes "Fairies."

In other words, the meaning of 'God' is included in the meaning of 'good.' So, even for pagan 'gods,' the 'good' that Steinbeck expresses generally becomes associated with 'Divine Protection.' What is the most important is that it is a word that is described in the condition of the natural qualities of a good person.

The opposite word is the word "bad." Roark and Katy the pig are also described with this adjective. However, other synonyms besides this "bad" are temporary or emotional, which express nothing more than a temporary and acquired feeling or condition, although the degree of "evil" may be greater.

I will analyze a scene in which "virginity" is mentioned.

> This definition [of virginity] is a grave danger to the basis of our religion since there is nothing to differentiate between the Grace of God knocking it out from the inside or the wickedness of man from the outside. (23)

Note the word "wickedness" used here, the word meaning "malicious." The fact that it is not a word "bad" should be focused on here. Regarding men impregnating women, it originally has the doctrine of "Original Sin." If it is "bad," it will be linked to the concept of "original sin," but here the word "bad" is not used to describe men's "wickedness" of impregnation. Since it is described as "wicked," the expression "from the outside" is ruled out. The reader is left with the option "the Grace of God knocking out from the inside."

975

This "choice" theory out of the two is a method of story development that Steinbeck excels most and considering his wordplay, "grave" may be "grace." By choosing this option, Katy's virginity is honored and will lead to the final happy ending, "Happily Ever After."

Therefore, this "divine protection" is regarded as Celtic magic analyzed from above. Thus, by interpreting this work from a Celtic viewpoint, the "virginity" of this work can be interpreted more deeply.

In conclusion, by reading "God" of this work from a Celtic perspective, and also the "pig" from a Celtic viewpoint and by deciphering its symbolism and magical nature from "Celtic Culture," this short story continues to deepen its meaning, elevated to a solid and profound masterpiece.

Woks Cited and Referred Bibliographies

Anonymous, trans. Lady C. Guest. *The Mabinogion, From the Welsh of the Llyfr Coch O Hergest.* Lomdon: Bernard Quaritch, 1877.

Arvel, Wirton. *Jack's Wagers (A Jack O' Lantern Tale): A Jack O' Lantern Tale for Halloween & Samhain.* London: Kentauron Publishers, 2014.

Brekilien, Yann. *La Mythologie Celtique.* Paris: Éditions du Rocher, 1993.

Cunliffe, Barry. *The Celtic World.* London: McCraw-Hill Book Company, 1979.

Curran, Bob. *The Creatures of Celtic Myth.* London: Cassel & Co., 2000.

Curtin, Jeremiah. *Myths and Folktales of Ireland.* New York: Dover Publications, 1975.

Frazer, James George. *The Golden Bough: A study in Magic and Religion.* New York: Oxford University Press, 1994.

Green, Miranda J. *Celtic Myths.* London: British Museum Press, 1993.

_____. *Exploring the World of Druids.* London: Thames & Hudson Ltd., 1997.

James, Simon. *Exploring the World of the Celts.* London: James and Hudson Ltd., 1995.

Lisca, Peter. *The Wide World of John Steinbeck.* Reprinted. New York: Viking Press, 1981.

Meillet, Antoine. *Introduction à l'étude comparative des langues indo-européennes,* Massachusetts: Murray Printing Company, 1973.

Steinbeck, John. *Saint Katy the Virgin*. New York: Covici-Friede, 1936.

_____. *The Pastures of Heaven*. New York: Brewer, Warren & Putnam, 1932.

_____. *Tortilla Flat*. New York: Covici-Friede, 1935.

_____. *In Dubious Battle*. New York: Covici-Friede, 1936.

_____. *The Pearl*. New York: Viking Press, 1947.

_____. *East of Eden*. New York: Viking Press, 1952.

_____. "The Affair at 7, rue de M—," in *The Portable Steinbeck*. Revised, Selected, and

Introduced by Pascal Covici, Jr. New York: Viking Press, 1971.

_____. *The Short Reign of Pippin IV: A Fabrication*. New York: Viking Press, 1957.

Zakzek, Iain. *Chronicles of the Celts*. London: Collins & Brown Ltd., 1996.

Hara, Kiyoshi. *Spiritual History of Ethnic Origins: Brittany and Modern France*. Tokyo:

Iwanami Shoten, 2003.

Kimura, Masatoshi. Ed. *65 Chapters for Understanding the Celts*. Tokyo: Akashi Shoten,

2018.

Nakazawa, Shinichi, Mayumi Tsuruoka et al. *Celtic Religion Druidism*. Tokyo: Iwanami

Shoten, 1997.

Tsuruoka, Mayumi and Kazuo Matsumura. *Illustrated Celtic History: Reading Culture,

Art, and Mythology*. Tokyo: Kawade Shobo Shinsha, 1999.

Green, Miranda J. *Dictionary of Celtic Myth and Legend*. London: Thames and Hudson,

1992.

The Oxford English Dictionary. First Edition. Oxford: At the Clarendon Press, 1933.

Chapter 6

Celtic Music, Land, and Diaspora in *The Grapes of Wrath*

When reading some of Steinbeck's works, we notice they reveal some Irish elements. This is a study of the Irish elements found in *The Grapes of Wrath*, featuring three aspects: Irish music, the land problem transplanted into American Culture, and the Irish Diaspora.

Professor Inazawa was the first scholar in Japan who pointed out the close link between Steinbeck and his Irishness. He noted in his excellent work *Sutainbekku No Sekai: The Grapes of Wrath and East of Eden* that "It is indisputable that Steinbeck's being of Irish stock consciously or unconsciously greatly influenced his work. This at times erupts with roars of laughter in *Tortilla Flat*, at other times it takes the form of a heavy contemplative mood in *East of Eden*. The origin of this tinge of sweet sentimentality that hovers over so many of his works is also partly to be found here ... " (Inazawa 17: Translation Mine).

As many critics and scholars have pointed out, *East of Eden* is an Irish-based novel and Steinbeck himself described some of the Irishness in this work. During his lifetime, after the publication of *East of Eden*, he visited Londonderry on a pilgrimage as stated in *A Life in Letters* (below *LL* 454). Many Americans seem to observe this custom, as did the former US President Clinton.

It is true that Steinbeck's attitude toward writing, the formation of his thinking and character formed in his childhood were mainly influenced by his mother, of Irish origin, who taught him how to read and write. Therefore, one hypothesis might be that in *The Grapes of Wrath* also, some Irish elements could be embodied in some way or other.

I

The 'Dance' plays a very important role in *The Grapes of Wrath* (below

GOW, although critics and scholars have not evaluated the dance scene in the chapters 22, 23, and 24. It is at a dance that Tom Joad "smacked'im [Herb] over the head" with a shovel (*GOW*56: Subsequent quotations from this work will be noted by page number in the parentheses following the quotations)—a fact that obsesses Tom from the beginning (from chapter 2 to chapter 30).

Steinbeck had used this 'dance' image in his former works. For example, in *In Dubious Battle* (1936), the word 'bird-like' (used as a dance-style in Broadway Musical Dancing) is introduced (Steinbeck 343) and in *Of Mice and Men* (1937), the word 'shift' (an image of moving from one position to another, thus linking to the dance image) is used in the scene Curley and Lennie met each other for the first time (Steinbeck 27).

In *GOW*, the main theme of enjoying a full human life, a life essentially human, is featured in the dancing scenes of the chapters 22, 23, and 24 at Weedpatch. The following is one of them.

> The music snarled out "Chicken Reel," shrill and clear, fiddle skirling, harmonica nasal and sharp, and the guitars booming on the bass strings. The caller named the turns, the square moved. And they danced forward and back, hands'round, swing your lady. The caller, in a frenzy, tapped his feet, strutted back and forth, went through the figures as he called them. (357)

With an "essentially human life" here is meant a life indispensable and fruitful to the human being: a life full of joy and comfort. The Joads suffered from the "dust" (29) and left their land and their house in Oklahoma by truck "loaded with implements" (94). On their way to California, Grampa died of "a good quick stroke" (144) and Granma also passed away when they would "get acrost" (239) the desert. However, after having overcome such hardships and several difficulties, they managed to slip into the Weedpatch camping field. Thus this "Chicken Reel", the same equivalent of the American traditional folk music "Turkey in the Straw" which has its origin in the Irish tune "Auld Rose

Tolly" (Nakamura and Noguchi 14) could be regarded as the "Song of Manself" evolved out of the "Song of Myself". So much so in fact that this chapter may be one of the climaxes of this novel considering that the Joads enjoy the true meaning of their life while dancing to the fiddle after having overcome several difficulties.

The dancing style of "reel" is originally a four-beat Irish mode of dancing which became popular during the 18th century in Ireland and it is a typical Irish style of dancing as is the "jig" a three-beat Irish dancing style.

One of the fountainheads of American Popular Music is probably the old Celtic folk music presently still existing in Scotland and Ireland. American popular music in general was developed on the basis of these Celtic dances and musical forms. Many of the Irish emigrated to North America just after the so-called "Potato Famine" in the mid-19th century in Ireland. It is clear from Clarke's description that "Of around thirty thousand settlers in 1817, two-thirds were from the British Isles, and most of these were Irish" (Clarke 14-5) that by the mid-19th century the number was skyrocketing when among those emigrants was Samuel Hamilton, Steinbeck's maternal grandfather, born in Northern Ireland. He "left the old country for the United States and married an American girl of Irish ancestry, Elizabeth 'Liza' Fagen, in New York in 1849" (Tessitore 14).

It seems that Steinbeck in describing these dancing scenes in detail, is representing his Irish identity. For example, the description of Jule watching at the gate who says, "These here dances done funny things. Our people got nothing, but jes' because they can ast their frien's to come here to the dance, sets' em up an' makes' em proud" (355). The description of Ma Joad who leaned her head close to her daughter and says, "'Maybe you wouldn' think it, but your Pa was as nice a dancer as I have ever seen, when he was very young" (357). And the description of the caller who directs the dance, saying: "Swing to the right an' lef'; break, now—break—back to—back" (357). Besides these, there are plenty more descriptions of dancing in this work.

The Irish originally have a custom of dancing on the occasion of some rituals.

See Woodham-Smith's statement:

> The custom [of dancing and fiddling] on such occasions [as in pre-famine period] is for the person who has the work to be done to hire a fiddle, upon which engagement all the neighbors joyously assemble and carry in an incredibly short time the stones and timber upon their backs to the new site; men, women and children alternately dancing and working while daylight lasts, at the termination of which they adjourn to some dwelling where they finish the night, often prolonging the dance to the dawn of day. (Woodham-Smith 24)

Woodham-Smith's indication of the Irish dance rituals runs parallel with the situations of the Joads and the dance at Weedpatch in *GOW*. Therefore we consider that Steinbeck uses the motif of Irish dancing as an indicator of life in its real meaning: life full of joy and comfort.

II

Another Irish element seen in this work is the "Irish Diaspora" linked to the Irish land problem. It seems better to discuss these matters not separately but collaterally because these problems are two sides of the same coin.

As to the "migration" theme of this novel, there have been many criticisms just after *GOW* was published in 1939. Taylor introduced and analyzed this migration in *Forum*, CII (November 1939) as follows: "The migrants' trek dates back to 1925, when cotton first became a major crop in California" (Taylor 649). Lisca stated in the article "*The Grapes of Wrath* as fiction" that "Because Steinbeck's subject in *The Grapes of Wrath* is not the adventures of the Joad family so much as the social conditions, ..." (Lisca 734). Brasch studied *GOW* from the Biblical viewpoint and concluded: "assumptions that Casy is a Christ figure and the Joads (read Judah) represent the Children of Israel returning from exiles in Egypt" (Brasch 45).

More criticisms followed on the theme of "migration" of the Joads from the philosophical, allegorical, symbolical, social and naturalistic viewpoint after the ones discussed above but the following seems to be the first criticism that attempted an interdisciplinary approach: both literary and cultural.

Salter described in his essay the human mobility as a dominant force both in Cultural Geography and in *The Grapes of Wrath* and concluded that "By sorting out several of the most significant subthemes in this universe of movement, an orderly analysis of both the novel and this aspect of cultural geography becomes possible" (Salter 140).

This approach was prominent at the time of the advent of "Multiculturism" in the 80s in the United States and it is in this context that the concept of "Irish Diaspora" seems to have developed.

"Diaspora" originally means "dispersion" (Appiah and Gates eds. 178), a concept only applied to the Jewish recently "spreading to almost every group that has had a history of widespread out-migration" (Connoly ed. 267); a concept that "during the 1990s became fashionable in world history and the specific Irish context as well" (Connoly ed. 267).

Gladstein describes the "American appeal, the theme of the eternal immigrant" (Gladstein 134) in her article "Steinbeck and the Eternal Immigrant" as the reason why *GOW* became famous worldwide and considers "economic and political problems creating migrations" demonstrating the fact that "The Oklahomans in California are like the Chinese in Malaysia, the Indians in South Africa, the Turkish in Germany, or the Algerians in France" (Gladstein 134).

She does not refer to the Irish in America but her statement implies the problem of the "Irish Diaspora" when saying that "Faced with seemingly insurmountable obstacles, immigrants the world over not only survive, but prevail" (Gladstein 144). This statement also holds true in the case of the Joads where they survive natural disasters.

Supposing the Joads were the Irish, it would be meaningful to analyze that

"American appeal" of the emigrants from Ireland from this point of view. See the disaster scene of the corn destroyed by the dust storm in the first chapter of *GOW*.

> The people came out of their houses and smelled the hot stinging air and covered their noses from it. And the children came out of their houses, but they did not run or shout as they would have done after a rain. Men stood by their fences and looked at the ruined corn, drying fast now, only a little green showing through the film of the dust. (5)

The corn here could be replaced by the potato in mid-19th century Ireland. During three years (1846 to 1848), more than one million Irish emigrated from Ireland owing to the "Potato Famine". This image neatly overlaps with the hardships experienced by the Joads in *GOW*.

In this work, more than three hundred thousand "Okies" trek from Oklahoma toward California because of the "Dust Storm", as is seen in the description "the dispossessed, the migrants, flowed into California, two hundred and fifty thousand, and three hundred thousand" (244). Many hunger situations evoking the "Potato Famine" are pictured in the descriptions like "a homeless hungry man, driving the roads with his wife beside him and his thin children in the back seat" (245).

The tragedies of the "Okies" are often described in this way. Steinbeck's eye seems to witness not only disasters in Oklahoma but to look also far beyond toward Ireland.

The Irish land problem is firmly implanted into American Culture in this work. There are many descriptions of land problems in this work. This is one of them.

> Then crop failure, drought, and flood were no longer little deaths within life, but simple losses of money. And all their love was thinned with money, and all their fierceness dribbled away in interest until they were no longer at

all, but little shopkeepers of crops, little manufacturers who must sell before they can make. Then those farmers who were not good shopkeepers lost their land to good shopkeepers. (242-3)

This is only one of the descriptions Steinbeck makes but in chapter 19, the land problem in California when still Mexican territory, is given a pretty detailed description. The land situations in both California and Oklahoma were almost identical.

In the United States, when distributing land to the 'boomers' for common use, the Federal Government made a good application of the "Homestead Act" (established in 1862) but still some capitalists emerged who derived much capital from the land and lived on the interest from the capital.

In Ireland, the situation on the land was much worse. In the mid-19th century, during the O'Connell period, when the "Potato Famine" occurred, the farmers were considered villains and were obliged to pay taxes to the landlord. Woodham-Smith says: "The land was divided and sub-divided, again and again, and holdings were split into smaller and still smaller fragments, until families were attempting to exist on plots of less than an acre, in some cases half an acre" (Woodham-Smith 32) or that "The owner of one acre ground manured the soil and prepared it for the reception of seed; the hirer provided the seed, planted it, and performed all subsequent operations. Rent was high" (Woodham-Smith 34).

The land situation in Oklahoma was much better than in Ireland because some of the 'boomers' had already managed to possess their own land by the end of the 19th century.

According to the 1990 census, there are 641, 733 Irish-Americans in Oklahoma, about twenty percent of the total population (Gall et al, eds. 488). Their immigration dates are uncertain. All that is known to us is that "the longer the journey westwards into Texas or up the Mississippi River to the frontier lands, the higher the fare, and that choice was not open to many" (Laxton 28). Among these were also some Irish who had managed to possess land

and settle soon after having emigrated from their own country under difficult circumstances.

Considering these facts, there seem to have been many Irish among the "Okies". The Joads can be considered representative of these. The Federal Government had opened up the land of the native Indian tribes at end of the 19th century which led to the invasion of the 'boomers'. It is in this context we have to view the emigrants from Ireland as typified by the Joads.

<h2 style="text-align:center">III</h2>

As is well known, *GOW* deals with the big problem of unity of the 'family' as a form of "Group Dynamism", particularly after the fourteenth chapter, a chapter that moves from the so-called " 'I' to 'we'" (158) philosophy.

French indicated the "education of the heart" in this work and tried to analyze it to work out the universal problem of the 'family' resolving the important scenes and the speeches of almost all the characters, from Tom Joad to Rose of Sharon (French 94-100). French's analysis that "the first significant change in the family's attitude occurs in the Weedpatch government camp where the Wallaces share their work with Tom, although they may thereby cut their meager earnings" (French 97) is an important statement leading to a solution of the 'family' problem, because the 'family' Steinbeck describes here also seems to have its origin in Ireland.

Woodham-Smith's statement: "The Irish are fond of children, and family feeling is exceptionally strong" (Woodham-Smith 31) well reveals this Irish trait parallel to situations in the Joad-family. As a case in point, Steinbeck describes Ma Joad as a strong and gentle woman at Bakersfield in chapter 20, a woman who evolved out of only 'herself' and gave what little food the Joads had: "Before Ma had finished with the plates they were back, silent and foolish. Ma shook her head. "I dunno what to do. I can't rob the fambly. I got to feed the fambly. Ruthie, Winfiel', Al," she cried fiercely" (269).

Chapter 6

There is an abundance of descriptions where the Joads as a 'family' share their miserable life with the other "Okies", but the most important scene representing this Irish element of the 'family' is in chapter 30. Here Ma Joad speaks to Mrs. Wainwright about giving a hand in a severe situation; "Or anybody. Use'ta be the fambly was fust. It ain't so now. It's anybody. Worse off we get, the more we got to do" (466).

This Ma Joad's scene "Use'ta be the fambly was fust" leads to the Irish family element because it reminds us of Steinbeck's maternal grandfather and grandmother who were of Irish stock.

Considering the 'dance' in terms of the 'family', the joy and comfort of life Steinbeck describes in this work as Irish elements are all the more reinforced and persuasive to the reader together with the group concept of the 'family'.

Second, as for the "Irish Diaspora", it is also well embodied in this work as mentioned above adjacent to the land problem. The words "westward", "western" and "migration" in the context of "Westering" (meaning "going westward") are used many times in this work. Here it might be necessary to clarify these words.

Steinbeck seems to use the word "migration" not only from the 'translocal' viewpoint (as a trek from Oklahoma to California) hut also from the 'transnational' viewpoint (as an emigration from Ireland to Oklahoma, then toward California). See Grampa's speech in chapter 10.

> Me—I'm stayin'. I give her a goin'-over all night mos'ly. This here's my country. I b'long here. An' I don't give a goddamn if they's oranges an' grapes crowdin' a fella outa bed even. I ain't a-goin'. This country ain't no good, but it's my country. No, you all go ahead. I'll jus' stay right here where I b'long. (116)

The reason why Grampa would not like to go to California is that he had come to Oklahoma from Ireland toward the end of the 19th century and settled there; Oklahoma was Eden because there were fertile lands at that time. In this situation, Steinbeck seems to regard this Grampa as his Irish ancestor and describes him from the Irish level by using his suggestive phrase "pilgrimage was over" (94) in the same chapter. So much so that this "migratory" concept is leveled up to the 'transnational': the Grampa he describes might have gone into exile from Ireland to Oklahoma.

'Hybridization', another aspect of "Diaspora", is well embodied in Ma Joad's speech: "Woman, it's all one flow, like a stream, little eddies, little waterfalls, but the river, it goes right on. Woman looks at it like that. We ain't gonna die out. People is goin' on—changing' a little, maybe, but goin' right on" (443) in chapter 28. This shows how useful a life she led in California and how well she perceived the real meaning of life mentally and physically by picking cotton. If they hadn't gone to California, the Joads could not have attained such kind of mental attitude. In this sense, the Joads were well hybridized into an excellent "Manself".

We may conclude that *GOW* is an excellent novel in which Steinbeck defines his identity as 'Irish', and 'transnational' thus giving the reader a more refined idea of the "Irish Diaspora" and in addition, the three above-mentioned Irish aspects could perhaps be said to comprise only one of the "five layers" (*LL* 178) to which Steinbeck himself refers in his letter to Pascal Covici, but even these aspects alone are adequate to certify the greatness of John Steinbeck as a writer who won a Nobel Prize—an author who created a genre of Irish-American literature in the same manner as his contemporary writer Margaret Mitchell who wrote the great masterpiece *Gone With the Wind* in 1936.

Acknowledgement:

This paper was completed thanks to TRAVEL GRANT conferred by The English Literary Society of Japan in 2001.

Chapter 6

Works Cited

Appiah, Kwame Anthony and Henry Louis Gates, Jr. eds. *The Dictionary of Global Culture*. New York: Quality Paperback Book Club, 1997.

Brasch, James D. "*The Grapes of Wrath* and Old Testament Skepticism." *John Steinbeck's The Grapes of Wrath*. Harold Bloom, ed. New York: Chelsea House Publishers, 1988.

Clarke, Donald. *The Rise and Fall of Popular Music*. New York: St. Martin's Press, 1995.

Connolly, S. J. ed. *The Oxford Companion to Irish History*. New York: Oxford University Press, 1998.

French, Warren. *John Steinbeck*. 2nd ed. Boston: Twayne Publishers, 1975.

Gall, Tomothy L. et al. eds. *Worldmark: Encyclopedia of the States*. Detroit: Gale Research Inc., 1995.

Gladstein, Mimi Reisel. "Steinbeck and the Eternal Immigrants." *John Steinbeck: The Years of Greatness, 1936-1939*. Tetsumaro Hayashi, ed. Tuscaloosa: University of Alabama Press, 1993.

Inazawa, Hideo. *Sutainbekku No Sekai (The World of John Steinbeck): The Grapes of Wrath and East of Eden*. Tokyo: Shicho-sha (Shicho Publishing Company), 1978.

Laxton, Edward. *The Famine Ships: The Irish Exodus to America*. New York: Henry Holt and Company, 1997.

Lisca, Peter. "*The Grapes of Wrath* as Fiction." *John Steinbeck. The Grapes of Wrath: Text and Criticism*. Peter Lisca, ed. London: Penguin Books, 1977.

Nakamura, Toyo and Hisamitsu Noguchi. *CD plus Book: Amerikan Myuzikku No Genten (The Origin of American Music)*. Tokyo: Odibukku (Audio and Book), 1994.

Salter, Christopher L. "John Steinbeck's *The Grapes of Wrath* as a Primer for Cultural Geography." *Critical Essays on Steinbeck's The Grapes of Wrath*. John Ditsky, ed. Boston: G. K. Hall&Co., 1989.

Steinbeck, Elaine and Robert Wallsten eds. *Steinbeck: A Life in Letters*. New York: Viking Press, 1975.

Steinbeck, John. *The Grapes of Wrath*. London: Penguin Classics, 2000.

_____. *In Dubious Battle*. London: Penguin Classics, 2000.

_____. *Of Mice and Men*. London: Penguin Classics, 2000.

Taylor, Frank J. "The Great Migration." *John Steinbeck*. *The Grapes of Wrath: Text and Criticism*. Peter Lisca, ed. London: Penguin Books, 1977.

Tessitore, John. *John Steinbeck: A Writer's Life*. New York: Franklin Watts, 2001.

Woodham-Smith, Cecil. *The Great Hunger: Ireland 1845-1849*. London: Penguin Books, 1991.

Chapter 7

Celtic Use of Music in *The Grapes of Wrath*

This is a critical essay based on the Symposium Presentation delivered at the annual conference of the John Steinbeck Society in May 2019. As a chairperson, the author appeared at the symposium wearing his hair in the wild manner of Beethoven, and controlled the timing of the arrangement of the symposium in the style of Brahms as if he had imitated his composing style as an improvisation. The theme, which the author treated, resembles the style of Mozart: some optimistic musical tune of the theme in the pessimistic passages as in the second movement of K.488. This musical structure is like the story-telling structure in chapters 22, 23 and 24 of *The Grapes of Wrath*.

When reading some of Steinbeck's works, we notice they reveal some Celtic elements. This is a study of the Celtic musical elements found In *The Gropes of Wrath*, including Irish music.

Professor Inazawa was the first scholar in Japan who pointed out the close link between Steinbeck and his Irishness. He noted in his excellent work *Sutainbekku No Sekai: The Grapes of Wrath and East of Eden*: "It is indisputable that Steinbeck's being of Irish stock greatly influenced his work, consciously or unconsciously. This at times erupts with roars of laughter in *Tortilla Flat*, while at other times it takes the form of the heavy contemplative mood in *East of Eden*. The origin of this tinge of sweet sentimentality that hovers over so many of his works is also partly to be found here ... " (Inazawa 17: trans. Mine).

As many critics and scholars have pointed out, *East of Eden* is an Irish-based novel and Steinbeck himself described some of the Irishness in this work. After the publication of *East of Eden*, be visited Londonderry on a pilgrimage as stated in *A Life in Letters* (below *LL* 454). Many Americans seem to observe this custom, as did the US President, Bill Clinton.

It is true that Steinbeck's attitude toward writing, the formation of his thinking and character in his childhood were mainly influenced by his mother, a lady of Irish origin, who taught him how to read and write. Therefore, one hypothesis might be that in *The Grapes of Wrath*, some Irish elements could also be embodied.

I

Steinbeck makes a comment about his strong belief in a small essay "About Ed Ricketts" included In *The Log from the Sea of Cortez* (1951, below *LFSOC*), as follows:

> When the book *Studs Lonigan* came out, Ed read it twice very quickly. "This is a true book," he said. "I was born and grew up in this part of Chicago. I played in these streets. I know them all. I know the people. This is a true book." And of course, to Ed <u>a thing that was true was beautiful</u> (*LFSOC* lviii: Underline: Mine).

This idea coincides with Walter Pater's philosophy. Pater states in his writing titled *The Renaissance* (1873): "To see the object as in itself it really is," has been justly said to be the aim of all true criticism whatever; ... The objects with which aesthetic criticism deals—music, poetry, artistic and accomplished forms or human life ... (Pater xxv). Pater's philosophy seems to be greatly linked to Steinbeck's view of music as was already indicated by Kiernan, the first Steinbeck student of his music: " ... Steinbeck told me that his goal as a writer of fiction had been 'to cut up reality and make it more real ... This is the intricate music of the art of fiction. It's the music I have always tried to play" (Kiernan xvii).

As it is well known, Pater was the first aesthetic critic who introduced Schopenhauer's philosophy on music to the English world. He revised this philosophy in his own way or interpretation as follows:

> *All art constantly aspires towards the condition of music.* For while in all

kinds of other kinds of art it is possible to distinguish the matter from the form, and the understanding can always make this distinction, yet it is the constant effort of art to obliterate it (Pater 111).

Schopenhauer stressed the power of music as an immediate art style: "The effect is so very much more powerful and penetrating than is that of the other arts, for these others speak only of the shadow, but music of the essence" (Schopenhauer 257). He seems to consider music to be a most superior kind of art. As for Steinbeck, between fiction and reality, he seems to have strove to rewrite fiction as reality more than any other writer. This reveals that he won both Pulitzer Prize and Nobel Prize by linking to his philosophy of non-teleological thinking: music as non-teleological thinking from the viewpoint of "thinking as it really is."

II

The "Dance" plays a very important role in *The Grapes of Wrath* (below *GOW*), although critics and scholars have not evaluated the dance scene in the chapter 22, 23, and 24. It is at a dance that Tom Joad "smacked'im [Herb] over the head" with a shovel (*GOW* 56: Subsequent quotations from this work will be noted by page number in the parentheses following the quotations)—a fact that obsesses Tom from chapter 2 to chapter 30.

Steinbeck had used this 'dance' image in his former works. For example, in *In Dubious Battle* (1936), the word 'bird-like' (used as a dance-style in Broadway Musical Dancing) is introduced (Steinbeck 343) and in *Of Mice and Men* (1937), the word 'shift' (an image of "moving from one position to another" [*OED* 694], thus linking to the dance image) is used in the scene where Curley and Lennie met each other for the first time (Steinbeck 48).

In *GOW*, the main theme of enjoying a full human life, a life essentially human, is featured in the dancing scenes of the chapters 22, 23, and 24 at Weedpatch. The following is one of them.

The music snarled out "Chicken Reel," shrill and clear, fiddle skirling, harmonica nasal and sharp, and the guitars booming on the bass strings. The caller named the turns, the square moved. And they danced forward and back, hands'round, swing your lady. The caller, in a frenzy, tapped his feet, strutted back and forth, went through the figures as he called them (466).

An "essentially human life" means a life indispensable and fruitful to the human being: a life full of joy and comfort. The Joads suffered from the "dust" (37) and left their land and their house in Oklahoma by truck "loaded with implements" (122).

On their way to California, Grampa died of "a good quick stroke" (188) and Granma also passed away when they would "get acrost" (311) the desert. However, after having overcome such hardships and several difficulties, they managed to slip into the Weedpatch camping field. Thus, this "Chicken Reel," which has its origin in the Irish tune, could be regarded as the "Song of Manself" evolved out of the "Song of Myself." So much so, in fact, that this chapter may be one of the climaxes of this novel considering that the Joads enjoy the true meaning of their life while dancing to the fiddle after having overcome several difficulties. Here is a tune of "Chicken Reel":

(Musical Notes Described by the Author, Viewing Chubby Wise's Performance in 1936 on YouTube)

The dancing style of "reel" is originally a four-beat Irish mode of dancing which became popular during the 18th century in Ireland, and it is a typical Irish style of dancing as is the "jig," a three-beat Irish dancing style.

One of the fountainheads of American Popular Music is probably the old Celtic folk music presently still existing in Scotland and Ireland. American popular music in general was developed on the basis of these Celtic dances and musical forms. Many of the Irish emigrated to North America just after the so-called "Potato Famine" in the mid-19th century in Ireland. It is clear from Clarke's description that "Of around thirty thousand settlers in 1817, two-thirds were from the British Isles, and most of these were Irish" (Clarke 14-5) and that by the mid-19th century, the number was skyrocketing and among those emigrants was Samuel Hamilton, Steinbeck's maternal grandfather, born in Northern Ireland. He "left the old country for the United States and married an American girl of Irish ancestry, Elizabeth 'Liza' Fagen, in New York in 1849" (Tessitore 14).

Furthermore, it is evident that over a period from 1900 to 1950 most of the important developments in the field of Irish music did take place in the USA; as a case in point, Chubby Wise first performed "Chicken Reel" with a fiddle in 1936, and Leroy Anderson arranged this "Chicken Reel" and released it as a record style in 1946. Irish music is traditionally played by improvisation, not by the musical notes. Nuala O'connor indicates as follows:

The years after the famine up until the late 1930s were important years for Irish traditional music, particularly for the instrumental or dance music tradition. In those years over four million people left Ireland for America; each ship carried with it a cargo of music. Irish music transplanted itself in the new country and by so doing ensured its survival as a living tradition. It renewed and changed itself in a way that affected the subsequent development of the music in both its adopted country and its country of origin (O'Connor 62).

It seems that, in describing these dancing scenes in detail, Steinbeck is representing his Irish identity. For instance, watching at the gate, Jule says, "These here dances done funny things. Our people got nothing, but jes' because they can ast thair frien's to come here to the dance, sets'em up an' makes'em proud" (464). Leaning her head close to her daughter, Ma Joad also says, "Maybe you wouldn' think it, but your Pa was as nice a dancer as I have ever seen, when he was very young" (467). Meanwhile, the caller directs the dance, saying, "Swing to the right an' lef; break, now—break—back to—back" (467). Besides these, there are plenty more descriptions of dancing in this work.

The Irish originally have a custom of dancing on the occasion of some rituals. See Woodham-Smith's statement:

> The custom [of dancing and fiddling] on such occasions [as in pre-famine period] is for the person who has the work to be done to hire a fiddle, upon which engagement all the neighbors joyously assemble and carry in an incredibly short time the stones and timber upon their backs to the new site; men, women and children alternately dancing and working while daylight lasts, at the termination of which they adjourn to some dwelling where they finish the night, often prolonging the dance to the dawn of day (Woodham-Smith 24).

Woodham-Smith's indication of the Irish dance rituals runs parallel with the situations of the Joads and the dance at Weedpatch in *GOW*. Therefore we consider that Steinbeck uses the motif of Irish dancing as an indicator of life in its real meaning: Life full of Joy and Comfort.

III

As is well known, *GOW* deals with the big problem of unity of the 'family' as a form of "Group Dynamism," particularly after the fourteenth chapter, a chapter that moves from the so-called "I to 'we'" (206) philosophy.

Warren French indicated the "education of the heart" in this work and tried to analyze it to work out the universal problem of the 'family' resolving the important scenes and the speeches of almost all the characters, from Tom Joad to Rose of Sharon (French 94-100). French notes, "The first significant change in the family's attitude occurs in the Weedpatch government camp where the Wallaces share their work with Tom, although they may thereby cut their meager earnings" (97) is an important statement leading to a solution of the "family" problem, because the "family" Steinbeck describes here also seems to have its origin in Ireland.

Woodham-Smith's statement "The Irish are fond of children, and family feeling is exceptionally strong" (Woodham-Smith 31) well reveals this Irish trait parallel to situations in the Joad family. As a case in point in chapter 20, Steinbeck describes Ma Joad as a strong and gentle woman at Bakersfield, a woman who evolved out of only 'herself' and gave what little food the Joads had: "Before Ma had finished with the plates they were back, silent and foolish. Ma shook her head. 'I dunno what to do. I can't rob the fambly. I got to feed the fambly. Ruthie, Winfiel', Al,' she cried fiercely" (351).

There is an abundance of descriptions where the Joads as a "family" share their miserable life with the other "Okies," but the most important scene representing this Irish element of the "family" is in chapter 30. Here Ma Joad speaks to Mrs. Wainwright about giving a hand in a severe situation. "Or anybody. Use'ta be the fambly was fust. It ain't so now. It's anybody. Worse off we get, the more we got to do" (606).

This Ma Joad's scene "Use'ta be the fambly was fust" leads to the Irish family element because it reminds us of Steinbeck's maternal grandfather and grandmother who were of Irish stock.

Considering the "dance" in terms of the "family," the joy and comfort of life Steinbeck describes in this work as Irish elements are all the more reinforced and persuasive to the reader together with the group concept of the "family."

Second, as for the "Irish Diaspora," it is also well embodied in this work as mentioned in chapter 6 adjacent to the land problem. The words "westward," "western" and "migration" in the context of "Westering" (meaning "going westward") are used many times in this work. Here it might be necessary to clarify these words.

Steinbeck seems to use the word "migration" not only from the "translocal" viewpoint (as a trek from Oklahoma to California) but also from the "transnational" viewpoint (as an emigration from Ireland to Oklahoma, then toward California). See Grampa's speech in chapter 10:

> Me—I'm stayin'. I give her a goin'-over all night mos'ly. This here's my country. I b'long here. An' I don't give a goddamn if they's oranges an' grapes crowdin' a fella outa bed even. I ain't a-goin'. This country ain't no good, but it's my country. No, you all go ahead. I'll jus' stay right here where I b'long (152).

The reason why Grampa would not like to go to California is that he had come to Oklahoma from Ireland toward the end of the 19th century and settled there; Oklahoma was Eden because there were fertile lands at that time. In this situation, Steinbeck seems to regard this Grampa as his Irish ancestor and describes him from the Irish level by using his suggestive phrase "pilgrimage was over" (122) in the same chapter. So much so that this "migratory" concept is leveled up to the 'transnational': the Grampa he describes might have gone into exile from Ireland to Oklahoma.

'Hybridization,' another aspect of "Diaspora," is well embodied in Ma Joad's speech: "Woman, it's all one flow, like a stream, little eddies, little waterfalls, but the river, it goes right on. Woman looks at it like that. We ain't gonna die out. People is goin' on—changin' a little, maybe, but goin' right on" (577). This shows how useful a life she led in California and how well she perceived the real meaning of life mentally and physically by picking cotton. If they hadn't gone to California, the Joads could not have attained such kind of mental attitude. In this sense, the Joads were well hybridized into an excellent "Manself": "Chicken Reel," the same level with "Song of Manself" and with Music as Non-Teleological Thinking.

We may conclude that *GOW* is an excellent novel in which Steinbeck defines his identity as 'Irish' and 'transnational,' thus giving the reader a more refined idea of the "Celtic Diaspora." In addition, the above-mentioned Celtic aspects of music could perhaps be said to comprise only one of the "five layers" (*LL* 178) to which Steinbeck himself refers in his letter to Pascal Covici, but even these aspects alone are adequate to certify the greatness of John Steinbeck as a writer who won a Nobel Prize and an author who created a genre of Irish-American literature in the same manner as his contemporary writer Margaret Mitchell, who wrote the great masterpiece *Gone with the Wind* in 1936.

Acknowledgement:

This paper was completed on the basis of the sixth chapter's essay "Celtic Music, Lard, and Diaspora in *The Grapes of Wrath*," featuring especially "Celtic Music."

Works Cited

Appiah, Kwame Anthony, and Henry Louis Gates, Jr. eds. *The Dictionary of Global Culture*. New York: Quality Paperback Book Club, 1997.

Brasch, James D. "*The Grapes of Wrath* and Old Testament Skepticism." Harold Bloom ed. *John Steinbeck's The Grapes of Wrath*. New York: Chelsea House Publishers, 1988.

Clarke, Donald. *The Rise and Fall of Popular Music*. New York: St. Martin's Press, 1995.

Connolly, S. J. ed. *The Oxford Companion to Irish History*. New York: Oxford University Press, 1998.

French, Warren. *John Steinbeck*. 2nd ed. Boston: Twayne Publishers, 1975.

Gall, Tomothy L. et al. eds. *Worldmark: Encyclopedia of the Stats*. Detroit: Gale Research Inc., 1995.

Gladstein, Mimi Reisel. "Steinbeck and the Eternal Immigrants." *John Steinbeck: The Years of Greatness, 1936-1939*. Ed. Tetsumaro Hayashi. Tuscaloosa: University of Alabama Press, 1993.

Inazawa, Hideo. *Sutainbekku No Sekai (The World of John Steinbeck: The Grapes of Wrath and East of Eden*. Tokyo: Shicho-sha (Shicho Publishing Company), 1978.

Kiernan, Thomas. *The Intricate Music*. Boston: Little Brown and Company, 1979.

Laxton, Edward. *The Famine Ships: The Irish Exodus to America*. New York: Henry Holt and Company, 1997.

Lisca, Peter. "*The Grapes of Wrath* as Fiction." *John Steinbeck. The Grapes of Wrath: Text and Criticism*. Ed. Peter Lisca. London: Penguin Books, 1977.

O'Connor, Nuala. *Bringing It All Back Home: The Influence of Irish Music*. London: BBC Books Ltd., 1991.

Pater, Walter. *The Renaissance*. New York: Random House, 1873.

Salter, Christopher L. "John Steinbeck's *The Grapes of Wrath* as a Primer for Cultural Geography." *Critical Essays on Steinbeck's The Grapes of Wrath*. John Ditsky, ed. Boston: G. K. Hall&Co., 1989.

Schopenhauer, Arthur. *The World as Will and Presentation*. Trans. by E. F. J. Payne. Volume I. New York: Dover Publications Inc., 1969.

Steinbeck. Elaine, and Robert Wallsten, eds. *Steinbeck: A life in Letters*. New York: Viking Press, 1975.

Steinbeck, John. *The Grapes of Wrath*. New York: Viking Press, 1939.

_____. *In Dubious Battle*. New York: Covici-Friede, 1936.

_____. *Of Mice and Men*. New York: Covici-Friede, 1937.

_____. *The Log from the Sea of Cortez*. New York: Viking Press, 1951.

Taylor, Frank J. "The Great Migration." *John Steinbeck. The Grapes of Wrath: Text and Criticism*. Ed. Peter Lisca. London: Penguin Books, 1977.

Tessitore, John. *John Steinbeck: A Writer's Life*. New York: Franklin Watts, 2001.

Woodham-Smith, Cecil. *The Great Hunger: Ireland 1845-1849*. London: Penguin Books,

1991.

The Oxford English Dictionary. Volume IX. First Edition. Oxford: At the Clarendon Press, 1933.

Chapter 8

The Wayward Bus:
Juan Chicoy's Allegorical Journey

Introduction

Steinbeck published this work in 1947 after World War II. In the United States, this is the decade when the United States itself experienced an economic boom. This period witnessed the development of motorization, people's migration to the suburbs and the development of lodging facilities such as hotels and motels with a noticeable eye.

The story is set in Rebel Corners, a starting point for bus trips serving as a bus terminal and has accommodating facility. The writer anticipated this modern period after World War II and completed this work given this historical background with popular culture at that time. This slap stick novel contrasts with *The Pearl*, a fabulous story based on a Mexican folktale, released in the same year.

Steinbeck had already published works on the theme of "mobility" before the war. To say nothing of *The Grapes of Wrath*, in the novel *The Pastures of Heaven* (1932) the heroes as a catalyst moved to the fictitious place named Corral del Cielo but were unable to settle down for some reason or other and were obliged to leave the place as the story progressed.

After the war, the writer began to express his characteristic "Versatility" more than ever before. While it is commonly said that the use of "big words" and their simple symbolism; thus, to put it in a negative way, we could say that he has become a cheap writer.

It is commonly said that *Cannery Row* and *Sweet Thursday* (the sequel of *Cannery Row*) are the two greatest masterpieces of Steinbeck's literature after World War II, although the author of this book will consider the "Celticity" seen in this work, *The Wayward Bus*: especially from the viewpoint of "Druidism," then "Twilight" Imagery, and finally the story as a whole. I would like to try to examine the concept of "allegorical journey" flowing deeply in the whole story.

I

The story begins with a description of "oak trees," which are abundant in California.

> To the east the tops of the mountains were just becoming visible in outline with the dawn. Pimples came out carrying the lighted hand lamp and unkinking the cable behind him on the ground. The light made the great trees stand out, and it was reflected on the yellow-green of the new little oak leaves. (18)

This scene marks the first appearance of pimple-faced Pimples, who is preparing for the bus' departure. The writer is best at depicting scenes with oak trees standing out clearly in the morning sun.

In this way, the writer lets the narrator hint to the reader about the outcome of the story. Steinbeck uses this kind of description scene in almost all of his works including the great and world-famous masterpiece *The Grapes of Wrath*. The exquisite use of color at the beginning of the story hints at the ending of the story as is seen in the first scene of "The Chrysanthemums" in *The Long Valley*.

As Louis Owens points out (Owens 109), the depiction of December in the opening section "fog and rain do not go together" (9) in "The Chrysanthemums" can also be said to hint at the sad ending of the story.

In *The Wayward Bus* also, we will consider this depiction of the scene based on the following facts. The expression "stand out," focusing on "Ambiguity," connotes the "conspicuousness" of "oak trees" and another meaning of "deviating from the standard and positioning it outside." If we can perceive this connotation, we can deeply read the meaning of the sentence "It was a quick grouping of a Camel advertisement on the wall—another blonde on a poster with balloon-like breasts—and a tree [oak tree] she [Camille Oaks] could see through a window" (128). The secret behind Camille Oaks is that she stands out and deviates from the norm. Furthermore, this name comes from the two meanings of oak trees symbolizing "Druidism" and the concept of "Druidism," which symbolizes God in Celtic culture.

In addition to the above quotation, this "light" is the twilight at the turning point from the darkness of night to the dim light of morning, and we understand that it means "dawn." Next, we consider the following cited passage.

> Light was creeping up the sky and over the mountains. The colorless dawn of grays and blacks moved in so that white and blue things were silver and red and dark green things were black. The new leaves on the big oaks were black and white, and the mountain rims were sharp. (24)

The expression "dawn of grays" that the narrator describes is an image of "Celtic Twilight." Also, by depicting "The new leaves on the big oaks were black and white," it can be thought of as hinting at the writer's eternal theme of "good and evil" of the work *The Pearl*, written and published in the same year 1947.

Steinbeck stated that "there are only good and bad things..." (*The Pearl* 2) and also expressed his own idea of "the story of good and evil" (*JN* 4) in *The Journal of a Novel: The East of Eden Letters,* as regards *East of Eden* published later.

As for the "Celtic Twilight," we will consider by quoting a poem "Into the Twilight" representative of W. B. Yeats; the third and fourth stanzas seem to be related to the interpretation of this work.

> Come heart, where hill is heaped upon hill:
> For there the mystical brotherhood
> Of sun and moon and hollow and wood

And river and stream work out their will;

And God stands winding His lonely horn,
And time and the world are ever in flight;
And love is less kind than the gray twilight,
And hope is less dear than the dew of the morn. (Finneran 59)

In this poem, the word 'mystical' appears in the third stanza and the last two lines, "Of sun and moon and hollow and wood/And river and stream work out their will;" a passage reminiscent of Romanticism, and in the fourth stanza, in this twilight, "love is less kind than the gray light," these lines of which seem to be comparable to the first vividly expressed part of the scene which the mysterious woman Camille Oaks tells us at the end of the story.

There was a little rim of lighter sky around the edge of a great dark cloud over the western mountains, and then as the cloud lifted the evening star shone out of it, clear and washed and steady.

"Star light, star bright, first star I see tonight, wish I may, wish I might, get the wish I wish tonight."

Camille turned her head sleepily. "What did you say?"

Norma was silent for a moment. Then she asked softly, "We'll see how it goes?"

"Yeah, we'll see how it goes," said Camille. (312)

An Irish-American film director Walt Disney created the similar lines that hinted at the completion of "Pinocchio," in a famous animation film entitled *Pinocchio* which was released around in the year the book *The Wayward Bus* was published. However, what is noteworthy is the scene where Camille Oaks speaks kindly for the first time. Here the gentleness of Camille Oaks reveals deeply in the "Celtic Twilight," in "a little rim of lighter sky." In the passage "We'll see how it goes" reflects Steinbeck's own philosophy of "non-teleological thinking."

This scene is depicted in the evening, when the sun is setting, and this is the "twilight" zone. This is the most important time period when talking about "Celtic Culture." As to why it can be said that these are Celtic depictions of the scenes, the "twilight" hours mentioned earlier, i.e., "the twilight hours when late afternoon changes into night," and "the twilight hours when night turns to dawn," are depicted as one aspect of "Celtic Culture." This is because it is thought to be a time period reminiscent of the Utopia "Tír na nÓg" and a time period in which fairies can regenerate.

According to Imura, for the Celts, the time when fairies begin to move is "the time before 'rebirth', namely, 'the twilight before dawn,' and the time after 'rebirth,' returning to 'darkness'" (Kamata and Tsuruoka 47, trans. Mine), and from this idea, this time period can be considered to be two "twilight hours" namely "before dawn and twilight" (Fujimoto 741), as is pointed out by Reiji Fujimoto.

Regarding the night which governs darkness, Imura said, "with the image of 'death' in the earth, the ethnic and mythological aspects of fairies are revived as 'eternal memories from the past to the present'" (Kamata and Tsuruoka 47-48, trans. Mine). Therefore, these two hours of the day, "the twilight hours before dawn" and "the twilight hours," are, as Fujimoto points out, "tired of this world dominated by the notions of good and evil. It can be thought of as the Utopia of the Celts, 'Tír na nÓg'" (Fujimoto 742, trans. Mine), where people escape from time and space. What Fujimoto considers here is, in short, a "mysterious period of time."

Now, since Camille Oaks appeared in Chapter 7, passengers around her have praised her for her beauty. Camille Oaks is described as a mysterious woman and as a sex symbol, and from the beginning of the story, Camille Oaks does not tell people about her real name and observes what is going on around her. In the words of Takahiko Sugiyama, she is depicted as an "existence" that "stands out" (Sugiyama 576). I will list up as many expressions and depictions related to Camille Oaks as possible here. Similar expressions and depictions will be omitted.

> blonde, dish, smelled of sex, hustler, dental nurse, right and dainty and fine, tramp, giant wine glasses and the stags, goddess, etc.

In this way, although Camille Oaks is often portrayed in a negative image, there are some quotations that portray her in a slightly positive way. This is summarized in the scene Camille Oaks speaks to Norma at the end of the story, as if she had realized the logic of things, as follows:

> "Look, kid," she said. "You [Norma]'ll just have to believe this until you find it out for yourself—everybody's a tramp some time or other. Everybody. And the worst tramps of all are the ones that call it something else." (302)

This passage seems to be what Camille Oaks thinks is the essence of humanity. People must hide their true nature. If we don't live like that, people around us won't respect us. Camille herself lives her life by being kind to those around her by putting on a so-called good face. But the real evil is, as Camille Oaks says, instead of bringing it to the surface, it seems to be a way of living by "calling it something else" and hiding it from others. At this point Camille Oaks can be said to be a "goddess" (224) who sees everything through.

II

There are at least 11 characters in this story. Louie, a bus driver and womanizer; Juan Chicoy, a guide and driver; Alice, his wife; Pimples Carson, Juan's assistant with a pimpled face; Norma, the former employee of the bus terminal at Rebel Corners; Elliott Pritchard, a businessman; Bernice Pritchard, his wife; Mildred, Pritchard's daughter; Camille Oaks, a mysterious woman; Ernest Horton, an inventor and lastly, Van Brunt, an old man suffering from a cerebral vascular disorder.

In the story development, many scenes are described with the imagery of light and color, used as a lighting device for stage plays, creating an exhibition that is applied to both a novel and a dramatic play.

This is why Steinbeck himself chose the title of this work. The first few lines quoted in the back cover are from *Everyone*, a medieval play with the theme of morality. The story progresses like this medieval morality play in this work. In the past, this statement was often pointed out by various critics and researchers, but Takahiko Sugiyama, in particular, has pointed out that "The writer does not sufficiently convince our readers that this work is an allegory or a moral novel. He hasn't been able to do that. The reason is that these devices are so-called *deus ex machina*. They were placed too abruptly in this story, as if they were a makeshift solution and they were often inserted too suddenly" (Sugiyama 570, trans. Mine).

Rather than categorizing this work a "morality novel," it may be put into a genre of a "morality play" like a medieval morality play *Everyone*. However, as a "morality novel," this work seems to be an interestingly attempted genre to give a new spotlight to the reader. In addition to this idea, the value of the writer Steinbeck's "Versatility" will be more evaluated, although Steinbeck's using the devices like *deus ex machina* mentioned above was inserted and juxtaposed "suddenly" on a "whim" as if they were carefully exposed. This is the humor of the writer's carefully calculated usage.

One of the most important characters in the development of this story is Camille Oaks as was mentioned before and I would like to explain it in more detail.

Camille Oaks worked at night business in the past, and in the eyes of the public, it can't be said that she has a good status. However, she has a sensitivity that quickly perceives the evil ugliness of the people belonging to the upper class. This can be understood from various expressions in the text. According to the following quotation, this is evident.

> Camille looked at Mr. Pritchard's face and her eyes flicked to the club button on his lapel. She knew where he had seen her. When she took off her clothes and sat in the bowl of wine she very carefully didn't look at the men's faces. There was something in their wet, bulging eyes and limp, half-smiling mouths that frightened her. She had a feeling that if she looked directly at one he might leap on her. To her, her audiences were blobs of pink faces and hundreds of white collars and neat four-in-hand ties. (129-130)

The upper class wears hundreds of "white collars" and "neat four-in-hand ties," which are associated with "high society." Mr. Pritchard can be said to be the representative. However, the reality is that he hides a very ugly side.

Camille, who can't believe others, gradually comes to regain her true self by Norma. Norma was once working at the bus terminal of Rebel Corners, but after an incident, she decided to quit her job, get on this bus and travel somewhere far away. It was Camille who gently and kindly comforted and treated Norma in great depression. We'll see the following quotation.

> Norma was flushed with pleasure. She had never been so happy in her life. This beautiful creature was nice to her. They were friends. And she [Camille] didn't say they'd live together. She said she'd see how things worked out. For some reason this gave Norma a great deal of confidence. (187)

"This beautiful creature" here refers to Camille, and the two of them get to know each other. This is a warmhearted scene where their friendship blooms for the first time. Even after this, their friendship remains strong.

In the same chapter, I will not quote it but Norma gently shows concern for

Camille, who is being courted by Pimples. It was Camille who took advantage of Norma and coaxed her into getting some fresh air. And the last scene of the story, their friendship connects to the scene quoted earlier.

Next, among the 11 characters, we will look at the characteristics of those who stand at the opposite of Camille Oaks. In this story, the persons who are the opposite of Camille Oaks are Mr. Pritchard, a successful businessman, his wife Bernice, and their daughter Mildred. Moreover, there is Ernest Horton, who believes himself to be an inventor and entrepreneur. I would like to analyze these people one by one.

First, about Mr. Pritchard, a president of the company. He takes pride in his success as a businessman and is quite self-confident, so his class is also superior to other peoples'. He is depicted as someone who belongs to the top, or so-called high society. This is clear from the next quotation.

> Mr. Pritchard had a whole series of tactics for getting on with people. He never forgot the name of a man richer or more powerful than he, and he never knew the name of a man less powerful. (152)

Pritchard's description goes on to be stated, "He had found that to make a man mention his own name would put that man at a slight disadvantage" (152). From this description of Mr. Pritchard, it seems that people who belong to so-called high society live their lives hiding their own true self. This kind of hiding true nature is depicted in the description of Camille mentioned earlier.

Next, I will consider Bernice, Mrs. Pritchard. Mr. Pritchard succeeds as a president and because of his success, his wife also feels like a celebrity. However, in the following situation, her true self as a woman is thought to be revealed. Consider the immediate aftermath of Camille's incredibly vulgar behavior.

> Mrs. Pritchard was beating herself with words. Her [Camille's] reaction had

frightened her. She said to herself, even whispering the words, "What a horrible, vulgar story. What animals those young girls are." (255)

The term "those young girls" used here refers to Norma and Camille, who have become good friends, but the term "animals" is used instead. In this way, she is portrayed as despising the two people who are of a lower status than her, but in reality, "Mrs. Pritchard's face was glowing. She breathed very rapidly" (254-255), and she is reminded of her former lover. The writer shows the situation in a way that evokes sexual excitement.

The daughter Mildred is struggling behind her parents' "high class" consciousness. As a 21-year-old university student in the prime of his youth, she ends up accompanying his father on his own vacation trip to Mexico.

> Now Mildred kept her own counsel, thought her own thoughts, and waited for the time when death, marriage, or accident would free her from parents. But she loved her parents, and she would have been frightened at herself had it ever come to the surface of her mind that she wished them dead. (67-68)

If you listen to Mildred's inner voice, which goes so far as to wish that her parents were dead, we will notice the word "surface." Mildred has seen the true nature of her upper-class parents and can see through their "essential" side. Toward the end of the story, Mildred temporarily develops an affair with Juan, a driver and guide. Here it seems that the woman's true nature, rather than the superficial, is being expressed. This is probably due to the cleverness of the way the story unfolds.

Ernest Horton is an inventor who supposedly makes a living from his patents, and it seems that he has succeeded so far by distinguishing between the front and back of things, observing his opponent, and using that strategy.

"Everything goes to show something. I have to laugh sometimes. You know, we're supposed to be a mechanical people. Everybody drives a car and has an icebox and a radio. I suppose people really think they are mechanical minded, but let a little dirt get in the carburetor and — well, a car has to stand there until a mechanic comes and takes out the screen. Let a light go off, and an electrician has to come and put in a new fuse. Let an elevator stop, and there's a panic." (276)

This scene expresses the fragility of modern people. With the progress of civilization, we pretend to know something. Even in scenes where we can read Steinbeck's warning to us modern people who wear a mask of hypocrisy. I would like to focus on the word "something" quoted in this part. Although it is an ordinary word, it has the meaning of "something important." One thing is certain. In this word "something," there is "the real truth." I can't help but find the important meaning of "authentic." It is because the theme of this work, as mentioned earlier, lies in the Camille's line, "the worst tramps of all are the ones that call it something else." (302)

III

Now, we will finally get to the core part of this novel: as to how this work uses the device of Celtic representation, I would like to consider how *Everyone* is well constructed into this modern morality novel.

Camille Oaks, which is the allegory indicated by the name "oak trees" symbolizing "Druidism," and furthermore, lighting equipment and the imagery of "twilight" I have already mentioned many times are widely used throughout this work.

I would like to consider the writer Steinbeck's religious views that flow throughout his works. His religious views are not specifically stated by himself, but they are clearly expressed throughout his works. We can get a glimpse of his religious views seen in his early works, one of which is *To a God Unknown* (1933) with his religious views very specifically expressed.

The idea of polytheism emerged in *To a God Unknown*, and in *The Pearl* (1947) there emerged frequent use of the lowercase plural "gods" instead of writing "God." When we think about it, it can be said that the writer Steinbeck creates works that make readers aware of "Celtic gods."

In the California history, since the Carmel Mission in the late 18th century, Christianity has been propagated by Hispanic settlers and furthermore by Irish immigrants. Mexican Indians and Irish immigrants came into contact with each other from the 19th century onwards. This is thought to be because they have coexisted with this idea of polytheism. Therefore, since the writer Steinbeck is greatly influenced by his mother who also has Scottish-Irish blood on her mother's side with this idea of polytheism, we may conclude that Steinbeck himself was born with this Celtic perspective consciously or unconsciously.

As various researchers and critics have pointed out, this work also uses allegorical techniques. We can see the evidence.

First, Juan Chicoy, who is depicted as a bus driver and guide, is described as an Irish-Mexican inherited from his Irish mother. The small metal of Virgin Guadalupe is placed near the bus driver's cab as a talisman. Various researchers and critics agree that Juan Chicoy symbolizes Jesus Christ. There are many scenes where Juan possesses this metal as a talisman. I would like to quote just one. A Mexican father worships and celebrates this metal of Virgin Guadalupe. The similar atmosphere Juan's father worships and celebrates this metal is well depicted in *Everyone*, several stanzas of which are collected in *The Wayward Bus*, following two medieval works from *Piers Plowman* to *Pilgrim Progress*. The following quotation corresponds to a scene reminiscent of *Everyone*.

> Skyrockets were by nature the way to celebrate Saints' Days. Who could think otherwise? The rising, hissing tube was obviously the spirit rising to Heaven, and the big, flashing bang at the top was the dramatic entrance

to the throne room of Heaven. Juan Chicoy, while not a believer in an orthodox sense, now he was fifty, would nevertheless have been uneasy driving the bus without the Guadalupana to watch over him. (20-21)

The way this quotation is described as "a dramatic entrance to the throne room of heaven" is thought to be a symbol of *Everyone* from *Piers Plowman* to *Pilgrim Progress*. It seems to be one aspect of the allegorical journey of the story.

"Oaks" incorporated in the name of Camille Oaks is symbolized as "Druidism" in Celtic representation. I have already mentioned this perspective many times, so I will refrain from discussing it here, In chapter 12 of this novel, a real "oak" floating up and down the San Isidro River is introduced. It is thought that by being drawn in parallel as a real "oak" tree, Camille Oaks, casting a mysterious light, plays a major role in the development of the work. Consider the following quotation.

As they [Breed and Juan] watched, a great old live oak tree came rolling heavily down the stream. When it struck the bridge and turned, the whole structure cried out and seemed to brace itself. The tree caught in the submerged underpinning and there came a shrill, ripping sound from under the bridge. (184)

This depiction is a scene that depicts the rain and river flooding as natural forces in more detail. In this depiction, despite old man Van Brunt's vehement objections, the bus continues along the old road to the destination San Juan de la Cruz with the help of the Oak Tree symbolizing Druidism. It seems that this is a foreshadowing depiction, aiming at the place of San Juan de la Cruz.

Another foreshadowing part that the bus successfully arrives is in chapter 10, which is right in the middle chapter of this work. We can also see this is also a depiction of the ferocity of nature, but it is also a depiction of an Angus cow floating up and down the San Ishidro River. Angus cow originally comes from

Scotland. The author of this book considers it to be one of the symbols of the gods that appear in Celtic mythology.

> And he [Breed] had seen a few planks of planed lumber come twisting down, and then a piece of roof with shingles still on, and then the drowned, bobbing body of McElroy's black Angus bull, square and short-legged. As it went under the bridge it rolled over on its back, and Breed could see the wild upturned eyes and the flapping tongue. (164)

This scene is also reminiscent of Celtic mythology. In Yeats' poem quoted earlier, the line "God stands winding His lonely horn" indicates that the Celtic god is an animal incarnate. The Celtic god is depicted as an incarnation of an animal with horns like a deer or cow symbolizing the Celtic gods.

Among many works written about "Celtic God," let me quote just one. Here is Green's explanation.

> Ireland had a predominantly pastoral economy in antiquity, and cattle figure prominently in the written mythological tradition. Bulls were important images here, having close associations with the supernatural. (Green 1992, 52)

Looking at it this way, this work incorporates many devices of Celtic representation. It seems that this representation makes the work more profound.

Next, comparing this work with *Everyone*, especially analyzing the essence of morality, I would like to give one conclusion.

Conclusion

Until now, various elements of Celtic representation have been witnessed throughout this work. As I have verified, comparisons with the medieval morality play in which this work uses several lines as its subtitle seems to have been few in research so far. In the previous Steinbeck research on this work, Peter Lisca, a leading Steinbeck researcher, interprets this work as the "actual journey by the allegorical bus" (Lisca 233). Richard Astro concludes, "Steinbeck focused directly on the specimen-types who people the modern world and attempted with little artistic success to drive these characters to penitence" (Astro 177).

Furthermore, the moral values that Steinbeck uses in his works, that is, "good and evil" seems, the author of this book believes, to be a deep-rooted theme in "Puritanism," an eternal theme in the whole American Literature, and it has been noted by scholars and critics of American literature that Steinbeck's idea on morality is rather lenient. That seems to be an almost unanimous opinion. For example, the consistent idea of "Puritanism" cannot be found in Steinbeck's works. The reason is, to put it simply, lies in the difference of length and depth of European and American history. The French Revolution changed the moral outlook of Europe, including Britain. It is generally said that the idea of "new morality" has sprung up; it seems that this idea is closer to the moral perspective that Steinbeck takes up.

Several lines of *Everyone* quoted in this work are as follows as a beginning:

> I pray you all gyve your audyence
> And here this mater with reverence,
> By fygure a morall playe;
> The somonynge of Everyman called it is,
> That of our lyves and endynge shewes
> How transytory we be all daye. (1)

I will refrain from giving a complete synopsis here. Everyman is summoned by Death. He is summoned and has to go to the graveyard. Everyone tries to borrow the aid of Friendship, Kindred, Cousin, Goods, Good Deeds, Knowledge,

Confession, Beauty, Strength, Discretion, and Five Wits. However, in the end, those who tried to help until the end were Good Deeds and Five Wits. Furthermore, when Everyman finally tried to enter the graveyard, Five Wits receded from Everyone and only Good Deeds stayed along with Everyone to the end.

I will consider the last lines of the morality play of Good Deeds' line, as follows:

> All erthly thynges is but vanyte,
>
> Beautc, Strengthe, and Dyscrecyon do man forsake,
>
> Folysshe frends and kynnesmen that fayre spake,
>
> All fleeth save Good Dedes, and that am I. (48)

Now, here is a scene in *The Wayward Bus* that responds well to the lines of this "Good Deeds." It is near the end, a scene of a conversation between Kit, also known as Pimples, and Camille Oaks. I will quote them and discuss them next.

> "Have you got a girl now?" Camille continued.
>
> "Well, kind of a one. But she's—er—well, she's kind of silly."
>
> "Is she true to you?"
>
> "Sure," said Pimples.
>
> "How do you know?"
>
> "Well, I never could—I mean—yeah, I'm sure." (282)

At a first glance, this is an ordinary conversation, but the phrase "is true" in this conversation is what makes this work so special. It seems that this will be the theme of this work. In the passage quoted above about Camille's line, "the worst tramps of all are the ones that call it something else." (302)

This line seems to be linked to the lines "All is nothing but emptiness. / Beautiful things alone can't cover everything in this world" (trans. Mine), as "Good Deeds" says at the end of the story of *Everyone*. In other words, even if we commit a crime, we can get along well by being "true."

By the way, the word that has a common image for "Good" and "True" in "Good Deeds" is "Virtue." It turns out that it is so from the descriptions of *Oxford English Dictionary*. I will quote them one by one and consider about them.

> Good: Applied to <u>God</u>, sometimes in the wide sense, as connoting moral perfection generally, and sometimes with more restricted reference to His benevolence. (IV. 288)
>
> True: In more general sense: Honest, honourable, upright, <u>virtuous</u>, trustworthy: free from decent, sincere, truthful; of actions, feelings, etc. sincere, unfeigned. (XI.417)
>
> Virtue: The power or operative influence inherent in a supernatural or <u>divine being</u>. (VII. 238)
>
> (Underlined, Mine)

As is well known, the word "true" which means "sincere" has a definition of "virtuous." The word "virtue" has the definition of "divine being." Therefore, in this sense, the meaning of "True" leads to the image that the literal meaning of "good" is "applied to God" and means "moral perfection." In short, "True" is well linked to "Good Deeds."

When we think like this, *The Wayward Bus* seems to be likened to the morality play of *Everyone*. It can well be thought of as a morality novel written in the way of Celtic Allegory.

Works Cited and Referred Bibliographies

Astro, Richard. *John Steinbeck and Edward F. Ricketts: The Shaping of a Novelist.* University of Minnesota Press, 1973.

Brekilien, Yann. *La Mythologie Celtique.* Paris: Édition du Rocher, 1993.

Cunliffe, Barry. *The Celtic World*. London: Constable, 1992.

Finneran, Richard J. ed. *The Collected Poems of W.B. Yeats*. New York: Simon & Schuster Inc., 1996.

Green, Miranda J. *Exploring the World of Druids*. London: Thames & Hudson Ltd., 1997.

_____. *Celtic Myths*. London: British Museum Press, 1993.

Lisca, Peter. *The Wide World of John Steinbeck*. Reprinted, New York: Gordian Press, 1981.

Moses, Monterose J. ed. *Everyman: A Morality Play*. New York: J.F. Taylor & Company, 1903.

Owens, Louis. *John Steinbeck's Re-Vision of America*. Athens: University of Georgia Press, 1985.

Steinbeck, John. *The Wayward Bus*. New York: Viking Press, 1947.

[Sugiyama, Takahiko ed., supervising trans. *The Pearl /The Wayward Bus*. Osaka: Osaka Kyoiku Tosho, 1999.]

_____. *The Pearl*. New York: Viking Press, 1947.

_____. *Journal of a Novel: The East of Eden Letters [JN]*. New York: Viking Press, 1969.

Tedlock, E.W. JR and Wicker, CV eds. *Steinbeck and His Critics*. Albuquerque: University of Mexico Press, 1957.

Yeats, W. B. "The Celtic Twilight" in *Mythologies*. London: Macmillan Press, 1959.

[W. B. Yates. *The Celtic Twilight*, translated by Kimie Imura. Tokyo: Chikuma Shobo, 1993.]

Zakzek, Iain. *Chronicles of the Celts*. London: Collins & Brown Ltd., 1996.

Fujimoto, Reiji. "Yeats," Fumiyo Uesugi, ed. *Light Imagery: English Poetry in Tradition*. Tokyo: Kirihara Shoten, 1985.

Hara, Kiyoshi. *Celtic Water Veins*. Tokyo: Kodansha, 2007.

Kamata, Toji and Mayumi Tsuruoka eds. *Celt and Japan*. Tokyo: Kadokawa Shoten, 2000.

Kimura, Masatoshi ed. *65 Chapters for Understanding the Celts*. Tokyo: Akashi Shoten, 2018.

Sonoi, Hidetoshi. *English Literature and Morals*. Fukuoka: Kyushu University Press,

2005.

Green, M. J. *Dictionary of Celtic Myth and Legend*. London: Hudson and Thames, 1992.

The Oxford English Dictionary. First Edition. Oxford: At the Clarendon Press, 1933.

Chapter 9

Cannery Row and *Sweet Thursday:*
"A Midautumn-Twilight's Dream" from "Gregorian Music" to "Polyphony"

Introduction

Steinbeck is often said to be a "versatile" writer. In 1930s in America, his works reflect the background of socialism ideology and the Great Depression in the US. He is a great Nobel Prize-winning writer with his characteristic way of creating fabulous works based on narrative/mythological as well as biological/ecological ideas.

Steinbeck himself described *Cannery Row* as full of nostalgia, stating "It [*Cannery Row*]'s written on four levels and people can take what they can receive out of it. One thing—it never mentions the war—not once" (*SLL* 273), and regarding *Sweet Thursday*, he said, "It [*Sweet Thursday*] is a continuation concerned not with what did happen but with what might have happened" (*SLL* 474).

As many researchers and critics have pointed out, both works depict Steinbeck's philosophies such as "non-teleological thinking," "phalanx theory," "holistic" concept and more. The idea of "group-man" is well illustrated, and as for *Cannery Row*, despite the bad reputation of Malcolm Cowley's "a poisoned cream puff" (Fontenrose 101), we can discern many deep themes hidden behind in the work.

Fontenrose stated "While men admire the virtues, they love the products of the vices" (Fontenrose 107), recognizing the "ambivalent" aspect of this work and Lisca stated "an adequate statement of the 'reverence for life' which pervades *Cannery Row* and the frame of mind into which Steinbeck retreated following his experience of war" (Lisca 217), analyzing the way Doc recites the three Sanskrit poems narrated at the end of the work.

123

Meyer also notes that "The book's conclusion with Doc's paradoxical joy/ sorrow is therefore appropriate to the reality of *Weltschmerz* (world sorrow)" (Meyer 61).

In *Sweet Thursday*, Timmerman highly praised the construction of the work as a "farce," stating "none is so carefully or successfully arranged as the party in *Sweet Thursday*" (Timmerman 179) and DeMott states "When Doc fully admits the subjective and objective poles of humanity are necessary to live and to create, he learns the most valuable lesson of his life" (DeMott 178).

The author of this book focuses on Frankie, a socially vulnerable person who has not been the subject of much criticism so far in *Cannery Row* although it is not mentioned in the text, while adding consideration to the idea of "reformation" from the perspective of "Celtic Twilight." Furthermore, in the sequel *Sweet Thursday*, the true value of Steinbeck's literature featuring "phalanx" theory, "holism" philosophy and "group-man" theory will be well clarified, considering the "music" that appears in many parts of the two works as a metaphor for Doc's reformation, and changes his true self from an "individual" perspective to the "whole" perspective analyzing the process of his sublimation.

I

Steinbeck's *Cannery Row* is a myth that is the writer's original style: It is a masterpiece that has both a metaphorical and allegorical aspect, in addition to a "holistic" element. In this chapter, we will consider Frankie, a boy who has not been discussed much so far.

Young Frankie appears in Chapter 10, and the scene in which he appears is not very cool. He is depicted as this quotation that "For a week or so he stood outside the basement door and looked in. Then one day he stood inside the door. Ten days later he was in the basement" (*CR* 58). As a result, it follows that "They didn't want him in school. There was no place for him" (*CR* 59). The most important passage is the statement that "He wasn't an idiot, he wasn't dangerous, his parents, or parent, would not pay for his keep in an institution" (*CR* 59).

Despite this, criticisms of Frankie are harsh, calling him a "criminally insane" (Lisca 210), a "mentally defective boy" (Metzger 24), and even "mentally retarded" (Meyer 42). However, compared with Tularecito, a boy of about the same age who appears in Chapter 4 of *The Pastures of Heaven*, Frankie does not harm others. Frankie is rather "a nice, good, and kind boy" (*CR* 60). However, as is stated at the end of chapter 10, the thing happened that "Tray and beer collapsed forward into the young woman's lap" (*CR* 62). However, this was rather an act Frankie did out of the extreme stress, and it can be interpreted as an unavoidable blunder because he is a boy.

Franky's biggest mistake is in Chapter 28, when he holds a party for his beloved Doc by stealing a watch from a store as a present for Doc.

> "What's the matter, Frankie?" Doc asked.
>
> "He broke into Jacob's last night," the chief said. "Stole some stuff. We got in touch with his mother. She says it's not her fault because he hangs around your place all the time.
>
> "Frankie—you shouldn't have done it," said Doc. (*CR* 185)

Of course stealing is bad, but if you compare it with Tularecito, a boy about the same age as Frankie who appears in Chapter 4 of *The Pastures of Heaven* mentioned earlier, Tularecito is a boy who hits a person with a shovel and hurts him. Frankie's crime seems to be much lighter than Tularecito's, since the latter ended up being sent to a criminal insane similar to a juvenile detention center just like Hazle. Rather, other than Mack and Frankie, Doc's friends drink "alcohol," while Doc is away, go on a rampage, and destroy facilities in Doc's laboratory, even though they are friends (*CR* Chapter 20). Therefore, this should be considered to be a much more serious offense.

By narrating Frankie's childhood in parallel with Hazle's, the writer succeeds in making Frankie's future more reassuring. This is Steinbeck's excellent specialty in depicting foreshadowing. However, Steinbeck's style is quite predictable and, to say the worst, it can be a little simple.

For example, the death of the old dog predicts Lennie's death in *Of Mice and Men*, and the disappearance of the eldest son Noah predicts Tom Joad's "dropout" in *The Grapes of Wrath*. If we count them, there is no end to them.

> Hazel grew up—did four years in grammar school, four years in reform school, and didn't learn anything in either place. Reform schools are supposed to teach viciousness and criminality but Hazel didn't pay enough attention. He came out of reform school as innocent of viciousness as he was of fractions and long division. (*CR* Chapter VI 32-33)

In this way, as is mentioned earlier, by overlapping 26-year-old Hazle and 11-year-old Frankie, Steinbeck seems to present readers with his unique and excellent method of foreshadowing. The way the last part is written in Chapter 28, "...maybe he [Frankie] had a reason (that he loves Doc)" (*CR* 186) suggests that Frankie, like Hazle, will return as a "good person" who is free from so-called "evil." Hazel's hard work at Doc's laboratory is mentioned throughout the text, including in Chapter 6. Therefore, even though Frankie and other characters appear in this work, despite their failures, there is not even a hint of sadness.

This may be one point of view for interpreting the work, but I believe that one of the clues to deciphering this work lies in the way in which "dusk" and "dawn" are depicted at the beginning of chapters 4 and 14 respectively. It is during this "magical" time that the "original joy" of party-hosting persons emerges.

> In the evening just at dusk, a curious thing happened on Cannery Row. It happened in the time between sunset and the lighting of the street light. There is a small quiet gray period then. (*CR* Chapter IV 22)

> Early morning is a time of magic in Cannery Row. In the gray time after

the light has come and before the sun has risen, the Row seems to hang suspended out of time in a silvery light. (*CR* Chapter XIV 88)

Twilight is the time when the sun goes down in the evening and when the sun rises at dawn, and this time of twilight is the most important time when considering Celtic culture. In Ireland, the sun often sets after 9pm. Therefore, we must consider that night, as we know it, overlaps with "twilight." The time when the party is held is just in this "twilight."

According to Kimie Imura, for the Celts, the time when fairies begin to move is "the time before 'rebirth', namely, 'the twilight before dawn,' and the time after 'rebirth,' returning to 'darkness'" (Kamata and Tsuruoka 47, trans. Mine), and from this idea, this time period can be considered to be two "twilight hours" namely "before dawn and twilight" (Fujimoto 741), as is pointed out by Reiji Fujimoto.

Regarding the night which governs darkness, Imura said, "with the image of 'death' in the earth, the ethnic and mythological aspects of fairies are revived as 'eternal memories from the past to the present'" (Kamata and Tsuruoka 47-48, trans. Mine). Therefore, these two hours of the day, "the twilight hours before dawn" and "the twilight hours," are, as Fujimoto points out, "tired of this world dominated by the notions of good and evil. It can be thought of as the Utopia of the Celts, 'Tír na nÓg'" (Fujimoto 742), where people escape from time and space. What Fujimoto considers here is, in short, a "mysterious period of time."

At the same time, I would like to note that this work is set at a party held on Doc's birthday (October 27th), which is close to Halloween (October 31th). In the Celtic calendar, the year begins on the day when fairies go from the depth of the earth to the surface of the earth via the caves, and this day is commonly known as *Samhain*. In the Celtic world, this *Samhain* is "a dangerous time; a period in which the conventional boundaries of space and time were temporarily suspended and where the spirits of the Otherworld mingled freely with the living; a time of immense spiritual energy, when monstrous events were liable to take place" (Green 1997, 36).

In this work, the power of Doc, Mack, and his friends will reach their full potential in the lead-up to October 27th. If we pay attention to the word "ghosts" uttered by Doc (*CR* 144 and many others) and the use of the word "gray" at the beginning of chapters 4 and 14 that I pointed out earlier, we can see that this "gray" is the Celtic word "gray," not "grey" in its spelling. This is an image of the light from the Celtic Utopia "Tír na Nóg." The work begins with a depiction of a scene filled with the "gray" imagery of Cannery Row, and concludes with the word "dusty" (*CR* 208: gray imagery), which represents the eyes of a rattle snake.

We will discuss Yeats' poem "Into the Twilight" by quoting the third and fourth stanzas, which seem to be relevant to my consideration.

Come heart, where hill is heaped upon hill:
For there the mystical brotherhood
Of sun and moon and hollow and wood
And river and stream work out their will;

And God stands winding His lonely horn,
And time and the world are ever in flight;
And love is less kind than the gray twilight,
And hope is less dear than the dew of the morn. (Finerran 59)

In this poem, the word 'mystical' appears in the third stanza and the last two lines can be interpreted as "Even the sun, the moon, the caves, the forests, the rivers, and the streams live according to their own will." Furthermore, in the fourth stanza, it can be interpreted that in this twilight, there is a gentleness that even love can't surpass it, so if we apply this to all the characters in this work, we can see that all of them are "into the twilight."

It is an undeniable fact that this is the state of mind of "Tír na nÓg." In other words, it is important that the storytelling of this work proceeds during the "twilight" of the traditional "Celtic Culture." This "magic" time behind the

"Celtic Twilight," plays an important role as a metaphor for Frankie's "reforming" of his guilt. Although this is just one hypothesis, it is thought that the "phalanx theory" was born from Steinbeck's discussion of Celtic ethnicity. The word "phalanx" was used "when the men pulled their shields together and advanced in lockstep" (Benson 269) in the ancient Rome toward the battle of Celtic peoples. During this period, "battles were fought over and over again" (Hara 129, trans. Mine). I will refrain from going into details here, as I have discussed this in detail in Chapter 3, but the "turtle" depicted in Chapter 3 of his masterpiece *The Grapes of Wrath* has been mentioned many times. It would not be an exaggeration to say that Steinbeck's portrayal of the story, which is reminiscent of Celtic culture, is a wonderful example of how it continues to move forward despite facing obstacles and being turned upside down.

By the way, Hideo Inazawa was involved in the research on the relationship between Steinbeck and the Celtic people more than 50 years ago.

> In the end, the great thing about *Cannery Row* is the quality of the episodes that are scattered here and there and the quality of the stories. It will be able to focus on the points that can provide some clues to Steinbeck's mysterious connection with Lao Tzu. Will it be possible to accurately grasp Steinbeck's connection with Lao Tzu? Or can it only be expressed in vague abstract words such as "Oriental" and "Mystical," which the Celtic people are said to possess. (Inazawa 222-223, trans. Mine)

Lovejoy argues that this "vague" view of the universe was a process of gradual evolution from an immature one, citing Leibniz's writings from the late 17th century, "It is probable that the earliest animals were marine forms, and that the amphibia and land-animals are descended from these. And elsewhere Leibniz on metaphysical grounds extends this conception of gradual development to the entire universe" (Lovejoy 256), and Celtic thought is based on this idea. This is consistent with the idea of developmental stages. In other words, the Celtic view of life exists as a collective entity in the relationship between the earth and the underground. This is because when Christianity began to be propagated to the Celtic world, the Celtic gods were said to be "gods that were chased out by the newly arrived humans and came to live underground" (Hara 45, trans. Mine). As for this, many of the descriptions of the sea in *Cannery Row*, similar to the many descriptions of the "land" mountains and the earth in *The Pastures of Heaven*, *Tortilla Flat*, and *To a God Unknown* can be said to lead to Steinbeck's own philosophical view and ecology, Steinbeck's "holistic" view of life: a Celtic view of life representing Celtic myths and folktales. In other words, Steinbeck's "phalanx theory" was originally based on Celtic thought, but through his "meeting with Ed Ricketts in 1930" (Benson 184), the whole "collective body" of the earth and the underground and Ed Ricketts' view of life, in which he sees each marine animal "within the scheme of the shore as a whole" (Benson 187), led to the creation of a hypothesis that the "concept" of marine life extended to the "realm" of marine life. It is a well- known fact that the first work that dealt with the "phalanx theory" in marine life was a short story "The Snake" (first published in 1935), collected in *The Long Valley*.

Cannery Row is a slapstick comedy of "a dream story that unfolds with the imagery of one night's twilight" that echoes the story development of Shakespeare's masterpiece *A Midsummer-Night's Dream*. It will be engraved as a new milestone. In the sequel *Sweet Thursday*, the story develops into "the fate of Doc's love and its fulfillment," and this theme is similar to the theme of "the fate of love and its fulfilment" of *A Midsummer-Night's Dream*. It can be said to be the fairy version of *Cannery Row* and *Sweet Thursday*.

II

The story developing into Doc's love story as *Cannery Row* continues to the sequel *Sweet Thursday*. Doc worked as a sergeant during World War II, and the story begins when he returned to Cannery Row after his mission. A rough

summary of the story goes like this: "Lonesome" (*ST* 66 and many others:
described as a voice from the depths of Doc's heart) Doc says, "I don't want a
wife. I have all the women I want!" (*ST* 107), but he doesn't really mean it. He
hesitates and becomes lethargic about writing a paper on "Symptoms in Some
Cephalopods Approximating Apoplexy" (*ST* 32). In order to break out of this
lethargic state, Mac and his friends come up with a clever idea of Doc getting
married to a "dame" (*ST* 32). The idea was to make Doc get married to Susie.
Unlike the magical aphrodisiacs that appear in *A Midsummer-Night's Dream*,
here Doc and his friends band together to plan a party, and through the twists
and turns, via the drama presentation of "Snow White and the Seven Dwarfs"
(*ST* 175), Susie and Doc successfully fall in love and get married to each other,
and the story ends up happily.

In this work, towards the fulfillment of Doc's love, Steinbeck uses Celtic
imagery of light and color, moreover, the appearance of the Irish fairy
"leprechaun." He also changes the musical device from a single melody to a
compound melody ("Octopus" and "Snow White"). The main image is an octet
(because of both the "octopus" image and "Snow White plus Seven Dwarfs"
image), but it is developed into a trio to depict Doc's inner conflict. In other
words, the shift in perspective from the "individual" that appears in *Cannery
Row* to the "whole" (group man) that appears in *Sweet Thursday*, which gives
the story a profound finish. This is so-called Steinbeck's philosophy of "from 'I'
to 'we'": from the "individual" to the "whole."

First, regarding the imagery of light and color, the scene in Chapter 10 where
Doc meets a man called the seer is represented in a way that is reminiscent
of "Celtic Culture." First, the seer says, "I saw a mermaid last night. You
remember, there was a halfmoon and a thin drifting mist. There was color in the
night, not like the black and gray and white of an ordinary night" (*ST* 72). This
is exactly the situation I have pointed out. The scene described here leads to the
scene described as "the yellow light of the setting sun illuminated a cloud to the
eastward, a clot of gold" (*ST* 73).

By listening to the prophet's advice about love at the twilight, Doc begins to think more deeply about "love" than before, and he is able to overcome the difficulties associated with "love" in the future. The author of this book believes that this chapter has great significance.

Furthermore, in Chapter 19, the Irish fairy "leprechaun" (*ST* 122) that mends shoes appears in *Sweet Thursday* when the "the butterfly pageant in Pacific Grove" is held, and Chapter 21 is a very important chapter that determines whether or not the arrangements for the party are successfully made. In this important chapter the fairy is depicted in a way that is reminiscent of Irish fairies, as is shown below.

> By tacit agreement no one mentioned the raffle to Doc. To Doc's friends Mack and the boys mentioned the rigging of the lottery, but to strangers— who cared? It was a perfect example of the collective goodness and generosity of a community.
>
> But if communities have a group Good Fairy they also have an Imp who works parallel with and sometimes in collaboration with the Good Fairy. (*ST* 135)

It goes without saying that the "Good Fairy" here is an allusion to the Irish fairy "good people." In this way, Steinbeck can be considered to have skillfully blended "Celtic Culture" with the "group man" philosophy in the important scenes of the story.

This "group man" philosophy is equivalent to the "phalanx theory," according to *OED* and in Steinbeck's most important works, they are two sides of the same coin. They are also deeply connected to "holistic" thinking. In other words, we can read two "ambiguities" of the word "phalanx": "1. If they form "a body of heavy-armed infantry drawn up in close order, with shields joined" (*OED* VII 763), 2. It represents "a number or set of persons, banded together for a common purpose" (*OED* VII 763).

Next, let's consider "music." In this work, "music" (*ST* 18 and many others) appears as a key to understanding the work. For Doc, "music" is "man's loveliest achievement" (*ST* 21) and is "based on truth" (*ST* 33). In *Cannery Row*, it mainly appears as "Gregorian chants and Gregorian music" (28 and many others), but in *Sweet Thursday* it appears as *Die Kunst der Fuge* (21 and many others). It serves as a "sound effect" when depicting the psychology of Doc, which makes the work richer.

As to "Gregorian music", it is a religious music played with a "single melody" or so-called "monophony." In contrast, Bach's *Die Kunst der Fuge* is a "polyphony" with at least "three melodies." Look at the music score below and we will consider it.

Die Kunst der Fuge

Contrapunctus 1

(Bach 2)

According to *Music Encyclopedia* edited by Hiroshi Shimonaka, a "fugue" is "the highest polyphonic music form based on imitative counterpoint" (Shimonaka 2093, trans. Mine), and "After the theme is presented, the interludes are presented in turn, and the counterpoint phrases are combined contrapuntally as counterpoint melodies" (Shimonaka 2094, trans. Mine) to conclude the musical piece. In other words, it is a technique in which the same rhythm of the melody is "chasing each other" to compose a single piece of music, and as a case in point, in the above score, the middle part (second voice) presents four "half notes" first, and then one "half note." It presents two "quarter notes," one "half note," and then four "eighth notes," chasing the same pattern. Thus, the upper part (first voice) is played from the fifth measure of the first stanza, and the third part (third voice) is played from the third measure of the second stanza. All of these are not "accompaniments" but "melodies," which is why they are called "polyphony."

The "Gregorian music" that appears a lot in *Cannery Row* and *Die Kunst der Fuge* that appears a lot in *Sweet Thursday* are the structure of "monophony" versus "polyphony." The depictions are illustrated in the following contrasting ways in the work. First, let me quote from Chapter 18 of *Cannery Row*.

> And the girl's face went ahead of him[Doc]. He sat down on the beach in the coarse dry sand and pulled off his boots. In the jar the little octopi were huddled up each keeping as far as possible from the others. Music sounded in Doc's ears, a high thin piercingly sweet flute carrying a melody he could never remember, and against this, a pounding surf-like wood-wind section. The flute went up into regions beyond the hearing range and even there it carried its unbelievable melody, (114 -115)

The music depicted here is "mysterious" and "beyond the range of human hearing." The only thing I want to focus on is the single melody of the flute. It can be said that it symbolizes the single melody of Gregorian music. What

I would like to pay more attention to is that before and after the quotation, a woman appears when a marine creature is captured by chance. There are depictions of the girl, but the way the girl is depicted is mysterious. In particular, the similar image of the depiction of "the girl's eyes had been gray" (*CR* 115) is repeated in a row, giving the impression of "Celtic Twilight."

The same musical description, as is symbolized by *Die Kunst der Fuge* in *Sweet Thursday*, is represented in more than at least three voices. The music is also significant in this work. It also appears in many scenes of Doc's emotional turmoil and scenes of sexual arousal toward women. I won't go into details, but the most important scenes are the same as in *Sweet Thursday*. The scene is quoted from Chapter 3, which depicts a description of the "octopus."

> The top voice of his thinking mind would sing, "What lovely little particles, neither plant nor animal but somehow both—the reservoir of all the life in the world, the base supply of food for everyone. If all of these should die, every other living thing might well die as a consequence." The lower voice of his feeling mind would be singing, "What are you looking for, little man? Is it yourself you're trying to identify? Are you looking at little things to avoid big things?" And the third voice, which came from his marrow, would sing, "Lonesome! Lonesome! What good is it? Who benefits? Thought is evasion of feeling. You're only walling up the leaking loneliness." (24-25)

After this depiction, Doc takes a young lady to La Jolla to collect marine lives. However, the lady is disappointed with Doc's several explanations about the "octopus" and leaves Doc at last.

This incident leads to the fact that Mack gives an example of "every time he [a guy] gets feeling low he goes back to his wife" (32), which brings us the beginning of the story's greatest climax that Mack and his friends become eager to find Doc's sweetheart.

Conclusion

Frankie who has been considered so far and the other characters the writer tells to us readers through the narrator including Doc, are "gentle and good" characters, which in the Celtic world will represent "fairies." They are the persons with the image of "good fellows" (in the Celtic world, fairies are called "good people"). This will be discussed in Chapter 4 in this book. I once quoted and considered Yeats' works, and in *Cannery Row* and *Sweet Thursday*, there are countless references to "ghosts and fairies" (*CR* 144 and *ST* 68, and many others). Especially, as to Doc in *Cannery Row*, he is depicted as a "fine fellow" (13), which equals to "good people."

The fact that these two works considered in this chapter skillfully incorporate Celtic Fairy Culture seems to owe a great deal to the comical story development of Shakespeare's *A Midsummer-Night's Dream*, mentioned earlier. The struggle of the fairies who help the love accomplishment between Hermia and Lysander and between Helena and Demetrius, parallels the development of the love story of Doc. The characters' efforts are colored by the image of "King Arthur and the Knights of the Round Table" who help Doc fulfill his love as a human being.

This is nothing but an image of *A Midsummer-Night's Dream*. In Puck's line in Scene 1 of Act 2, the use of the Irish fairy "changeling" (Shakespeare 34) and British poet "Robin Good-fellow" (Shakespeare 35: In the text, it is divided into two syllables like Robin Good-fellow) can be interpreted as an "ambiguity" of "fairy" and "good fellow"). Therefore, it can be said that *Cannery Row* and *Sweet Thursday* adequately portrays the "good people" around Doc.

Why did Steinbeck think of good people at a time when America was experiencing such social unrest? The question is whether the characters were portrayed as kind or, at worst, weak. The unrest that the United States was experiencing domestically (*The Grapes of Wrath* was published in 1939). In the year 1939, the bad effects of the Great Depression, which had been lingering since 1929, remained unresolved. The year 1945, when *Cannery Row* was published, was the year when in the middle of World War II, Steinbeck used a means of depicting the unstable world situation as a propaganda.

The author of this book believes that this is the method used by Steinbeck. In the 1930s, America was in a weakened state during what was called the "political season." In order to promote America internationally, they must present an image of "strong America." Steinbeck was probably no exception. When the government, through the New Deal, demanded that artists, including W. Disney, create works that would give the people "dreams and courage," Steinbeck seems to have had no choice but to jump on the bandwagon

Once this "strength" reached its peak in American propaganda with the image of "the strong live; the weak die" suggesting the shooting death of Lennie depicted in *Of Mice and Men* (1937), then the external problem with the Nazis came up. Coincidentally, World War II broke out in 1939 with Germany's invasion of Poland, and when the American people's eyes turned to external affairs, the world suffered from poverty from the late 1920s through the Great Depression. It was probably *The Grapes of Wrath* that drew attention to domestic issues such as rural issues, and negative images such as concern and anxiety about "totalitarianism" called "Nazism" and "fascism." It seems that Steinbeck published *Cannery Row* and its sequel *Sweet Thursday* as a question to the American people in an attempt to dispel this "Nazism and Fascism" with his positive thought of "holism" and theory of "group man."

Therefore, in the author's opinion, in addition to *Cannery Row* and *Sweet Thursday* being read as "naturalistic" novels, these two works can also be read as a type of "romanticism" in the light of "fairy tales" of "only one-night dream." In this sense, so-called weak people that Steinbeck depicts, including Frankie, paradoxically present to us "strength, courage and hope" as "they are" of those who survive harsh times, based on Steinbeck's philosophy of "Non-teleological Thinking."

As a whole, it seems that *Cannery Row* and *Sweet Thursday* as "two slapstick comedies weaved with a dream story that unfolds with the imagery of twilight" are reminiscent of the story development of Shakespeare's masterpiece, *A Midsummer-Night's Dream*. In other words, *Cannery Row* and *Sweet Thursday* have become a new landmark in Steinbeck's literature.

Furthermore, the description of the "octopus" and the image of the conductor of "an orchestra" (*ST* 45) which suggests Doc, and the orchestration performed by most of the composers, including Mozart who appears in the main story, is the most standard one: a formation using seven instruments with one conductor.

Therefore, at least also from a "musical" viewpoint, Steinbeck's unique philosophy of "group man" is well depicted, and that the depiction of "music" is based on "Celtic Culture." It can be thought that these two works blend well with this "group man" theory born from Celtic philosophy, which makes these two works even more profound.

Works Cited and Referred Bibliographies

Bach, J.S. *Die Kunst der Fuge*. Ed. Davitt Moroney. Munich: G. Henle Verlag, 1989.

Balaswamy, Periaswamy. *Symbols for Wordlessness: A Study of the Deep Structure of John Steinbeck's Early Novels*. Chennai: Ramath Academic Publishers, 2005.

Benson, Jackson J. *The True Adventures of John Steinbeck, Writer*. York: Viking Press, 1984.

Britch, Carroll and Cliff Lewis, "Growth of the Family in *The Grapes of the Wrath*," in *Critical Essays on Steinbeck's The Grapes of Wrath*. Ed. John Ditsky. Boston: G. K. Hall & Co., 1989.

DeMott, Robert. "Steinbeck and the Creative Process: First Manifesto to End the Bringdown Against *Sweet Thursday*" in *Steinbeck: The Man and His Work*. Ed. Richard Astro and Tetsumaro Hayashi. Corvallis: Oregon State University Press, 1971.

Finneran, Richard J. ed. *The Collected Poems of W. B. Yeats*. New York: Simon& Schuster Inc., 1996.

Fontenrose, Joseph. *John Steinbeck: An Introduction and Interpretation*. New York: Holt,

Rinehart and Winston, Inc., 1963.

French, Warren. *John Steinbeck*. 2nd ed. Boston: Twayne Publishers, 1975.

Green, Miranda. *Exploring the World of Druids*. London: Thames & Hudson Ltd., 1997.

Hintz, Paul. "The Silent Woman and the Male Voice in Steinbeck's *Cannery Row*" in *The Steinbeck Question: New Essays in Criticism*. Ed. Donald R. Noble. New York: Whitston Publishing Company, 1993.

Levant, Howard. *The novels of John Steinbeck: A Critical Study*. Columbia: University of Missouri Press, 1974.

Lisca, Peter. "Escape and Commitment: Two poles of the Steinbeck Hero" in *Steinbeck: The Man and His Work*. Ed. Richard Astro and Tetsumaro Hayashi. Corvallis: Oregon State University Press, 1971.

_____. *The Wide World of John Steinbeck*. Reprinted, New York: Gordian Press, 1981.

Lovejoy, Arthur O. *The Great Chain of Being*. Harvard University Press, 1936.

Metzger, Charles R. "Steinbeck's *Cannery Row*" in *A Study Guide to Steinbeck: A Handbook to His Major Works*. Ed. Tetsumaro Hayashi. N.J.: Scarecrow Press, 1974.

Meyer, Michael J. "Steinbeck's *Cannery Row*" in *A New Study Guide to Steinbeck's Major Works, with Critical Explications*. Ed. Tetsumaro Hayashi. N.J.: Scarecrow Press, 1993.

Moore, Harry Thornton. *The Novels of John Steinbeck: A First Critical Study*. Chicago: Normandie House,1939.

Owens, Louis. *John Steinbeck's Re-Vision of America*. Athens: University of Georgia Press, 1985.

Shakespeare, William. *A Midsummer-Night's Dream*. Ed. Henry Cuningham. London: Methuen & Co., 1905.

Steinbeck, Elaine and Robert Wallsten eds. *Steinbeck: A Life in Letters*. New York: Viking Press, 1975.

(Written as *SLL* in the main text)

Steinbeck, John. *Of Mice and Men*. New York: Covici-Friede, 1937.

_____. *The Grapes of Wrath*. New York: Viking Press, 1939.

_____. *Cannery Row*. New York: Viking Press, 1945.

(As for sources from this text, only page numbers are added in parentheses or *CR*)

_____. *Sweet Thursday*. New York: Viking Press, 1954.

(As for sources from this text, only page numbers are added in parentheses or *ST*)

Timmerman, John H. *John Steinbeck's Fiction: The Aesthetics of the Road Taken*. Norman: Oklahoma University, 1986.

Fujimoto, Reiji. "Yeats" in Ed. Fumiyo Uesugi, *Light Imagery: English Poetry in Tradition*. Tokyo: Kirihara Shoten, 1985.

Hara, Kiyoshi. *Celtic Water Veins*. Tokyo: Kodansha, 2007.

Inazawa, Hideo. *Steinbeck View*. Tokyo: Shichosha, 1967.

Kamata, Toji and Mayumi Tsuruoka, eds. *Celt and Japan*. Tokyo: Kadokawa Shoten, 2000.

Kihara, Kenichi. *Yeats and the Mask: The Paradox of Death*. Tokyo: Sairyusha, 2001.

Takahashi, Masao. *20th Century American Novel 3: Political Season during 1930s*. Tokyo: Toyamabo, 1951.

Tatemoto, Hidehiro. "*Cannery Row*—Modern Personal Nostalgia" Ed. Kiyoshi Nakayama et al., *Rereading Steinbeck*. Tokyo: Kaibunsha Publishing Company, 2001.

Green, Miranda J. *Dictionary of Celtic Myth and Legend*. London: Thames and Hudson Limited, 1992.

Shimonaka, Hiroshi, ed. *Music Encyclopedia*. Tokyo: Heibonsha, 1991.

The Oxford English Dictionary. First Edition. Oxford: At the Clarendon Press, 1933.

Chapter 10

East of Eden:
"Kiss Me, Kate" — Will Cathy/Kate's soul be saved?

Introduction

East of Eden is said to be a masterpiece that Steinbeck put all his heart and soul into writing. As has been already said, there are Steinbeck's autobiographical elements that allow us to unravel the history of his own birth, and as a contrapuntal comparison to the episode, Cyrus, Adam, Aron, and Cal as major characters are fictionally depicted in three generation-saga with a total of over 600 pages.

Regarding the creation of *East of Eden*, Steinbeck himself said, "I will tell them [my sons] one of the greatest, perhaps the greatest story of all—the story of good and evil, of strength and weakness, of love and hate, of beauty and ugliness" (*Journal of a Novel* 4). In Steinbeck's works, there can be found a theme of so-called "binomial contrast" in almost all his works, but no matter who reads them, their symbolism is clear, easy to understand, and relevant to our real lives.

The author of this book believes that this work has a deep impact on our hearts. As many researchers and critics have pointed out, this work has a Biblical motif. There is no doubt that this work is based on the story of Cain and Abel. But because the theme is so complex, critical viewpoints vary very much.

If I focus on Cathy/Kate, which I am about to discuss, Lisca says "Cathy is too much like Satan to be a credible human being, and too much like a weak, pitiful human being to be properly Satanic" (Lisca 273), and he indicates a kind of criticism that there is a certain lack of absoluteness as a monstrous character.

French criticizes all of Steinbeck's characters as "it is too much to ask readers to 'go along' with a story when they're not sure whether the author is thinking of

141

his characters as laboratory specimens or as real folks" (French 148), and as to Cathy/Kate, he harshly criticizes: "Kate is not the only character that Steinbeck fails to manage consistently" (French 148).

The author of this book can't write down all the criticisms due to index constraints, but here are some comments regarding Cathy/Kate. Most of the criticisms, including those listed above, are negative. But in contrast to these criticisms, Gladstein protects Cathy/Kate in her affirmative opinion that "She [Cathy/Kate] is also a far cry from his usual whore with a heart of gold" (Gladstein 98).

As I have some sympathetic feeling about this phrase "with a heart of gold," this is considered to be an aspect of Cathy/Kate's "kindness." Therefore, *East of Eden* can be analyzed from the viewpoint of the "kindness" of this woman. I would like to consider and discuss this perspective in the following chapter.

I

Before discussing Cathy/Kate's "kindness," I will first consider Cathy/Kate as depicted in the image of a cat, and then examine Cathy/Kate from a Celtic perspective.

Both Cathy and Kate are originally named "Katharina," and the story revolves around the image of a "cat." The original meaning of the name comes from Greek and means "purity." Gladstein seems to have discovered the meaning of this term in *East of Eden*, but she does not elaborate on it. The author of this book first analyzes the imagery of a 'cat' in Cathy/Kate, who is depicted as the image of a "wild cat" (Shakespeare 62) in *The Taming of the Shrew*.

The introduction scene of Cathy/Kate is in Chapter 8, and Steinbeck depicts her through the narrator as a "devil" who is not of this world. Her "feet were small and round and stubby, with fat insteps almost like little hoofs" (73) and her voice is huskily soft, but "Cathy's voice could cut like a file when she wished" (73). It is also described as "She moved quietly" (73) and "Something looked out of her eyes, and was never there when one looked again" (73). These depiction methods of Steinbeck seem to be conscious of the image of a cat. This is the way the writer intended to write "the worship of the unearthly" (*JN* 79), and it is a witch-like way of description. Also, phonologically, the word "cut" is reminiscent of the word "cat." Although I will not go into details, such figurative expressions can be used in many scenes where Cathy/Kate appears.

"Cats" have their origin in Egypt, and in this work, in the opening scene of Chapter 11, where Cathy meets Adam and Charles for the first time, is a scene reminiscent of her origin. Adam's line suggests, "Charles, we could go to Egypt and walk around the Sphinx" (110), and in response to the sound of Cathy arriving at the front door of the house, Adam says, "Those goddam cats!" (110). Steinbeck's precisely calculated plot development can be seen in the lines of Cathy/Kate, which symbolically develop the work as an image of a "cat."

As are mentioned many times in the previous chapters, the image of the color of "gray" during "twilight," which is one of the Celtic symbols, can be summarized as "before dawn, the magical time when fairies begin to move." It is used extensively in this work, especially in the depiction of Cathy/Kate, and in the development of the storytelling. Since this time period is a "magical time period," it can also be interpreted as a mysterious time period where "good" (kindness) and "evil" (evilness) coexist; It can also be interpreted as a mysterious time period that goes beyond such concepts.

First, at the end of the scene in which Cathy/Kate sets her house on fire, kills her parents and escapes, there is a description that "the ache goes out of it [time], the colors melt together, and from the many separated lines a solid gray emerges" (89). As to the depiction about Edwards, a prostitute, who tries to kill Cathy/Kate who manages to escape with a narrow death. In the scene with Cathy/Kate, it is described as "gray rim of dawn" (99), and in the scene where Adam proposes to Cathy, the sparrow flies in the sky at "dawn," and the scene is described as "gray." It is a way of depicting the image of "gray twilight," in which the sparrows fly off like "a gray scarf twisting in the light" (120).

These perfect descriptions include the scene in which Cathy shoots Adam, the scene in which she enters her room during the imagery of time of "dusk," and she escapes from Adam with the passage of suggesting "Druids" of "crisp dry oak leaves on the path" (202). Moreover, there are countless examples of how the walls of her room are described as "gray" (462 and many others) when she runs a business.

The time when the sun goes down in the evening and the time when the sun rises at dawn signify the time of "twilight," although there are relatively few depictions about "dawn" in this work. These are the most important time span when we analyze "Celtic Culture."

According to Kimie Imura, for the Celts, the time when fairies begin to move is "the time before 'rebirth', namely, 'the twilight before dawn,' and the time after 'rebirth,' returning to 'darkness'" (Kamata and Tsuruoka 47, trans. Mine), and from this idea, this time period can be considered to be two "twilight hours" namely "before dawn and twilight" (Fujimoto 741), as is pointed out by Reiji Fujimoto.

Regarding the night which governs darkness, Imura said, "with the image of 'death' in the earth, the ethnic and mythological aspects of fairies are revived as 'eternal memories from the past to the present'" (Kamata and Tsuruoka 47-48, trans. Mine). Therefore, these two periods of the day, namely, "the twilight hours before dawn" and "the twilight hours," are, as Fujimoto points out, "tired of this world dominated by the notions of good and evil. It can be thought of as the Utopia of the Celts, 'Tír na nÓg'" (Fujimoto 742), where people escape from time and space. What Fujimoto considers here is, in short, a "mysterious period of time."

In the Celtic calendar, the year begins on the day of Halloween when fairies go from the depth of the earth to the surface of the earth via the caves, and this day is commonly known as *Samhain*. In the Celtic world, this *Samhain* is "a dangerous time; a period in which the conventional boundaries of space and time were temporarily suspended and where the spirits of the Otherworld mingled freely with the living; a time of immense spiritual energy, when monstrous events were liable to take place" (Green 1997, 36).

Rhodes states "In the Middle Ages, black cats were often portrayed as the familiars of witches, which is likely to be the origin of the distrust with which they are regarded in America, where early Puritan settlers rejected anything associated with the Devil and witchcraft" (Rhodes 31). It appears that many people, including those who came to America, believed that cats were responsible for the ominous omens and omens associated with "black magic," which is said to be of Celtic origin.

In this work, Liza is depicted as a typical Irish woman. Since her husband Samuel is described as "wide open to the devil" (11), she believed in the existence of the devil and "In that one book [the Bible] she [Liza] had her history and her poetry, her knowledge of peoples and things, her ethics, her morals, and her salvation" (43). This shows that she hated the existence of demons. In other words, she is depicted as a woman who is the opposite of Cathy/Kate.

Regarding the characteristics of the characters in this work who are Irish, the narrator classifies them into five types in addition to at least the characteristics mentioned above. First, there is a type that "The Irish do have a despairing quality of gaiety, but they have also a dour and brooding ghost that rides on their shoulders and peers in on their thoughts" (40). Next is the type that "They [The Irish] condemn themselves before they are charged, and this makes them defensive always" (41). The third type is that "he [an Irishman]'s all full of plans—a hundred plans a day. And he's all full of hope" (140). The fourth type is that "He [Samuel] looked in himself for envy and could find none" (177). And finally, the fifth type is that "they [the Irish including the Hamiltons] all half believed they had wings—and they got some bad falls that way" (275).

Other important Celtic concepts include "Druids" and the "oak" belief. Like his other works, in this work are also depicted many scenes concerning these concepts, and just as I have discussed them in detail in the former chapters, they are considered to play an important role in Steinbeck's carefully calculated story

145

development as well.

Furthermore, there are Celtic symbols including the rise of "automobiles" (suggesting Model T) with the introduction of "Henry Ford" (40), and "water" (166 and many others) symbolizing the source of life and the fountain of youth, which is used for irrigation. All of these are reminiscent of Irish mythology, folklore, and even Ireland itself.

II

As is mentioned before, Cathy/Kate's original name "Katharina" means "purity" in Greek. Therefore, her true self should be pure and gentle. In her introduction scenes of Cathy/ Kate, she has "from the first a face of innocence" (73), and her hair is described as "gold and lovely" (73), and she is "dainty and very sweet" (78), and the descriptions of her "delicate blooming skin, the golden hair, the wide-set, modest, and yet promising eyes, the little mouth full of sweetness" (78) prove her true beauty, which reflects her "purity." This is the evidence of Cathy/Kate's "innocence" in describing her face, and not a "devil" style of her depiction.

Then why has she grown into a "devil-like" being? This will be a problem with the family environment in which she has been raised since childhood. It appears that two incidents happened when Kathy was 10 years old.

In one incident Cathy/Kate, who originally seemed to have a stronger sexual desire than the others, had a sexual desire to increase even more when her mother, Mrs. Ames, "had to manipulate them [nipples] out when they became painful" (73) as Cathy/Kate's "nipples turned inward" (73). In another incident, Cathy/Kate's wrists "were tied with a heavy rope" by the boys (76).

These two incidents ignited the "sadism" and "masochism" that had always existed within Cathy/Kate, and she eventually became a prostitution operator and ran a brothel, after getting hired in a brothel where Mr. Edwards capture the girls who "begged for more whipping to wipe out their fancied sins" (92).

The biggest problem in the family environment is the presence of a father, Mr. Ames. He is described in Chapter 8 as an unreliable father because he is "uneasy about his daughter" (75), and he "rarely told the thoughts in his mind" (78).

From these situations, it can be seen that the father and Cathy/Kate is not on good terms with each other. Under such circumstances, there is no way that they will be able to understand each other even if Mr. Ames tries to "whip" (83) Cathy/Kate, which he is not good at. Rather, only feelings of resentment remain. This is clear from the way the writer depicts the father as being "frightened at the noise [of blowing] and hurt he was creating" (83) and "once she had learned she screamed, she writhed, she cried, she begged, and she had the satisfaction of feeling the blows instantly become lighter" (83).

This also applies to married Adam. Adam took care of Cathy/Kate's wounds, but he was unable to train her to be a lady. In short, it can be seen that because he was unable to train her, she lost all affection for him and left Adam. Of course, shooting Adam in the shoulder with a gun is "evil" and deserves a crime.

On the contrary, I will discuss the parts where Cathy/Kate's pure heart is best depicted. This is the scene in Chapter 45, where she thinks about her favorite elder son Aron and tries to come up with a party for his sons, hiding her own true self.

> Kate's lips were smiling sweetly and a gaiety was coming over her. Before she went it might be good to give a party for her sons. Just a simple little party with a circus afterward for her darlings—her jewels. And then she thought of Aron's beautiful face so like her own and a strange pain—a little collapsing pain—arose in her chest. (513)

This scene is a heartwarming scene in which Cathy/Kate (Kate here), who works as a prostitute, cares for her sons. From the first sentence, she is "smiling" and overflowing with cheerfulness, especially towards herself. She cares for her elder son Aron, who has similar pure and "beautiful face" like Kate's. After this,

Kate leaves to Aron "everything I [Kate] have to my son Aron Trask" (553) and commits suicide, but this is the best scene of Cathy/Kate's "pure and gentle" warmhearted hospitality.

W.B. Yeats' poem "Into the Twilight" generously expresses the image of "gray twilight," which can be used as a Celtic representation of this work, and can be considered to lead to the last scene of Adam Trask at the end of this work: that is, this seems to lead to the interpretation of "free will" in the phrase of "*Timshel!*" (602).

Into the Twilight

Out-worn heart, in a time out-worn,
Come clear of the nets of <u>wrong and right</u>;
Laugh, heart, again in the <u>gray twilight</u>,
Sigh, heart, again in the dew of the morn.

Your mother Eire is always young,
Dew ever shining and <u>twilight gray</u>;
Though hope fall from you and love decay,
Burning in fires of a slanderous tongue.

Come, heart, where hill is heaped upon hill;
For there the <u>mystical</u> brotherhood
Of sun and moon and hollow and wood
And river and stream <u>work out their will</u>;

And God stands winding His lonely horn,
And time and the world are ever in flight;
And love is less kind than the <u>gray twilight</u>,
And hope is less dear than the dew of the morn. (Finerran 59 Underline parts, Mine)

In this poem, the word 'mystical' in the third stanza and the phrase 'sun, moon, hollow, wood, river and stream work out their will' in the third stanza can be interpreted as "All living things in the whole universe, including humans, are able to live while respecting free will," judging from Steinbeck's "holistic" view of life. Furthermore, the word "gray twilight" in the second and in the fourth stanza, can be considered undeniable so that the characters that appear in this work will be in the same state of mind as "Tír na nÓg." It can be said that in this "twilight" hour, there is such a gentleness that even love cannot come close. In other words, it is important to assume that during this "Twilight," which is traditional "Celtic Culture," Steinbeck's storytelling that tells us of the "hidden side of Cathy/Kate's gentle heart" is also represented at the same time.

III

Steinbeck's interest in medieval Europe was nurtured by his mother Olive who read to him as a child. Steinbeck himself was very interested in Thomas Malory's *Le Morte D'Arthur*. Some of the titles of Steinbeck's works are borrowed from the works of medieval writings, including John Milton's *Paradise Lost*, William Shakespeare's *The Tragedy of King Richard III*. His other works seem to be reminiscent of the works of medieval writings, such as *Everyone* as was mentioned in the eighth chapter, and *A Midsummer-Night's Dream* as was analyzed in the ninth chapter.

Here, I will try to discuss *East of Eden* in the light of the story progression of Cathy/Kate to explain how Steinbeck reminds us of Shakespeare's *The Taming of the Shrew*.

In medieval literary works, stories about disciplining an overly strong-willed and nagging wife are many, such as the wife of Bath in Geoffrey Chaucer's *The Canterbury Tales*.

Masako Maekawa states "Katharina's final line in Act 5, in which she preaches that wives must be obedient, is by no means outlandish to the people of the time" (Maekawa 188, trans. Mine). Petruchio in *The Taming of the Shrew* gradually succeeds in dominating Katharina with his wisdom and strategy as are stated in the lines "Last night she [Katharina] slept not, nor to-night she shall not" (Shakespeare 105) while using the stick at one time and the carrot at another time, "Kate, eat apace: and now, my honey love, / Will we return unto thy father's house" (Shakespeare 116). At the end, the carrot and the stick are used repeatedly and Petruchio reprimands and dominates Katharina. Katharina is reborn as an obedient lady.

However, Cathy/Kate in *East of Eden* is the complete opposite, or rather, as I said earlier, Adam did not have the strength to make her reborn as an obedient lady like Katharina in *The Taming of the Shrew*. Adam's care, which is only "So good and kind" (118 and many others), is seen through, and in the end, Adam is deceived.

In Chapter 33 of this work, Tom killed his beloved wife Dessie with a drug he accidentally gave her. Regretful of what he had done, Tom rode a "blood-horse" (409) that could not be trained. There is a scene where he crosses a mountain with the horse. This mountain "crossing" symbolizes "Tom's suicide," and this is Steinbeck's good way of foreshadowing technique as is seen many times. As for Adam, who was unable to discipline Cathy/Kate, he eventually collapsed due to a "brain disorder." Therefore, just as Tom's suicide suggests that Adam eventually pass away, it constructs the parallel progression of the story development.

Katharina desperately endures Petruchio's treatment and is finally reborn as an "obedient" lady. On the contrary, Cathy/Kate ran away even after trying to kill Adam. The difference between the two is probably whether or not they saw a father figure in the men they married. Cathy/Kate has no respect for her father Mr. Ames, as is mentioned earlier. Cathy/Kate was unable to find her father figure in Adam, while Katharina managed to see in her husband Petruchio, the father figure of Baptista she respected very much. This is so much so in fact that as for Katharina, her father Baptista would have been one savior.

Chapter 10

Conclusion

"Into the Twilight" symbolizes the Celtic Utopian state of mind "Tír na nÓg" and this sentiment can be well applied to *East of Eden* as well. Not only this work but almost all of Steinbeck's works imply the theme of "good" and "evil." As the author of this book analyzed Steinbeck's techniques of storytelling in *The Wayward Bus*, the connotation of the word "good" that Steinbeck describes is considered a concept associated with "God," "grace," "truth," etc. It also covers the meaning of "virtue." Moreover, the meaning of "good" includes an "innate" aspect. However, as was mentioned in the analysis on *Saint Katy the Virgin*, the word "bad" connotes "inherent and original," and it is not on the same level as "evil" (*JN* 4) that is acquired after birth, essentially rather a temporary "evil" depicted in *East of Eden*.

Originally, people live their lives with both "theory of good nature" and "theory of bad nature," so the "good and evil" that Steinbeck describes are not distinguished by people but should be dealt with by time and place. Therefore, "*Timshel!*" (602 meaning "Thou canst") is an interpretation applied to Cathy/Kate who originally means "devil" (derived from "evil"). When she murders and commits a temporary but fatal "sin," asked whether her actions were right or not, in other words, when faced with a choice between "right or wrong," even if she is forced to make a "wrong" choice, it is still a personal decision: that is, the worst choice of "suicide" would be allowed to be made since it means a choice allowed, based on her "free will." Based on this "free will," we can choose any course of life no matter what different paths we take and how evil our choices are. And beyond this concept there is a "mystical" Celtic realm called "Tír na nÓg."

Steinbeck was of Irish stock inherited from his mother, and believed that he could have thought of every man and everything reaching a Celtic Utopian state of mind of "Tír na nÓg." It seems that he appeals this idea to us readers because of his Irish inheritance. This "mystical" state of mind is on the same plane as what Rose of Sharon shows at the end of *The Grapes of Wrath* in the scene of giving away her milk to a stranger, smiling "mystically."

If we think of it this way, the thought of "free will" will be well applied to Cal who indirectly killed Aron, to Cathy/Kate who also killed his parents and a prostitute and committed suicide due to the feeling of guilty, and even to Tom who gave his wife Dessie the wrong medicine and committed suicide due to the feeling of guilty for letting her drink the medicine to death.

This is because, as Reiji Fujimoto puts it, even those who committed a sin, "get tired of this world" (Fujimoto 742) but survive in "Tír na nÓg," a Utopia where we can escape and transcend the concepts of "good and evil." Furthermore, it is a Utopia of "immortality of the soul" that the Druids preach.

The author of this book do wish Adam forgives Cathy/Kate's sin and lives happily together, saying "Kiss me, Kate." in "Tír na nÓg."

Works Cited and Referred Bibliographies

Astro, Richard. *John Steinbeck and Edward F. Ricketts: The Shaping of a Novelist*. Minneapolis: University of Minnesota Press, 1973.

Benson, Jackson J. *The True Adventures of John Steinbeck, Writer*. New York: Viking Press, 1984.

DeMott, Robert. *Steinbeck's Typewriter: Essays on His Art*. New York: Whitson Publishing Company Troy, 1996.

Ditsky, John. "Essays on East of Eden" in *Steinbeck Monograph Series*, No.7. Ed. Tetsumaro Hayashi et al. Muncie: Ball State University, 1977.

Finneran, Richard J. ed. *The Collected Poems of W. B. Yeats*. New York: Simon & Schuster Inc., 1996.

Fontenrose, Joseph. *John Steinbeck: An Introduction and Interpretation*. New York: Holt, Rinehart and Winston, Inc., 1963.

French, Warren. *John Steinbeck*. 2nd ed. Boston: Twayne Publishers, 1975.

Gladstein, Mimi Reisel. *The Indestructible Woman in Faulkner, Hemingway, and*

Steinbeck. Michigan: University Microfilm, Inc., 1986.

Green, Miranda. *Exploring the World of Druids*. London: Thames & Hudson Ltd., 1997.

Heavilin, Barbara A. "Steinbeck's Exploration of Good and Evil: Structural and Thematic Unity in *East of Eden*" in *Steinbeck Quarterly*. Volume XXVI, Number 3 and 4. Ed. Tetsumaro Hayashi et al. Muncie: Ball State University, 1993.

Levant, Howard. *The Novels of John Steinbeck: A Critical study*. Columbia: University of Missouri Press, 1974.

Lisca, Peter. *The Wide World of John Steinbeck*. Reprinted, New York: Gordian Press, 1981.

Lovejoy, Arthur O. *The Great Chain of Being*. Harvard University Press, 1936.

McCarthy, Paul. *John Steinbeck*. Frederick Ungar Publishing Co., Inc., 1980.

Marks, Lester Jay. "East of Eden: 'Thou Mayest'" in *Steinbeck Quarterly*. Volume IV, Number 1. Ed. Tetsumaro Hayashi et al. Muncie: Ball State University, 1971.

Moore, Harry Thornton. *The Novels of John Steinbeck: A First Critical Study*. Chicago: Normandie House, 1939.

Noble, Donald R. Ed. *The Steinbeck Question: New Essays in Criticism*. New York: Whitson Publishing Company Troy, 1993.

Owens, Louis. *John Steinbeck's Re-Vision of America*. Athens: University of Georgia Press, 1985.

Peterson, Richard F. "Steinbeck's *East of Eden*" in *A Study Guide to Steinbeck (Part II)* Ed. Tetsumaro Hayashi. N. J.: Scarecrow Press, 1974.

Rhodes, Chloe. *Black Cats and Evil Eyes: A Book of Old-Fashioned Superstitions*. London: Michael O'Mara Books, 2014.

Shakespeare, William. *The Taming of the Shrew*. Ed. R. Warwick Bond. London: Methuen & Co.,1904.

_____. *A Midsummer-Night's Dream*. Ed. Henry Cunningham. London: Methuen & Co., 1905.

Simmonds, Roy. *A Biographical and Critical Introduction of John Steinbeck*. New York: Edwin Mellen Press, 2000.

Steinbeck, Elaine and Robert Wallsten eds. *Steinbeck: A Life in Letters*. New York:

Viking Press, 1975.

Steinbeck, John. *East of Eden*. New York: Viking Press, 1952.

_____. *The Grapes of Wrath*. New York: Viking Press, 1939.

_____. *Journal of a Novel: The East of Eden Letters*. New York: Viking Press, 1969.

(In the main text written as *JN*)

Timmerman, John H. *John Steinbeck's Fiction: The Aesthetics of the Road Taken*. Norman: Oklahoma University Press, 1986.

Watt, F. W. *Steinbeck*. New York: Chip's Bookshop, Inc., 1962.

Fujimoto, Reiji. "Yeats" in *Light Imagery: English Poetry in Tradition*. Ed. Fumiyo Uesugi. Tokyo: Kirihara Shoten, 1985.

Hara, Kiyoshi. *Celtic Water Veins*. Tokyo: Kodansha, 2007.

Inazawa, Hideo. *Steinbeck's View*. Tokyo: Shichosha, 1967.

Kamata, Toji and Mayumi Tsuruoka eds. *Celt and Japan*. Tokyo: Kadokawa Shoten, 2000.

Kihara, Kenichi. *Yeats and the Mask: The Paradox of Death*. Tokyo: Sairyusha, 2001.

Maekawa, Masako. "One Comment" in *The Taming of the Shrew* (in *The Complete Works of Shakespeare*). William Shakespeare/Translated by Tadashi Odajima. Tokyo: Hakusuisha, 1983.

Nakayama, Kiyoshi. *A Study of Steinbeck's Literature. Volume III: New York Period*. Osaka: Kansai University Press, 2002.

Tsuruoka, Mayumi. *Celtic Imagination: History, Mythology, and Art*. Tokyo: Seidosha, 2018.

Green, Miranda J. *Dictionary of Celtic Myth and Legend*. London: Thames and Hudson Limited, 1992.

The Oxford English Dictionary. First Edition. Oxford: At the Clarendon Press, 1933.

Encyclopedia of Criminal Psychology. Ed. Japanese Union of Psychological Associations. Tokyo: Maruzen Publishing Co. Ltd., 2016.

Chapter 11

The Winter of Our Discontent:
The Modern "Druid," Ethan Allen Hawley

Introduction

Steinbeck wrote about the tumultuous 1950s in America. It's more of a short
novel, written with sadness about the historical background of America in
the late 1950s. This work was written with a unique method. This work will
be examined from the perspective of "Celtic Culture." First of all, as I have
analyzed many times, "Celtic Twilight," which plays a very important role in the
development of the story, can be seen throughout this work as well. The "gray"
imagery and the "magic" time period appear in connection, adding depth to the
story. The work also explores Hawley's relationship with his son Ethan Allen
Hawley Jr. When we consider this viewpoint, we will find that there is more to
the relationship between the "Druids" than the simple parent-child relationship
of "father and son." We can also read the relationship between Hawley and his
wife Mary. Furthermore, Margie is on good terms with Mary. The relationship
between Hawley's wife and Margie, who are good "witches," can actually be
deeply connected to Celtic Culture. It is because Margie, who is depicted as a
"snake" image, is "loved by the Druids," when we predict Hawley's fortune with
the image of "a snake clinging to an oak tree" (Green 1997, 194). After fortune-
telling by tarot "cards" (94), Hawley is depicted as the "Druid." This can be
understood from the story development of Hawley becoming attached to Margie
and showing an interest in her.

   Steinbeck himself first began writing about the creation of *The Winter of
Discontent* in a letter dated November 5, 1959, the year before starting to write
and stated "It is very hard to raise boys to love and respect virtue and learning
when the tools of success are chicanery, treachery, self-interest, laziness and

cynicism or when charity is deductible" (*SLL* 653). Also, in the middle of writing, he seemed to have lost some confidence and said, "At worst it [a novel] should amuse, at half-staff move to emotion and at best illuminate" (*SLL* 676-677), as if he had lost confidence in his writing. Moreover, after the book review was released, he wrote "The reviews of Winter have depressed me very much" (*SLL* 698). It seemed that Steinbeck had completely lost confidence.

During the Cold War, the United States experienced a decline in morals and a change in values especially after the Korean War. The situations of the country changed in so short a period of time. Meanwhile, Steinbeck got married to Elaine, a woman of Irish descent, in the 1950s. It was his third marriage. There seemed to be a sense of frustration that nothing could be done about the declining morals of the people at that time.

Although he boasted that he would "write the best stories" (*JN* 4), he was not well received by those around him. *East of Eden* was not more accepted than was expected. The cause will be the extreme way of portraying "good" and "evil." It can be said that the true significance of "goodness" did not suit the times of the 1950s. Pure "goodness" did not signify the genuine "goodness" like in the period before World War II. Generally speaking, when it becomes rich, the country will expose a state of false "goodness" or hypocritical "virtue." At such deteriorated period when morals were declining, Steinbeck endeavored to express his mild disposition as a good "moralist" (French 160, Timmerman 265); that is, his excellent way of writing from the binary viewpoint of "good and evil."

As many researchers and critics have pointed out, there seems to be a lack of "Steinbeck-likeness." Fontenrose indicates that "This is not a non-teleological novel" (Fontenrose 137). Levant points out that "this last novel recapitulates Steinbeck's particular, mature conception of what a novel is, of how it is put together. The resulting strengths and weaknesses are typical rather than unique in Steinbeck's late fiction" (Levant 300).

However, no matter how less it is evaluated, the reason why this work won the Nobel Prize is because of its high level of evaluation: no doubt, this is a work of great value.

From now on, I will analyze the high value of this work. I would like to try to consider it from the perspective of Celtic representation.

I

Margie, who appears as a "witch-like" character in the text and is a close friend of Hawley's wife Mary. It reminds the reader of the word 'magic,' which is typical of Steinbeck's storytelling. Steinbeck's wordplay has appeared several times in his previous works such as "from Katy to Cathy/Kate." He uses many words with similar rhymes and ambiguity like "pun" in almost all his works. For example, the word 'register' (155) in *The Wayward Bus* (*WB*)means two connotations of "enrollment" and "a registered mail."

From her first appearance, Margie appears as a "witch." See the following quotation.

> Her[Margie's] tweed skirt clung lovingly in against her thighs and tucked up under her proud fanny, but it was in her eyes, her brown myopic eyes, that Ethan saw what his wife could never see because it wasn't there when wives were about. This was a predator, a huntress, Artemis for pants. Old Cap'n Hawley called it a "roving eye." It was in her voice too, a velvet growl that changed to a thin, mellow confidence for wives. (20)

This is how Margie depicts her "magic as a witch" seducing a man. The descriptions of her "skirt clung lovingly in against her thighs" and her "brown myopic eyes" are the ones which attract and even tempt Hawley. These depictions are written as an image of a "snake" that clings to itself and looks around. Also, her "voice" evokes animals and beasts of prey just like a witch. This is the similar way that Steinbeck portrays Cathy/Katy in *East of Eden* using the image of a "cat." That is, it can be thought that Margie is depicted with the image of a "snake" in this work. Both two animals are related to the significant effect on each work. Therefore, the author of this book believes that Margie is an important person.

Especially in *The Winter of Our Discontent*, Margie is an important character for Hawley. Actually, she plays an important role that can change the life of the protagonist. In this work, the word "snake" and its gestures are used many times to describe Margie. Descriptions such as a "rattlesnake" (101) and scenes in which Margie appears always have the image of a "snake." It is clear from the quotation mentioned above that this is the case.

Hawley is the "Druid" in modern times. The words of "Romans" (5) and "Calvary" (5) are used suddenly from the first chapter and the way of depicting these is reminiscent of Celtic Religion and Culture. Also, the story begins with Hawley's having a lot of wisdom and knowledge, which can be said to be linked to a book exposition. In short, as is seen among the Druids in general, Hawley can be thought with the image of the person "greatly esteemed in Celtic society — as mediators with the gods" (James 90).

One of the reasons for this is that Hawley graduates from that elite Harvard University. In addition, the modern Druids seem to leave great books that are handed down to the next generation in a written form, although "they [the Druids] passed their wisdom from one generation to the next in the form not of written texts but of memorized verse" (James 90).

This work introduces the method of handing down the tradition. The existence of these books is mentioned in Chapter 5, and is explained to his son Ethan Allen Hawley Jr. The son is informed of the existence of a huge collection of great books in the attic, which leads to his applying for an "essay contest." See the following quotation.

> A single unshaded light hung from a roof beam. The attic is floored with hand-hewn pine planks twenty inches wide and two inches thick, ample support for the neat stacks of trunks and boxes, of paper-wrapped lamps and

Chapter 11

vases and all manner of exiled finery. And the light glowed softly on the generations of books in open bookcases—all clean and dustless. (81)

As he introduces one of these great books to his son Allen, Hawley quotes one of famous verses of Irish-American patriot Patrick Henry (1736-99) and preaches to his son. This figure is exactly the modern "Druid," Ethan Allen Hawley. It is a manifestation of Hawley's dignity as the "Druid." It can be thought that Steinbeck is clearly conscious of the Irish-Celtic representation here as well. This is the quotation.

> "I see. Patriotic jazz. How's this for beat? 'Is life so dear or peace so sweet as to be purchased at the price of chains and slavery? Forbid it, Almighty God! I know not what course others may take, but as for me, give me liberty or give me death!'"
> "Great! That's the berries."
> "Sure is. There were giants on the earth in those days." (81)

As the "Druid," Hawley tends to think that he is doing a good job of preaching to his son, but as Hawley continues to preach for a while, his son hints at a quick way to win an essay contest, and he starts to think of some tricks. Hawley is told that in order to write an excellent essay, a prize will be won if a "trick" (82) is well used. Hawley, who does not notice his son's wrong doing of "plagiarism," which his son is about to commit, is exactly the pseudo-type of "good-natured person" in modern times. He does not perceive the "pretended good" and ends up converting "good" into "evil." He is devastated by his son's lack of morals.

However, the strong feeling that Hawley wants his son to inherit his will as is generally seen in the Druids, remains unchanged. Hawley's genuine affections for his son remain unchanged: as a case in point, "I hope we can live with him [Hawley Jr.]" (271) and "Go in peace—go with my [Hawley's] love" (216). Unlike in ancient times and the Middle Ages, when the Druids ruled

159

purely, in modern times we live no longer in a time when it is possible to clearly distinguish between "good" and "evil." It is expressed a lot in the story that Hawley himself does various cruel things behind the scenes.

Margie, with the "snake" imagery, becomes entangled with Hawley, the modern "Druid." According to Green, the "serpent" attaches itself to the Druid who prays in the oak tree, so Margie becomes a real helping hand for Hawley. The following passage, where the image of the "snake" is represented, is quoted here.

Similar imagery occurs in southern Gaulish representations of Sky-and Sun-god, for example at Seguret, where serpent is curled round an oak tree. (Green 1992, 194)

With this "snake" image, Margie carries out "Her project Ethan Allen Hawley" (195) and succeeds in captivating Hawley. It is exactly the image of the "snake" associated with the Druids, and as is predicted, it is responsible for the story development of "making Hawley rich." According to Margie's tarot cards' fortune-telling, Hawley ends up earning at least $4,000 in total: the sum of the "three thousand dollars" (269) Marullo gave to Hawley and the one thousand dollars that Danny "turned his back to you [Hawley]" (301) after his death.

II

There is a word in this work that has a particularly important meaning. It is the word "talisman" about Hawley's family and Hawley himself. The meaning of the word 'talisman' is "usually worn as an amulet to avert evil from or bring fortune to the wearer; also medicinally used to impart healing virtue" (*OED* 55). Steinbeck seems to create almost all of his works with the themes of "good" and "evil" encapsulated elaborately. The writer's use of this word in this last novel has great significance.

In addition, the sound of this word connotes the name of the Druid who was handed down to Wales. It is reminiscent of the word "taliesin," the name of the chief Druid priest. 'Taliesin' in Welsh is a compound word of 'tal-' (meaning "face") and '-liesin' (meaning "shining") (Nakazawa 89). The author of this book thinks that the word form of 'lis-' in the word "talisman" is reminiscent of 'liesin,' which means 'shining.' This fact seems to be Steinbeck's own "word play" method, and it is also represented about Grimm in the text, who devised "Grimm's Law," a grammatical theory that has been academically proven regarding the change of the words' forms. He also mentions "Grimm's Brothers" (80). Therefore, the writer uses this important word 'talisman' symbolizing various connotations and symbolism, which can be said that these "word plays" make this work profound.

As the original meaning suggests, this 'talisman' is used both in the middle of the story and at the end of the story.

In the last chapter, it is stated that "Then in my [Hawley's] hand it [the talisman] gathered every bit of light there was and seemed red—dark red" (311). From this way of depiction, the "talisman" as a stone symbolizes the "Philosophers' Stone." It is thought to have the symbolism and meaning of the "Philosophers' Stone." The interest of the writer Steinbeck in the medieval Europe has been discussed many times in this book and this is a statement that shows he also had knowledge of "alchemy."

Regarding the depiction of this "stone" as a "talisman," seen in Chapter 8, it is described in considerable detail, taking up most of one page.

I presume that every family has a magic thing, a continuity thing that inflames and comforts and inspires from generation to generation... The polished stone was not slick to the touch but slightly tacky like flesh, and it was always warm to the touch. You could see into it and yet not through it... It was magic—good to see, to touch, to rub against your cheek or to caress with your fingers. This strange and magic mound lived in the glass cabinet... And its color and convolutions and texture changed as my needs changed. (143)

Regarding its connection to "Celtic Culture," this talisman can be connected to the "Philosophers' Stone" depicted by J.K. Rowling's *Harry Potter* series and also the world of "immortality" depicted by Colin Wilson, etc. It goes without saying that this imagery is closely connected to the imagery of the "Legend of Holy Grail" depicted in *Le Morte D'Arthur*, which the writer has been familiar with since childhood.

According to Aromatico, this "Philosophers' Stone" is "characterized by its color, which is changeable red. Its color is a scarlet red shading to crimson, or ruby color shading to the color of garnet" (Aromatico 68). Moreover, as is well known, it can cure diseases of all living things. It is a panacea for healing and maintaining good health as Aromatico states "This acquisition of this gift promised riches, eternal health, and true knowledge" (Aromatico 70); thus, it truly represents "immortality."

Furthermore, in this work, a stone with a "serpent on" (260) is used as an amulet. This "talisman" in the story is undoubtedly the "Philosophers' Stone" itself, and this "serpent" pattern, if imagined as clinging to Hawley, symbolizes him as the "Druid." Its imagery as the "Philosophers' Stone" tells of the Hawley's fate. In this sense, the word "talisman" in this work is a very meaningful word, making this work profound both from an alchemical standpoint and from a Celtic perspective.

Next, we will consider why Hawley is the "Druid." This is because there appears a "Place" many times for contemplation and "prayer" (52 and many others). "The Place," which only Hawley knows, is used as a symbol of the Celtic Utopia "Tír na nÓg," the image of which is elaborately connected to "New Baytown" (181 and many others), which symbolizes "Celtic Forest." It will be that many "oaks" (181 and many others) inhabit the Druid's Places of prayer, and there are many passages reminiscent of the Druids in the beginning of Chapter 11 of the main text. In other words, New Baytown is depicted as if it were a "Celtic Forest."

The color image of "gray" during the "twilight," which is one of the Celtic symbols, can be summarized as "the magical hours before dawn and twilight when fairies begin to move," as I have mentioned many times before. It is used extensively in this work, especially in the depiction of Hawley and Margie, and also in other parts of this work. Since this time period is a "magical time period," it can also be interpreted as a mysterious time period where "good" (kindness) and "evil" (evilness) coexist; It can also be interpreted as a mysterious time period that goes beyond the concepts. Many images of this "Celtic gray Twilight" appear in this work, but the climax is the most exciting and excellent, when Hawley learns of his son's plagiarism and is about to cost him his own life. "Celtic Twilight," which exudes a "gray" color, is depicted as a relief from the scene of his immersion in "The Place" in the sea.

> The tide was on the rise. I waded into the warm bay water and clambered into the Place. A slow ground swell moved in and out of the entrance, flowed through my trousers. The fat billfold in my [Hawley's] hip pocket swelled against my hip and then grew thinner under my weight as it water-soaked. The simmer sea was crowded with little jellyfish the size of gooseberries, dangling their tendrils and their nettle cells. As they washed in against my legs and belly I felt them sting like small bitter fires, and the slow wave breathed in and out of the Place. The rain was only a thin mist now and it accumulated all the stars and town lamps and spread them evenly—a dark, pewter-colored sheen. (310)

This "Place" can definitely be thought of as "Tír na nÓg," and the use of color in the last line "pewter-colored sheen" (light emitting with a dark, lead-colored image), can be symbolized in the essence of "Celtic Twilight." Thus, the image of "Twilight" is used many times in the later progression of the story development like in the depiction that "Then in my [Hawley's] hand it [the light-bearer] gathered every bit of light there was and seemed red—dark red" (311). It can be believed that Hawley has a very important role in the "light-bearer," the talisman, shining with a sort of Druid's power and saving his own life.

The "rising tide" at the beginning of the above quotation seems to symbolize the injustices of his son and the "evil" of the society. It is also thought to symbolize both Hawley's approaching death and an image of "immortality." In the end, Hawley was saved from death with the power of the "talisman." Therefore, this "amulet" unites the "Philosophers' Stone," which exudes "Celtic Twilight," and Hawley's own "Place," where he can pray and meditate as the "Druid." This is my suitable interpretation on Steinbeck's last novel.

Conclusion

According to Kimie Imura, for the Celts, the time when fairies begin to move is "the time before 'rebirth', namely, 'the twilight before dawn,' and the time after 'rebirth,' returning to 'darkness'" (Kamata and Tsuruoka 47, trans. Mine), and from this idea, this time period can be considered to be two "twilight hours" namely "before dawn and twilight" (Fujimoto 741), as is pointed out by Reiji Fujimoto.

Regarding the night which governs darkness, Imura said, "with the image of 'death' in the earth, the ethnic and mythological aspects of fairies are revived as 'eternal memories from the past to the present'" (Kamata and Tsuruoka 47-48, trans. Mine). Therefore, these two hours of the day, "the twilight hours before dawn" and "the twilight hours," are, as Fujimoto points out, "tired of this world dominated by the notions of good and evil. It can be thought of as the Utopia of the Celts, 'Tír na nÓg'" (Fujimoto 742), where people escape from time and space. What Fujimoto considers here is, in short, a "mysterious period of time."

In the Celtic calendar, the year begins on the day when fairies go from the depth of the earth to the surface of the earth via the caves, and this day is commonly known as *Samhain*. In the Celtic world, this *Samhain* is "a dangerous time; a period in which the conventional boundaries of space and time were temporarily suspended and where the spirits of the Otherworld mingled freely with the living; a time of immense spiritual energy, when monstrous events were liable to take place" (Green 1997, 36)

As we have seen in this work, when we pay attention to the way the word "gray" is used, this "gray" is the Celtic color imagery of 'Tír na nÓg.' In this work, "the Place" is depicted as a "cave," filled with a "gray" twilight; where Hawley prays and contemplates, just like the Steinbeck's view of Celtic device with the story development.

By the way, as the modern Druid, Hawley was unable to pass on the Druid tradition down to his son. I will discuss the fate of the Druids by quoting Kazuo Tsukikawa's view here.

> The fundamental unity is that of the father. The son receives the rules of things from his father. However, this son does not forget that he is not only the child of his father, but also that he was born from his mother's womb, which is also "Natural." What's more, the Druidic norm taught by his father is the very teaching that he received the secrets of "Nature," not by his mother. What a paradox! Here begins the son's deviation. A son cannot remain a copy of his father.
>
> (edited by Shinichi Nakazawa et al. trans. Mine, 102)

According to Tsukikawa, the son "steals the wisdom of the 'father' by means of an elixir accidentally splashed into the dwarf's hand" (Shinichi Nakazawa et al., eds. Trans. Mine, 101), and this is exactly applicable to Ethan Allen Hawley Jr. In other words, Hawley's son, Ethan Allen Hawley Jr. generously steals the Druid tradition that Hawley inherited from his father, the important "teachings" of great books, and submits them to an "essay competition" in the form of "plagiarism."

Steinbeck features so-called preachers in many of his works. As a case in point, Merlin in *Cup of Gold*, Jim Casy in *The Grapes of Wrath*, Doc in *Cannery Row* and *Sweet Thursday*, and even Lee in *East of Eden* fall into this lineage. For the first time in this last novel, Hawley takes on the role of a preacher, both as the main character and as the "Druid."

In this final novel, Steinbeck tells the story from the eye of the first person "I" in a "novelette" style, telling the story through the eyes of the main character, Ethan Allen Hawley. The story seems to depict the contradictions of the United States in the 1950s, which cannot be divided simply by considering the dichotomy of "good and evil" or "binomial contrast," or the various situations in the world. In Reloy Garcia's words, this novel is "the record of the country's malaise, of the country's unfulfilled dreams and unmet obligations, and of what happens to principles, to dreams, and to ideals in the care of the moneylenders" (Garcia 245).

Also, in their real life, Steinbeck sent eight continuous letters to his wife Elaine, in which humorous and various story-like jokes such as "Bogworthy" (*SLL* 677) and "Merlin" (*SLL* 684) were written to her. Similar jokes can be thought of being frequently used in the main text of this work; implying a new age arrival of "minimalism" in American Literature, represented by Raymond Carver in the 1970s, suggesting the beginning of so-called "personal novel" style in American Literature.

As a pioneer of "minimalism" before Raymond Carver, Steinbeck reveals friendly life with his wife, depicting their happy marriage life in the work, and the first-person narrator Ethan Allen Hawley, is the "Druid" in modern times: John Steinbeck himself.

Works Cited and Referred Bibliographies

Aromatico, Andrea. *Discoveries: Alchemy: The Great Secret*. New York: Harry N. Abrahams, 2000.

Benson, Jackson J. *The True Adventures of John Steinbeck, Writer*. New York: Viking

Press, 1984

DeMott, Robert. *Steinbeck's Typewriter: Essays on His Art*. New York: Whitson Publishing Company Troy, 1996.

Finneran, Richard J. ed. *The Collected Poems of W. B. Yeats*. New York: Simon & Schuster Inc., 1996.

Fontenrose, Joseph. *John Steinbeck: An Introduction and Interpretation*. New York: Holt, Rinehart and Winston, Inc., 1963.

French, Warren. *John Steinbeck*. 2nd ed. Boston: Twayne Publishers, 1975.

Garcia, Reloy. "Steinbeck's *The Winter of Our Discontent*" in *A Study Guide to Steinbeck: A Handbook to his Major Works*. Ed. Tetsumaro Hayashi. Metuchen, N.J.: Scarecrow Press, Inc., 1974.

Green, Miranda J. *Exploring the World of the Druids*. London: Thames & Hudson Ltd., 1997.

_____. *Celtic Myths*. London: British Museum Press, 1993.

Jackson, Robert. *The Alchemists*. London: Weidenfeld Nicolson Illustrated, 1997.

James, Simon. *Exploring the World of the Celts*. London: Thames & Hudson Ltd., 1995.

Levant, Howard. *The Novels of John Steinbeck: A Critical study*. Columbia: University of Missouri Press, 1974.

Kerrigan, Michael. *Celtic Legends: Heroes and Warriors, Myths and Monsters*. London: Amberbooks Co., 2016.

Lisca, Peter. *The Wide World of John Steinbeck*. Reprinted, New York: Gordian Press, 1981.

Lovejoy, Arthur O. *The Great Chain of Being*. Harvard University Press, 1936.

Owens, Louis. *John Steinbeck's Re-Vision of America*. Athens: University of Georgia Press, 1985.

Shakespeare, William. *The Tragedy of King Richard the Third*. Ed. A. Hamilton Thompson. London: Methuen and Co., 1907.

Simmonds, Roy. *A Biographical and Critical Introduction of John Steinbeck*. New York: Edwin Mellen Press, 2000.

Steinbeck, Elaine and Robert Wallsten eds. *Steinbeck: A Life in Letters*. New York:

Viking Press, 1975.   (Written in the main text as *SLL*)

Steinbeck, John. *The Winter of Our Discontent*. New York: Viking Press, 1961.

_____. *The Wayward Bus*. New York: Viking Press, 1947.

(Written in the main text as *WB*)

_____. *Journal of a Novel: The East of Eden Letters*. New York: Viking Press, 1969.

(Written in the main text as *JN*)

Timmerman, John H. *John Steinbeck's Fiction: The Aesthetics of the Road Taken*. Norman: Oklahoma University Press, 1986.

_____. "The Shameless Magpie: John Steinbeck, Plagiarism, and the Ear of the Artist" in *Steinbeck Question: New Essays in Criticism*. Ed. Donald R. Noble. New York; Whitman Publishing Company Troy, 1993.

Fujimoto, Reiji. "Yeats" in *Light Imagery: English Poetry in Tradition*. Ed. Fumiyo Uesugi. Tokyo: Kirihara Shoten, 1985.

Hara, Kiyoshi. *Celtic Water Veins*. Tokyo: Kodansha, 2007.

Inazawa, Hideo. *Steinbeck View*. Tokyo: Shichosha, 1967.

Kamata, Toji and Mayumi Tsuruoka eds. *Celt and Japan*. Tokyo: Kadokawa Shoten, 2000.

Kihara, Kenichi. *Yeats and the Mask: The Paradox of Death*. Tokyo: Sairyusha, 2001.

Kotsuji, Umeko. *Celtic Thoughts on the Celts*. Tokyo: Shakai Shiso-sha, 1998.

Matsuoka, Toshitsugu et al. eds. *Celtic Bible Stories*. Tokyo: Iwanami Shoten, 1999.

Nakayama, Kiyoshi. *A Study of Steinbeck's Literature Vol. III: New York Period*. Osaka: Kansai University Press, 2002.

Nakazawa, Shinichi et. al. *Celtic Religion Druidism*. Tokyo: Iwanami Shoten, 1997.

Tsuoka, Mayumi. *Celtic Imagination: History, Mythology, and Art*. Tokyo: Seidosha, 2018.

Abraham, Lyndy. *A Dictionary of Alchemical Imagery*. Cambridge: Cambridge University Press, 2001.

Green, M.J. *Dictionary of Celtic Myth and Legend*. London: Hudson and Thames, 1992

The Oxford English Dictionary. First Edition. Oxford: At the Clarendon Press, 1933.

Part II

On the Compound Particle "iwa" in Kunten Materials

Ōsuke Tsujimoto

(Kansei Gakuin University)

1. Introduction

In ancient Japanese, the form "iwa," composed of the particle "i" and the binding particle "wa" is observed; however, examples of this usage are scarce in early literary works, such as the Manyoshu, making it challenging to conduct thorough investigations. Only few studies have delved into its meaning and usage.

(1) 夢に〔見〕三の鳩の雛あり、小なる<u>いは</u>〔者〕是レ愛子なり、忽に鷹に奪は被て去（き）ヌと見たり。（金光明最勝王経・197-10）

Yume ni san no iebato no hina ari. Shōnaru iwa kore aishi nari. Tachimachini taka ni ubawa-re-te shirizoki-nu to mi-tari. (Konkomyōsaishō. ōkyō, 197-10)

dream LOC three GEN dove GEN chicks appear small NOM namely cute.child COP suddenly hawk snatch-PASS-GER dissapear-PRF COMP see-PRF

In a dream, three doves appeared. The smallest one was the child I was fond of; but suddenly, a hawk snatched it away.

(2) 若（し）我<u>いは</u>是（れ）常（な）らは則（ち）業無く報無く苦を解脱すること無（く）なりぬべし。（成実論・二十三・39-16）

Moshi ware iwa kore tsunenara-ba sunawachi gyō naku hō naku ku o gedatsusuru koto nakunari-nu-beshi. (Jōjitsuron, 23, 39-16)

if I NOM namely ordinary COND namaly karma disappear reward disappear worry escape NMLZ disappear-PRF-PRESUM

If I were an ordinary person, I would neither suffer any consequences of my past actions nor be liberated from my worries.

In this study, we observe the occurrence of "iwa" in kunten materials during the early to middle Heian period. We explore its characteristics by comparing its usage with that of "i."

2. Previous Research

There has been limited prior research on the compound particle "iwa" in kunten texts. Traditionally, it is only known that the order of "i" and "wa" is fixed in "iwa," such that it cannot become "wai" (Hamada 1967:49). According to Ōtsubo (1961:113) and others, the "i" in the compound particle indicates the subject, suggesting that "iwa" is presumed to be attached to the subject of the sentence. Thus far, there has been no explicit refutation of this presumption.

In the case of the simple particle "i," Whitman and Yanagida (2012) and Bundschuh (2018) proposed functions similar to the contemporary "ga," expressing broad focus or acting as a referential pronominal, respectively. However, Tsujimoto (2023) presents counterexamples, rejecting these claims. In Tsujimoto (2023), I elucidate that the "i" in kunten texts attaches to nouns representing existing entities.

The following section reports the findings on the compound particle "iwa" in kunten texts. A preemptive conclusion is that "iwa" fundamentally attaches to nominalized forms of conjugated words, and the entities represented by these nominalized forms can either exist or not. Unlike "i," known to predominantly co-occur with predicates expressing actions, "iwa" exhibits no such bias and can also co-occur with predicates expressing states. Compared to "i," the constraint of "iwa" on the expression of subjects and predicates is more relaxed, except for its attachment to nominalized forms of conjugated words.

This study focuses on the instances of "iwa" in kunten materials from the early to middle Heian period. The materials investigated are those compiled by Tsujimoto (2023), which, due to space constraints, have not been included in this manuscript.

3. Characteristics of Preceding Terms

This section describes the characteristics of the vocabulary that precedes the compound particle "iwa."

3.1 Connection to Nominalized Forms of Conjugated Verbs

The most important characteristic of "iwa" is that it fundamentally connects to nominalized forms of conjugated verbs.

(3)　衆生若（し）聞（く）こと<u>得るイ</u>は、悉（く）諸の悪業を離せむ。（大方広仏華厳経・384-15）

Shujō moshi kiku koto uru iwa kotogotoku moromorono akugyō o rise-mu.

public if hear NMLZ gain NOM all every misdeeds ACC escape-CONJEC

Those who hear those words may be able to escape the consequences of the misdeeds they committed in their past lives. (Daihōkōbutsukegonkyō, 384-15)

(4)　若（し）<u>苦ナルい</u>は即（ち）是（れ）無我なり。（成実論・十八・26-7）

Moshi kunaru iwa sunawachi kore muganari.

if suffering NOM that.is.to.say namely selfless

The state of suffering is, in essence, a state of selflessness. (Jōjitsuron・18・26-7)

(5)　愚癡懈怠の根下劣なるガ、二乗の法の於に〔不〕勤（め）て修セヌ<u>イ</u>ハ、定（め）て大乗の輪（を）具すること能（は）不。（地蔵十輪経・聖語蔵本・203-10）

Guchi kedai no ne geretsunaru ga nijō no hō no ueni tsutome-te shūse-nu iwa sadamete daijō no wa o gusuru koto atawa-zu.

Ignorance laziness GEN base.nature ignoble APPOS nijo GEN Dharma GEN above practice-GER engage.in.discipline-NEG NOM in.no.wise daijo GEN wheel ACC carry NMLZ CAP-NEG

Among humans whose base nature is ignoble, characterized by ignorance and laziness, those who neither diligently practice nor

173

engage in the discipline based on Nijo's Dharma can never carry the wheel of the Mahayana, the Great Vehicle. (Jizōjūrinkyō, Shōgozōhon, 203-10)

(6) 大乗を修行するいは、宝器を作（る）が如（し）。（妙法蓮華経玄賛・294-23）

Daijō o shugyōsuru iwa hōki o tsukuru ga-gotoshi.

Daijo ACC practice NOM precious.object craft ACC SEEM

Engaging in the practice of Mahayana is akin to crafting a precious object. (Myōhōrengekyōgensan, 294-23)

(7) 同（じく）五濁なりと雖（も）、但、一乗（の）機有（る）いは則（ち）聞（く）。无きいは則（ち）聞（か）不。（法華義疏・436-15）

Onajiku gojokunari toiedomo tada ichijō no ki aru iwa sunawachi kiku. Naki iwa sunawachi kika-zu.

Same five.turbidities ADVRS only Ekayāna GEN opportunity possessor NOM immediately hear non-posessor NOM immediately hear-NEG

Even amidst the five turbidities, those who have the opportunity of Ekayāna (One Vehicle) can hear, while those without such an opportunity cannot. (Hokkegisho, 436-15)

These instances of "iwa" are interpreted as marking the subject; thus, they maintain the nominative particle characteristic inherited from "i." However, when attached to conjugated verbs, "iwa" is transformed, losing its case-marking nature and becoming a quasinominal particles[1]. It is thought that particles exhibiting such unique characteristics are likely exclusive to "iwa."

---

1 Instances of "iwa" following a noun are observed to a certain extent in the discourse on 成実論 (jōjitsuron). Outside of the context of 成実論 , only three instances were found, in the 願経四分律（聖語蔵本）(GankyōShibunritsu, Shogozohon), the 金光明最勝王経 (Konkomyōsaishō.ōkyō), and the 地蔵十輪経（東大寺図書館本）(Jizōjūrinkyō, Tōdaijitoshokanbon), with each having only one example.

Conventionally, subject noun phrases marked by "i" are noted for expressing the sense of a "...thing/person" rather than an "...action/state" (Kondo 2000:381). These instances appear acceptable when interpreted in this way. However, the following "iwa" appears to be more naturally understood as an "...action/state." Thus, it might be reasonable to consider it to have a distinct characteristic from "i."

(8) 他人を欺誑するいは必（ず）口業に由（り）て妄語の罪を得（る）が如（き）なり。（成実論・十二・2-56-4）

Tanin o gikyōsuru iwa kanarazu kugyō niyorite mōgo no tsumi o uru ga-gotoki nari.

others ACC deceive NOM surely words through faisehood GEN sin ACC gain SEEM COP

Deceiving others is surely akin to committing the sin of falsehood through words. (Jōjitsuron, 12, 2-56-4)

(9) …非時語し无益語し无義語するいは則（ち）唯綺語なり。（成実論・十二・1-54-8）

Hijigoshi muekigoshi mugigosuru iwa sunawachi tada kigo nari.

make.inappropriate.remarks make.pointless.remarks make.meaningless.words NOM namely only speaking.against.the.truth COP

Making inappropriate remarks, speaking without purpose, or uttering meaningless words is speaking against the truth. (Jōjitsuron, 12, 1-54-8)

(10) …詐（り）て大乗と号し、名利の為にするイは、弊の驢の師子の皮を披ガ如し。（地蔵十輪経・聖語蔵本・204-9）

Itsuwari-te daijō to gōshi, myōri no tameni suru iwa, hē no ro no shishi no kawa o kazuku ga-gotoshi.

falsely.claim-GER daijo COMP state fame GEN PURP do NOM attachiments GEN donkey NOM lion GEN skin ACC wear SEEM

Falsely stating that one is practicing Mahayana to gain fame and wealth is akin to a donkey wearing the skin of a lion as an attachment.

(Jizōjūrinkyō, Tōdaijitoshokanbon, 204-9)

3.3 Concerning the Prefixation of "mu"

The above understanding appears to be generally sufficient. However, when observing the types of preceding conjugated verbs, it is noteworthy that "mu" appears to some extent.

(11)　有（ら）ム善男子・善女人の、阿耨多羅三藐三菩提の心を発して、是の相似の般若波羅蜜（を）聞（か）<u>ムいは</u>、正道を失（ひ）てム。（大智度論・623-8）

Ara-mu zendanshi zennyonin no anokutarasammyakusambodai no kokoro o hasshi-te, kono sōji no GEN hannyaharamitsu o kika-mu iwa, sēdō o ushinai-te-mu.

Every male.believer female.believer APPOS anokutarasammyakusambodai GEN heart ACC occur-GER this similar hannnyaharamitsu ACC hear-HYP NOM right.path ACC lose-PERF-CONJEC

Every male and female believer, claiming to have reached the state of "anuttara samyak sambodhi" (the highest ideal enlightenment), may lose the right path upon hearing something resembling "prajna-paramita" (the highest wisdom).　(Daichidoron, 623-8)

(12)　若〔有受持〕此の正義と相応する経を受持すること有（ら）<u>むいは</u>、魔の所行に随（は）ず〔不〕して、魔の悪業を浄除（せ）む。（金光明最勝王経・207-7）

Moshi kono sēgi to sō.ōsuru kyō o jujisuru koto ara-mu iwa, ma no shogyō ni shitagawa-zushite, ma no akugyō o jōjose-mu.

If this righteousness COM accord scriptures ACC receive.and. memorize NMLZ experience-HYP NOM evil.spirit GEN deeds DAT obey-NEG evi.spirit GEN mischief ACC eliminate-CONJEC

If there is someone who can receive and memorize the teachings of the scriptures in accordance with this righteousness, they will not be misled by the deeds of evil spirits; instead, they will be able to eliminate the

evil actions of the one who commits mischief.　(Konkōmyōsaishō.
ōkyō, 207-7)

In Tsujimoto (2023:55-56), it is argued that the solitary "i" attaches to noun
phrases representing existing entities, and the difficulty of the preceding noun
being adnominally modified by "mu" is considered supporting evidence. In the
following examples, "mu" does not appear.

(13)　〔非〕十の悪不律儀に住セル者イ、能（く）是（の）如き无上正等
　　　菩提の大願を満するものにはアラズ。(地蔵十輪経・東大寺図書館本・
　　　109-19)

Jū no akufuritsugi ni jūse-ru mono i, yoku kono gotoki mujōshōtōbodai
no taigan o mansuru mono ni-wa-ara-zu.

ten GEN wrongful.deeds LOC stay-PERF someone NOM capably this
SEEM mujoshotobodai GEN great.wish ACC attain someone COP-
NEG

One who continues to engage in the ten wrongful deeds is not someone
capable of fulfilling the great wish to attain the highest enlightenment
this way. (Jizōjūrinkyō, Tōdaijitoshokanbon, 109-19)

(14)　黄鳥イ白キ形に作リ、黒キ烏イ変して赤ク為りナムヤ。（金光明最
　　　勝王経・12-17）

Ōchō i shiroki katachi ni tsukuri, kuroki karasu i henshi-te akaku nari-
namu ya.

yellow.bird NOM white appearance COP turn black crow NOM
transform-GER red become-CONJEC QP

Will the yellow bird turn white, and will the black crow transform and
become red? (Konkōmyōsaishō.ōkyō, 12-17)

(15)　故に但（し）此（の）如き説い善（なりといふことを）知る。（妙
　　　法蓮華経玄賛・216-1）

Yueni tadashi kono gotoki setsu i zennari toyū koto o shiru.

therefore indeed this SEEM theory NOM good COMP NMLZ ACC
know

Therefore, I have come to understand that this theory is indeed good.
(Myōhōrengekyōgensan, 216-1)

These examples present the basic occurrence pattern of "i." Various conjugated words, as illustrated, can adnominally modify nouns preceding "i." However, adnominal modification by "mu" is generally not possible. In contrast, "iwa" is distinct from "i" in that it allows the free occurrence of "mu," as seen in examples (11) and (12).

Tsujimoto (2023) reported that nouns preceding "i" are limited to those with an existential presupposition. However, no such constraint is observed in the case of expressions preceding "iwa." Although "iwa" is used under a syntactic constraint of attaching itself only to conjugated words, making its usage more limited than "i," it is versatile in that it can be used without considering the presence or absence of an assumption of existence.

3.4 Occurrence Conditions of Conjugated Verbs Other Than "mu"

There also appear to be noteworthy aspects regarding the occurrence conditions of conjugated verbs other than "mu." While I have identified the following phenomena in the context of such verbs, it remains unclear how these relate to the characteristics of "iwa" at this point.

First is the frequent appearance of the negation auxiliary verb "zu."

(16) 若（し）人の善を修せむか為の故に食せ<u>不いは</u>〔則〕唐 に怨属
を養（ふ）なり。（成実論・二十一・78-下15）

Moshi hito no zen o shūse-mu gatame no yueni shokuse-nu iwa itazurani onzoku o yashinō nari.

alternatively person APPOS goodness ACC practice-INT PURP GEN CSL eat-NEG NOM meaninglessly enemy ACC nurture COP.

Alternatively, perhaps when a person refrains from eating to practice goodness, it is nothing more than meaninglessly nurturing an enemy. (Jōjitsuron, 21, 78-b15)

(17) 言（フコト）を慎マ<u>ヌイは</u>〔者〕沙弥に非（ズ）〔也〕。（沙弥十戒

威儀経・104-9）

Yū koto o tsutsushima-nu iwa shami niara-zu.

speech NMLZ ACC guard-NEG NOM practitioner COP-NEG

Those who do not guard their speech cannot be called practitioners.

(Shamijikkai.igikyō, 104-9)

In the case of a noun preceding "i," examples of adnominal modification by the negation auxiliary verb are scarce, which might be due to the inherent scarcity of examples in which the negation auxiliary verb adnominally modifies a noun.

Additionally, among the auxiliary verbs other than "mu" and "zu," "ri" occurs to some extent.

(18) 若善く光（を）除滅せるいは則（ち）明浄なり。（成実論・十一・17-上16）

Moshi yoku hikari o jometsuse-ru iwa sunawachi mējōnari.

aternatively skillfully light ACC eliminate-PERF NOM namaly pure

Alternatively, a situation skillfully dimmed is, in essence, pure.

(Jōjitsuron, 11, 17-t16)

(19) 若人重き罪を造るいは善を脩すれば滅除すること得つ。（百法顕幽抄・93-20）

Moshi hito omoki tsumi o tsukure-ru iwa zen o shūsure-ba jometsusuru koto e-tsu.

alternatively person grave sin ACC commit-PERF NOM goodness ACC practice- CSL redeem NMNL gain-PERF

Alternatively, one who has committed a grave sin could have redeemed that sin by practicing goodness. (Hyappōkenyūshō, 93-20)

However, it is advised to be cautious in determining whether the frequent occurrences of examples like the ones mentioned above should be considered a characteristic of "iwa," as "ri" is also occasionally observed as an adnominal modifier of nouns preceding "i."

(20) 瞋心を懐せ（ケる）者い必（ず）能（く）惣を行す。（成実論・

十八・29-11)

Shinshin o kaise-ru hito i kanarazu yoku kotsu o gyōsu.

anger ACC harbor-PERF person NOM inevitably capably dazed.state ACC occur

A person harboring anger will inevitably end up in a profoundly dazed state. (Jōjitsuron, 18, 29-11)

When comparing the usages of "iwa" and "i," another phenomenon that deserves attention is that "iwa" does not connect with words using an adjectival conjugation. In the case of "i," it is possible for adjectival-conjugated words to perform adnominal modification on nouns preceding "i," and examples can be found where "i" connects with the adnominal form of adjectival-conjugated words.

(21) 若（し）実に功徳無キものい人を（し）て有りと謂（は）令（めむ）と欲ふ。(成実論・十三・69-33)

Moshi jitsuni kudoku naki mono i hito oshite ari to iwa-shime-mu to omō.

alternatively truly merit lack person NOM person ACC exist COMP say-CAUS-INT COMP think

Alternatively, those truly lacking in merit try to make others tell stories about their virtues. (Jōjitsuron, 13, 69-33)

(22) 是（の）如キ衆生い能ク深キ義を解ル。(金光明最勝王経・94-7)

Kono gotoki shujō i yoku fukaki gi o shiru.

This SEEM public NOM capably deep righteousness ACC understand

This type of public deeply understands righteousness. (Konkomyōsaishō. ōkyō, 94-7)

(23) …亦分別も無キい、聖の修行（し）たまふ所なり。(金光明最勝王経・29-23)

Mata fumbetsu mo naki i, hijiri no shugyō shi-tamō tokoro nari.

and discrimination ADD not.have NOM holy NOM practices do-HON place COP

Here, people without discrimination (vikalpa) are engaged in holy practices. (Konkomyōsaishō.ōkyō, 29-23)

(24) 真善の国王の等きイ、我ガ正法を興隆す。(地蔵十輪経・聖語蔵本・
186-8)

Shinzen no kokuō no-gotoki i, waga shōbō o kōryūsu.

Truly.good GEN king SEEM NOM his righteous.teachings ACC aphold

A truly good king upholds his own righteous teachings. (Jizōjūrinkyō, Shōgozōhon, 186-8)

In (23) and (24), we observe the attachment of "i" to adjectives. A valid interpretation might be that this supplements the particle "wa," forming "iwa." However, instances of the compound particle "iwa" directly attaching to adjectival inflections are scarce; indeed, this investigation identified only one example.

(25) 无きいは則（ち）聞（か）不。(法華義疏・436-15)

Naki iwa sunawachi kika-zu.

not.have NOM namaly hear-NEG

The one without an affinity for Ekayāna (the One Vehicle) does not hear the teachings of Ekayāna. (Hokkegisho, 436-15)

Unfortunately, there is no prepared explanation for the above phenomena. In this paper, I would like to highlight these phenomena as features requiring attention without delving into the principles behind their manifestation.

4. Characteristics of Predicates

Finally, we present the observational results regarding predicates that correspond to "iwa."

While indicating the difference in the number of examples remains a task for future research, one distinction from the case of "i" lies in the tendency for predicates expressing states to appear more frequently.

(26) 有る人の能く般若波羅蜜を説（く）いは〔者〕、大福徳有（り）。
（大智度論・762-10）

Aru hito no yoku hannnyaharamitsu o toku iwa, daifukutoku ari.

certain person GEN capably hannnyaharamitsu ACC expound.on

NOM great.merit attain

Those who can expound on prajna-paramita (the perfection of wisdom)

attain great merit. (Daichidoron, 762-10)

(27) 世尊は金剛の体なり、権現せる<u>いは</u><ruby>於<rt>こ</rt></ruby>レ<u>化身なり</u>。（金光明最勝王
経・14-1）

Seson wa kongō no tē nari. Gongense-ru iwa kore keshin nari.

Buddha TOP diamond-like GEN body COP manifest-PERF NOM

namely provisional.form COP

The Buddha has a diamond-like body. Its manifestation is a provisional

form. (Konkōmyōsaishō.ōkyō, 14-1)

(28) 菩薩摩訶薩の心を発（し）て布施する<u>イは</u>、大慈悲<u>有リ</u>。（地蔵十
輪経・東大寺図書館本・113-11）

Bosatsumakasatsu no kokoro o hasshi-te fusesuru iwa, daijihi ari.

bodhisattva GEN heart ACC generate-GER offer.material.possessions

NOM great.passionate.heart have

Those who attain the heart of a bodhisattva and offer material

possessions and teachings to others possess a great, compassionate

heart. (Jizōjūrinkyō, Tōdaijitoshokanbon, 113-11)

(29) 八億万の戸有て其（の）王舎城（に）属せる<u>いは</u>〔者〕、八萬の聚
落<u>有（る）</u>なり〔也〕。（法華義疏・323-19）

Hachiokuman no ko ari-te sono ōshajō ni zokuse-ru iwa, hachiman no

shūraku aru nari.

800.million GEN house exist-GER its Rajgir LOC belong.to-PERF

NOM 80,000 GEN settlements exist COP

There are 800 million houses, meaning there are 80,000 settlements in

Rajgir. (Hokkegisho, 323-19)

Takeuchi (2012) notes that, in Old Japanese, the particle "i" indicates the
agent of the action. I have observed this trend in Tsujimoto (2023) and have

demonstrated that such a tendency is discernible even in the kunten materials of the Heian period. Considering "iwa" as a form where these constraints have been alleviated seems reasonable.

5. Conclusion

In this study, I have highlighted the characteristics of "iwa" while comparing its usage with that of "i." The form "…muiwa," which involves non-real entities as subjects and the use of predicates expressing states, suggests a relaxing of the usage constraints observed with "i." However, explaining why "iwa" exclusively connects to inflecting words is a challenge. A more detailed observation of examples of "iwa" may reveal features unaddressed in this paper. In any case, research on "iwa" is still in its early stages.

References

Ōtsubo, Heiji (1961) *Kuntengo no kenkyu*. Kazama shobō, Tokyo.

Kondō, Yasuhiro (2000) *Nihongokijutubunpō no riron*. Hitsuji shobō, Tokyo.

Takeuchi, Shirō (2012) "Kodaigo no dōsashu hyōshiki o megutte – joshi -i to Ishigaki hōsoku –" in: Takayama, Yoshiyuki/Aoki, Hirofumi/Fukuda, Yoshiichirō, eds. *Nihongo bunpōshi kenkyū 1*, Hitsuji shobō, Tokyo.

Tsujimoto, Ōsuke (2023) "Joshi -i to sonzai zentei" *Kokugo kokubun*, Vol. 92. No.7, 44-62.

Hamada, Atsushi (1967) "Fukujoshi nado" *kokugo kokubun*, Vol. 36. No.1, 46-53.

Bundschuh, John (2018) "Japanese Particle -I -A Study in Early Middle Japanese" *Buckeye East Asian Linguistics*, Vol. 3, 11-20.

Whitman, John/Yanagida, Yuko (2012) A Korean Grammatical Borrowing in Early Middle Japanese Kunten Texts and its Relation to the Syntactic Alignment of Earlier Korean and Japanese. *Japanese/Korean Linguistics* 21, ed. Seungho Nam, Heejeong Ko and Jongho Jun, 121–135. Stanford:

The Works of John Steinbeck: In the Magic Light of "Celtic Twilight"

CSLI Publications.

[Note] This work was supported by JSPS KAKENHI Grant Number JP22K00578.

Travels with *Travels with Charley*—
In Search of America Now and Then

Kiyoshi Yamauchi

(Niimi University)

Introduction

There was a trend of publication in the first half of 2010s, in which authors traveled the similar routes to John Steinbeck's travels with his dog, Charley, and published books about the travel. Steinbeck traveled around in America in 1960 and published *Travels with Charley—In Search of America* in 1962. Half a century after the historic travel, many drove the Steinbeck's road, with or without their dogs, and wrote road narratives, while other nameless travelers only wrote blogs, posted in social media or maybe only kept their own travel logs.

Included in this category of books are: Bill Barich's *Long Way Home—On the Trail of Steinbeck's America—*(2010), Gregory Zeigler's *Travels With Max—In Search of Steinbeck's America Fifty Years Later—*(2010), John R. Olson's *Down John's Road—Recreating John Steinbeck's 1960 American Road Trip* (2011), Bill Steigerwald's *Dogging Steinbeck—Discovering America and Exposing The Truth About 'Travels With Charley'* —(2012), Vicki Cain's *Travels with Judy— In search of Steinbeck's America* (2012), Geert Mak's *In America—Travels with John Steinbeck—* (first published in Dutch in 2012, and translated into English in 2014) and Benoit Denizet-Lewis's *Travels with Casey—My Journey Through Our Dog-Crazy Country—* (2015). Out of these seven books, I will discuss four books: Zeigler's, Olson's, Steigerwald's and Denizet-Lewis's.

Gregory Zeigler, *Travels With Max—In Search of Steinbeck's America Fifty Years Later*

The theme of Zeigler's travel, and thus of his travel log, is "how Americans had changed" (1) or "what Americans are like today" (6) fifty years after John Steinbeck traveled and wrote his book *Travels With Charley*. As Zeigler put it, "America has come a long way in fifty years" (26); this book could be titled *America and Americans Fifty Years Later*.

Of course it is difficult to observe and record something accurately and objectively just like Steinbeck wrote in *The Log from the Sea of Cortez*, "We could not observe a completely objective Sea of Cortez anyway, for in that lonely and uninhabited Gulf our boat and ourselves would change it the moment we entered" (3). Zeigler also quoted from Steinbeck when he wrote about differing perspectives on travel: "What I set down here is true until someone else passes that way and rearranges the world in his own style" (241). But Zeigler tried to describe what he saw, what he felt, while he talked with many people along the way. During his nine-week and "fifteen-thousand-mile trip" (262), he hit the roads in 35 states, "met hundreds of people on this journey and observed hundreds more" (263), and created his narrative of *America and Americans Fifty Years Later*. In his narrative he made at least three mentions of a bald eagle (135, 143, 261), the national bird and a symbol of the United States. That helps what Zeigler described in this book as becoming symbolic of what America is like today.

Steinbeck started his journey from his then home Sag Harbor, New York, but Zeigler started his from his "permanent" (15) home in Jackson, Wyoming. Both of Steinbeck's and Zeigler's routes are shown on the maps (4-5, 48-49, 238-239). Zeigler tried to make as much the same route as Steinbeck's as possible. Steinbeck made his journey from September to December in 1960, while Zeigler's journey took place from September to November in 2009. Steinbeck's third wife Elaine visited John three times during the tour in Chicago, California and Texas, while Zeigler's second wife Dimmie visited Gregory just as many as times in Georgia, Chicago and California. He was not the only one who took Steinbeck's route 50 years later. Zeigler just saw a man (named "Tom") who also took Steinbeck's route like him and "was staying in the room right next to" (89) his room at Boyce's Motel in Deer Isle, Maine. Perhaps because of Zeigler's identical ancestry to Steinbeck's, "German and Irish" (81), he "felt a powerful sense of being right in Steinbeck's tracks" (74).

Zeigler visited several places in honor of Steinbeck. His visit to Sag Harbor was described in Chapter Five "Sag Harbor: At the Beginning at Last." He visited Steinbeck's house in Sag Harbor and its neighborhood, and met some of the people who knew Steinbeck. In California, Zeigler visited Steinbeck Country: Salinas, Monterey and Pacific Grove. In Salinas, Steinbeck's hometown, Zeigler visited Steinbeck House, Steinbeck's and Elaine's grave in Garden of Memories and the National Steinbeck Center. Zeigler also visited John Steinbeck's son, Thomas Steinbeck and his wife Gail in Santa Barbara, California.

Just like Steinbeck depicts his political conversation with his sisters about J. F. Kennedy and Richard Nixon (173), Khrushchev's visit to the United Nations in New York (32) and the historical events of the time in *Travels with Charley*, Zeigler's narrative deals with the issues of September 11, 2001 (75, 137), Hurricane Katrina (in New Orleans). Zeigler often talks about the impact of the recent economic recessions and/or President Obama's Administration with the people he met in various places. Zeigler also wrote about gay marriages (95), the decrease in the numbers of farmers in the US (97), intermarriages (234-235) and the two wars (in Iran and Afghanistan) (264). He mentioned the Fort Hood shooting tragedy which happened on November 5, 2009 as well.

Zeigler observes the changes of society and has introduced the expression of the "microwave society" (32) in which "we want everything right away." Zeigler met brothers of a white boy and a black boy in Rabun Gap School in Virginia, something "that Steinbeck could not have seen fifty years ago in the South" (51).

As society has changed, so has the style of traveling. Zeigler has used GPS which navigates the best traveling routes most of the time. Steinbeck used maps and he wrote in *Travels with Charley* that "maps are not reality at all—they can be tyrants" (26). If Steinbeck could have used GPS, what would he have written about the system?

What makes Zeigler's travel book so unique is that he also wrote blog articles along the way at "Travels With Steinbeck. Comparison of blog articles with the description in the book is also interesting, and a blog could be a new style of road narrative literature. I read his blog articles after I read the book, but if I had known about Zeigler and his travels with his dog when he was doing it, I could have enjoyed his historic travel in the making.

Cell phones made Zeigler's travel easier and merrier. Steinbeck had to use a pay phone to call home or friends, or write letters to them, but Zeigler used his cell phone to call home or friends, and his family members could reach him along the way. Zeigler sent postcards from each of the states to the school kids he met at the schools he visited during his travel. I believe he used emails and text messages to connect his family members and friends, and sometimes people he met along the way. These modern technologies certainly made Zeigler's trip less lonelier, as Zeigler wrote "[c]ell phones are a pretty good defense against loneliness" (107). Speaking of modernity, he mentions "Google" (76), "Wi-Fi" (82) and "a fleece blanket" (125), none of which was not used by Steinbeck, but all of which are necessary for Zeigler's modern driving trip using the internet. He even used *emoji* pictogram in the text "c(-:"(132).

In this book, Zeigler wrote about his two sons, perhaps like Steinbeck did when he wrote *East of Eden*, and his daughter Jamie and her child to be born (then while he was traveling, and now grandson Theo). He also wrote about John Steinbeck and his two sons, John IV and Thomas. Aaron and Cal in *East of Eden* are said to be modeled after Steinbeck's own sons, John and Thomas, and Steinbeck is said to have written *East of Eden* for his two sons. This book of Zeigler's is also meant to be a story from a father to his children and to his grandson. This book is dedicated to his children, Jamie, Alex and Wil and grandson, Theo.

John R. Olson, *Down John's Road—Recreating John Steinbeck's 1960 American Road Trip—*

John Olson wrote news articles for newspapers and radios, and retired in 2003. He lives in Poulsbo, Washington, which made his travel start in Washington, the northwest state of the mainland USA, and clockwise, which is compared with the counterclockwise travel of Steinbeck's, and also compared to the counterclockwise Zeigler's travel route starting in Wyoming.

John Olson had many things in common with John Steinbeck, not just first name John. Olson had some arguments with his sister like Steinbeck had "fighting over politics" (173) with his sister in *Travels with Charley*. Olson "reasoned a barber's chair was a good place to take a town's pulse" (131) compared to Steinbeck's theory about hairdresser as in "women tell a hairdresser things they wouldn't dare confess to a priest, and they are open about matters they'd try to conceal from a doctor" (*Travels with Charley*, 153). In New Orleans, Olson "decided to call a taxi as John Steinbeck had done in his 1960 visit" (212).

Olson, however, has different things from Steinbeck's. Olson is "insisting on traveling light" (22), which opposed to Steinbeck who "traveled weighted down" (22). In Steinbeck's time, it was easier to talk to a stranger, but now, "[p]eople are so tethered to cell phones, Bluetooth, MP3 players, iPods and laptops, that real conversation with someone two feet away can't be bothered with" (35). Their ways of writing are different too written as:

> Steinbeck said he could not "write hot"—the same day an event happened. He could afford to wait until he returned to Long Island to begin writing.
>
> That was not an option for me. Daily I would need stories, people and events to populate the pages of my future book. I had to write hot. (40)

Olson is a journalist and Steinbeck is a fiction writer basically.

As a retired journalist, Mr. Olson has shown his journalistic attitudes and skills in various parts of the book. His interviewing techniques are perhaps superb because of his background as a journalist, and make this book a present *America and Americans*. Steinbeck has "always admired those reporters who can descend on an area, talk to key people, ask key questions, take samplings of opinions, and then set down an orderly report" in *Travels with Charley* (70), although he does "not trust it as a mirror of reality" (70).

This book is dotted with pieces of information that Steinbeck scholars enjoy reading. For example, Olson surmised that the store in which Steinbeck bought a jacket in Livingston, Montana in 1960 was The Mercantile (48). Olson contacted Thomas Steinbeck, John Steinbeck's second son. Thomas Steinbeck gave Olson pieces of advice (312). Olson also mentions what Steinbeck's own son said about his father's famous road tour, which are very interesting to read for us Steinbeck scholars.

Once again, this book by John R. Olson is a great addition to the books written 50 years after John Steinbeck's *Travels with Charley* and it certainly is searching of America.

Bill Steigerwald, *Dogging Steinbeck—Discovering America and Exposing The Truth About 'Travels With Charley'*

The author of this book, Bill Steigerwald, was formerly a journalist for the *Los Angeles Times* in the 1980s, the *Post-Gazette* in the 1990s and the *Pittsburgh Tribune-Review* in the 2000s. His freelance articles, interviews and commentaries have appeared in many of the major newspapers in the USA and in magazines. In this book, he often refers to himself as a "drive-by journalist," probably by which he means he is trying to bust or "shoot down" the Steinbeck myths as a "drive-by" killer.

In his childhood his house was filled with hundreds of books, but Steigerwald did not know if there were any written by John Steinbeck (85). In his younger days he traveled across the USA a lot behind the wheel, including a dozen times on Route 66. Steigerwald mentions the names of his younger brothers, John and Paul in the book. John is a sports reporter and Paul is a sportscaster, by the way. Bill is the eldest of the Steigerwald media brothers.

He wrote in the "Introduction" (6) that he discovered two important and surprising truths when he retraced the route John Steinbeck took around the country in 1960. First, he found out the great author's iconic "nonfiction" road book was a deceptive, dishonest and highly fictionalized account of his road trip. Then he found out that America was still a big, beautiful, empty, healthy, rich, safe, clean, prosperous and friendly country. This introduction was dated "April 1, 2013," but it is no April fool's joke.

He wrote "that everything in 'Travels With Charley' was fiction until proved otherwise" (72), and he later asserts that his "rough guess is 90 percent of the humans in 'Travels With Charley' were made up in whole or in part" (248).

He pointed out some of the fabricated scenes in the text of *Travels with Charley*. He wrote that "Long before [he] reached the boondocks of eastern North Dakota [he] knew Steinbeck's encounter with that (traveling Shakespearean) actor never happened in the real world. It was pure fiction" (10). Steigerwald also writes:

"He [Steinbeck] described camping on a farm that night (of Sunday, September 25, 1960) and talking with the landowner about Nikita Khrushchev reportedly pounding his shoe on his desk that day at the United Nations. Khrushchev's tantrum at the U.N. actually happened nearly two weeks later. In 2010, a local writer searched hard for Steinbeck's farm and Yankee farmer near Lancaster and concluded both never existed. (43-44)

He also states that "[t]he extended family of Canucks jamming into Rocinante is a favorite scene in 'Charley.' But like other favorite scenes in the book, it most likely never happened—certainly not in the protracted, theatrical way Steinbeck described" (61). Steigerwald goes on to say:

Switching two nights around or combining two nights into one, which Steinbeck also did later in "Charley," are petty literary crimes in a nonfiction book. So is inventing a character—or two. So is creating a composite character from two real people. Honest journalists never want to see facts fiddled with for any reason. But fudging reality for the sake of drama is not rare and it's not new. It's been done forever in movies and TV shows about real people and real places. And it's been done in nonfiction books since they were invented. (61)

Steigerwald also doubts Steinbeck's encounter with the father and his son near the Idaho-Washington border. He states that "[i]f this caricature of a young gay man trying to escape the mountain-man culture of Idaho sounds like something Steinbeck-the-great-novelist made up, it's because he almost certainly did. Steinbeck said the young man even subscribed to The New Yorker, which to me was the most unbelievable thing of all" (142).

He also thinks that Steinbeck's visit to Fremont Peak is dubious. In *Travels with Charley*, Steinbeck takes Charley to Fremont Peak, which "overlooks the whole of my childhood and youth" (*Travels*, 179). Steigerwald admits the literary merit of the scene as he writes, "His brief goodbye to what would soon become 'Steinbeck Country' was some of the best writing in "Charley" (185). But Steigerwald "could no longer assume [Steinbeck] actually came up to Fremont Peak in November of 1960" (186), because "[b]y late October 2010 [Steigerwald] knew how much of [Steinbeck's] 'nonfiction' book was faked or dubious" (186). Steinbeck was able to write this very artistic scene, "because he had been on Fremont Peak so many times he knew its vista by heart" (186).

Steigerwald praises the scene in which Steinbeck described the "Cheerleaders" shouting out at Ruby Bridges walking to William Frantz Elementary School in New Orleans in 1960:

Going to New Orleans to see the Cheerleaders in action was the only deliberate act of journalism Steinbeck made on his entire trip, and it paid off. It gave his book of fictional encounters, musings and memories some needed punch and passion and a newsy edge. Not to mention a welcome dose of reality. Being where real people are doing real things always has a way of producing strong writing, whether you're a newspaper reporter covering a house fire or a great novelist covering race war. Steinbeck's Cheerleaders scenes, unlike any other in the book, prove it. In probably less than an hour, he found a powerful ending for "Charley" without having to rearrange the real world much at all. (219)

But he continues, "[t]he lineup of Central Casting All-Stars Steinbeck says he met before and after his visit to William Frantz Elementary is another matter. The characters he quotes when he arrives in New Orleans—a parking lot guy and a taxi driver—are no more believable or less wooden than the other fictional people he paraded through his book" (219). In other parts of the book, Steigerwald calls these fictional people "cardboard characters" (244).

Steigerwald professes, "[w]hen Steinbeck writes about something he really did on his trip, you can usually tell. Instead of inventing pages of wooden dialogue, he delivers detail" (210). Regarding the dialogues, Steigerwald guesses that "he [Steinbeck] may have created or embellished the scene to generate some laughs or tension or to show off his dialogue skills" (110).

It has been generally believed that "Elaine Steinbeck joined him [John] for a few days at a time along the way *(Steinbeck: A Life in Letters*, 690), but Steigerwald believes that Elaine joined her husband for "actually 28 straight days, from Seattle to Monterey, and then another 10 or so in Texas" (262), because Steigerwald believes that "[Elaine] protected the myth that Steinbeck was alone most of the time" (262). But "she had been cut out of the first draft of 'Travels With Charley'" (262) just as Carol, Steinbeck's first wife was cut out in *The Log From the Sea of Cortez* even if she was cruising with John and the crew members.

Steigerwald also thinks that Steinbeck spent fewer nights camping out than he wrote he did in *Travels with Charley*:

> Of his estimated 75 nights away from New York, about nine are unaccounted for. Three or four of them occurred on his final non-stop marathon from New Orleans to New York City. Four other mystery nights were spent in Maine on the coast near Calais, in northern Ohio or Indiana on the way to Amarillo. It's possible Steinbeck stopped and did a leisurely and lonely campout on one or several of those mystery nights. It's just highly unlikely, or he would have written about it. Plus, since he was usually hurrying to rejoin his wife, he probably either made motel stops or no stops at all. So how often did Steinbeck live up to the "Travels With Charley" Myth and actually sleep in his camper under the stars in the middle of the American nowhere? Not very often—if ever. (251)

Steigerwald calls this controversy "Charleygate" (273), and he thinks "that Steinbeck's son, John Steinbeck IV—who was often around when Steinbeck wrote the book—was right when he made the remark that his father 'just sat down in his camper' and made up most of the stories he wrote" (270).

Steigerwald cautions us Steinbeck scholars about our ignorance as he writes, "Inventing characters and making up their conversations in a nonfiction book was nothing new or rare or even necessarily wrong. Steinbeck's fictional quartet was harmless and obviously imaginary. It's just too bad for 50 years scholars didn't notice or care enough to point that out" (220). He also states that "scholars who liked Steinbeck apparently were too busy looking for deeper meaning in the conversations of a French poodle or trying to prove Steinbeck was a great writer or a prescient environmentalist. If they had been more critical, more skeptical, more scholarly, they might have saved me [Bill Steigerwald] a lot of work" (249). His comments to the scholars might be to the point to some degree. We should have been more critical, more skeptical, and more scholarly, just as

Steigerwald advised.

Steigerwald went to New York City, and "did something no one in the world had done in four years" (20), namely checking Steinbeck's handwritten first draft of *Travels With Charley* in Morgan Library & Museum in Manhattan. Steigerwald writes, "Few scholars or grad students had bothered to study it" (20). "According to the Morgan's curator of literary manuscripts, fewer than six people had looked at the manuscripts since 2000. [He] was the first since 2006" (21). Thanks to his visit to the library, we can read his original draft describing "Cheerleaders" in New Orleans.

On the road trip along Steinbeck Highway, Steigerwald was writing a "Travels Without Charley" road blog each day for the *Pittsburgh Post-Gazette*. Steigerwald's blog, which I read through along with my reading of this book, is comparable to John Steinbeck's letters to his wife Elaine in that, as Jay Parini points out, they were "later used as notes for writing the book" (Parini, 509).

This book is partly intended to show its readers the falseness of Steinbeck's "non -fiction" travel book, but since Steigerwald himself traveled along the Steinbeck Highway "dogging Steinbeck" and wrote about his own road trip, the reader can enjoy this as another good book about traveling by car.

Compared to Steinbeck's travel, which took 75 days, Steigerwald's trip took 38 days, about half as long as Steinbeck's. Steigerwald visited 26 states, compared to 34 states by Steinbeck. Steigerwald drove 11,276 miles, an average of 296 miles a day. Five hundred and ninety seven miles in Texas "was the farthest [he] had driven in a single day" (212). Steigerwald kept precise records of how much gas, meals, accommodations and other things cost. What allowed him to save his money for lodging was parking lots in Wal-Marts around the U.S. He slept in his Toyota RAV4 parked in the parking lot of Wal-Marts quite often. He utilized another chain, McDonald's as well. He "count[ed] on every McDonald's to have strong free Wi-Fi that you can use for as long as you want any time of day. And you [could] count on finding a gang of 4 to 6 wise old guys in bad hats who [would] be thrilled to answer a stranger's questions about what their local world was like in 1960" (68).

As Steigerwald put it, Steinbeck "left no notes, no journal and no expense records from the road" (8). He only wrote letters along the way, to his wife Elaine and his editors. Before the start of his journey for *Travels with Charley*, he wrote:

> I thought I might do some writing along the way, perhaps essays, surely notes, certainly letters. I took paper, carbon, typewriter, pencils, notebooks, and not only those but dictionaries, a compact encyclopedia, and a dozen other reference books, heavy ones. I suppose our capacity for self-delusion is boundless. I knew very well that I rarely make notes, and if I do I either lose them or can't read them. I also knew from thirty years of my profession that I cannot write hot on an event. It has to ferment. I must do what a friend call 'mule it over' for a time before it goes down. And in spite of this self-knowledge I equipped Rocinante with enough writing material to take care of ten volumes. (*Travels With Charley*, 16)

After reading this passage, do you still think he wrote along the way? Before his cruise with Ed Ricketts and crew members for *Sea of Cortez—A Leisurely Journal of Travles and Research* in 1940, twenty years before his travels with Charley, they prepared pens, pencils, erasers, typewriter paper, and a portable typewriter (*The Log from the Sea of Cortez*, 10-11). But it is known now that Steinbeck wrote *The Log from the Sea of Cortez* the next year based on Ed Ricketts journal.

In this voyage they took a camera, but it was never used: "The camera equipment was more than adequate, for it was never used.... we had no camera-man.... It was an error in personnel. There should be a camera-man who does nothing but take pictures" (*Log*, 11-12). The paper, carbon, typewriter, pencils, notebooks for the land cruise in 1960 are, like the camera on the boat in 1940, unused. It was an error in personnel again in 1960. There should have been someone who did nothing but write a journal, or if Ed Ricketts had been with Steinbeck and had written a journal along the way, we would be able to see a much different and more "accurate" version of *Travels with Charley*, or "Travels with Ricketts." In *The Log from the Sea of Cortez*, specific dates are written down, but there is no entry of dates in *Travels with Charley*. I think it is one of the evidences Steinbeck "fabricated" the travel episodes after the journey was all done.

I think Steigerwald is right in stating Steinbeck was not a journalist. As Steigerwald also points out, Steinbeck was fired by the *New York American*, a Hearst paper in 1926, when he was 24.

As I wrote earlier, I am aware of the controversy this book created. I have also noticed Steigerwald's journalistic way of sensationalizing things (sometimes too much) in order to get readers' attention. I, however, recommend *Dogging Steinbeck* to anyone who has already read John Steinbeck's *Travels with Charley*, but not otherwise. I also highly value his extensive and intensive research and journalistic attitude and philosophy throughout this book.

Benoit Denizet-Lewis, *Travels with Casey—My Journey Through Our Dog-Crazy Country*—

The author of this book, Benoit Denizet-Lewis is a *New York Times* best-selling author. He has published three books including this book, the other two are: *America Anonymous: Eight Addicts in Search of a Life*, and *American Voyeur: Dispatches From the Far Reaches of Modern Life*. He teaches in the department of Writing, Literature and Publishing at Emerson College in Boston, Massachusetts. According to the Wikipedia article about him, he was born in 1975. He writes in this book that he is gay (65), and that he had some addiction problem before (231).

The author "used to be a flight attendant" (293). His alma matter is Northwestern University in Chicago (296). Two of his favorite books are *My Dog Tulip*, by J. R. Ackerley, and *Dog Years*, by Mark Dory (242). They "happen to have been written by gay men" (242), and both of them are about dogs.

Denizet-Lewis writes in the beginning of the book that "Steinbeck had traveled the country to tell the story of America's soul: I was traveling the country to tell the story of America's dogs. Charley was an accessory; Casey would have a starring role"(9). He also writes:

> I wanted to write a different kind of dog book, one that would explore and celebrate the breadth of human-dog relationships in contemporary life. To do that, I planned to travel across America—the country with the highest rate of dog ownership on the planet—and hang out with as many dogs (and dog-obsessed humans) as I could. (9)

So "[o]n [his] journey [he] planned to meet therapy dogs, police dogs, shelter dogs, celebrity dogs, farm dogs, racing dogs, stray dogs, show dogs, hunting dogs, dock-diving dogs, and dogs with no discernable "job" other than lounging around the house and terrorizing the mailman" (9).

Compared with the Steinbeck's book, which often describes the time with his French poodle named Charley in the camping-truck named Rocinante, Denizet-Lewis's book puts greater emphasis on depicting the author's and his dog's encounters with other dogs and their owners in the places he and Casey visited, rather than on their time in the RV named Chalet.

As Steinbeck highly regarded Montana in *Travels with Charley*, Denizet-Lewis also thinks highly of Montana, writing, "It's difficult not to get philosophical under the stars of Montana ranch, and before long David and I were chatting like the oldest of friends" (264).

Like Steinbeck, who offered a ride to an old African American trudging with heavy heels in Texas(, who was not hitchhiking, though), Denizet-Lewis "stopped for a middle-aged man who looked remarkably like Harrison Ford" (273). The man was hitchhiking and he had a dog named Hyper.

Denizet-Lewis writes, "[o]ne of the challenges of driving around the country for months in an RV is that seemingly everyone—friends, Facebook followers, long-lost lovers—expects a visit" (155). I wondered if Steinbeck had the similar challenge. Denizet-Lewis also mentioned another RV traveling challenge of "bed bugs in motorhome" (184). Did Steinbeck have this problem when he traveled?

Denizet-Lewis and the other travel writers who took Steinbeck route about 50 years later had similar challenges and experiences like Steinbeck, but writers in the years of technology have gadgety inventions such as picture/movie-taking smartphones, blogs, YouTube and social media such as Facebook, the then twitter (present X) and so on. Denizet-Lewis used Facebook when he traveled. He posted some photos onto Facebook along the way. He also posted movies onto YouTube. We can still enjoy his photos and movies. Those posts really help us read this book and understand his travel.

This would be a good book, if you love traveling, dogs, or John Steinbeck. If you are not a dog lover, it would still be a fun read/travel. As Benoit Denizet-Lewis puts it, this truly is "a different kind of dog book" (9).

Conclusion

Reviewing the four of the books written by authors who followed Steinbeck's 1960 route, I would like to admit the publication of such books was a phenomenal thing. I also would like to admire the literary merits of Steinbeck's *Travels with Charley*. There is no telling whether or not there will be this kind of publishing trend like in 2035, which is 75 years after Steinbeck's travel with Charley, or in 2060, the commemorative 100th anniversary year of Steinbeck's journey. Whether this travel book by Steinbeck is a fiction or a non-fiction is of no great importance. The fact that this book attracts a lot of pilgrimage is of true value.

Acknowledgement

I would like to make my acknowledgement with thanks to Professor Emeritus Yasuhiro Sakai for his heartfelt encouragement to write this article.

Works Cited

Barich, Bill. *Long Way Home*, New York: Walker & Company, 2010. Print.

Denizet-Lewis, Benoit. *Travels with Casey*, New York: Simon & Schuster, 2014. Print.

Mak, Geert. *In America—Travels with John Steinbeck*, London: Harville Secker, 2015. Print.

Olson, John. Down John's Road — *Recreating John Steinbeck's 1960 American Road Trip* — . CreateSpace Independent Publishing Platform, 2011. 328pp. Print.

Parini, Jay. *John Steinbeck A Biography*, London: Heinemann, 1994. Print.

Steigerwald, Bill. *Dogging Steinbeck—Discovering America and Exposing The Truth About 'Travels With Charley.'* Pittsburgh, Pa.: Fourth River Press, 2012. Print.

Steinbeck, Elaine, and Robert Wallsten. *Steinbeck: A Life in Letters*, 1975. Harmondsworth: Penguin, 1976. Print.

Steinbeck, John. *The Log from the Sea of Cortez*, 1951. Harmondsworth: Penguin, 1976. Print.

_____. *Travels with Charley—In Search of America*, 1961. London: Pan Books, 1974. Print.

Yamauchi, Kiyoshi. Rev. of *Travels With Max—In Search of Steinbeck's America Fifty Years Later*, by Gregory Zeigler. *Steinbeck Studies* 36 (2013): 36-40. Print.

_____. Rev. of *Dogging Steinbeck—Discovering America and Exposing The Truth About 'Travels With Charley*, by Bill Steigerwald. Steinbeck Studies 37 (2014): 39-49. Print.

_____. Rev. of *Down John's Road—Recreating John Steinbeck's 1960 American Road Trip—*, by John R. Olson. *Steinbeck Studies* 39 (2016): 30-35. Print.

_____. Rev. of *Travels with Casey: My Journey Through Our Dog-Crazy Country*, by Benoit Denizet-Lewis. *Steinbeck Studies* 42 (2019): 54-59. Print.

Zeigler, Gregory. *Travels With Max—In Search of Steinbeck's America Fifty Years Later*. Salt Lake City, UT: Blaine Creek Press, 2010. Print.

_____. "Travels with Steinbeck," http://travelswithsteinbeck.wordpress.com/ . Accessed 29 Dec. 2023.

About the Author and Contributors

Yasuhiro Sakai: Professor Emeritus of English at National Institute of Technology, Yonago College, Tottori, Japan. His articles on Steinbeck, especially discussing Steinbeck's modes of depicting American culture in comparison with Celtic culture, have appeared in *Steinbeck Studies* and other academic journals. A recent article has appeared in the book titled *Sutainbekku To Tomoni: Botsugo 50-Nen Kinen Ronshu* (*With Steinbeck: Articles in Commemoration of the 50th Anniversary of John Steinbeck*, 2019)

Ōsuke Tsujimoto: Associate Professor of Japanese Language at Kansei Gakuin University, Hyougo, Japan. His major article is "On Quotative Structures with Stative Predicate in Early Middle Japanese" in *Language and Literature* No.234. (The Association for the Study of Japanese Language and Literature, 2022)

Kiyoshi Yamauchi: Professor of English at Niimi University, Okayama, Japan and the former President of the John Steinbeck Society of Japan. His major article is "The Last Scene of *The Grapes of Wrath*" in *Steinbeck Studies* Vol. 27, 2004.

The Works of John Steinbeck: In the Magic Light of "Celtic Twilight"

2024 年 4 月 24 日　初版第 1 刷発行
　　著　者　　酒井　康宏
　　発行者　　横山　哲彌
　　印刷所　　岩岡印刷株式会社

発行所　　大阪教育図書株式会社
　　　　　　〒 530-0055　大阪市北区野崎町 1 -25
　　　　　　TEL　06-6361-5936
　　　　　　FAX　06-6361-5819
　　　　　　振替　00940-1-115500
　　　　　　email　daikyopb@osk4.3web.ne.jp

ISBN 978-4-271-21086-3　　C3098　落丁・乱丁本はお取り替えいたします。